A WINTER Affair

MINNA HOWARD has had
an exciting career in fashion
journalism and now writes full
time, whilst enjoying time with
her grandsons and working as an
occasional Film and TV extra. She
lives in London.

Also by Minna Howard

Mothers and Daughters

Second Chances

A WINTER Affair

Minna HOWARD

First published as an ebook in 2016 by Aria,
an imprint of Head of Zeus, Ltd.

First published in print in the UK in 2017 by Aria.

9 7 5 3 1 2 4 6 8

A catalogue record for this book is available from
the British Library.

ISBN (PB): 9781788541053
ISBN (E): 9781784975869

Typeset by Divaddict Publishing Solutions Ltd.

MIX
Paper from
responsible sources
FSC® C020471

Printed and bound by CPI Group (UK) Ltd,
Croydon, CR0 4YY

Head of Zeus Ltd
First Floor East
5–8 Hardwick Street
London EC1R 4RG

WWW.HEADOFZEUS.COM

In affectionate memory of Maurice Gard who taught us to ski and love and respect the mountains.

Eloise had written three Christmas cards before she realized her mistake, but old habits die hard.

Love from Eloise, Harvey and the twins. But Harvey wasn't here and would not be coming back. She tore up the cards and threw them into the bin and then gave up on the whole idea; she would not be sending cards this year.

She sat at her desk in the still unfamiliar room of her new home in Wimbledon, struggling to repress the ache in her heart. Through the window she saw the driver of the supermarket delivery van wheeling cases of wine and boxes of goodies to number twenty-seven ready for the Christmas celebrations. She better go and buy her turkey breast, pudding for one and wine and chocolate to eat while she immersed herself in box sets, she thought wryly. This year she'd be home alone for Christmas for the first time in her forty-three years.

The telephone rang, cutting through her thoughts. It could be the twins calling from Tibet. She answered it full of hope. Her spirits fell a little when she realized it was not them but Desmond Maynard, her godfather, calling from his sunny home in Antigua.

'What are you doing for Christmas, my dear?' his voice boomed from across the world.

She'd told him all about her divorce. Perhaps he was going to ask her to stay with him for Christmas. Her heart rose as she pictured warm beaches and soft seas. She hadn't seen Desmond, her father's best friend, for a couple of years, he was good company and she'd always been fond of him. Knowing him, he'd even offer to pay for her ticket, which he could well afford, so she wouldn't feel bad about accepting. Now he was alone without Maddy, his beloved partner, he probably yearned for company at this emotional time of the year. She'd be happy to read to him, go on walks in the lush countryside and swim in the sea with him. So maybe her Christmas wouldn't be so bad this year after all.

'I haven't decided yet, Desmond. The twins are in Tibet. I'm going to catch up with them in the summer when I visit my parents in New Zealand and...' She was about to accept the invitation he had not yet given when he interrupted.

'Good, there's trouble at the chalet. Lawrence is tearing his hair out, he's had to sack two already and he has a big Christmas party for very important clients and is at his wit's end and doesn't know what to do.'

'Sack who... and what's it to do with me?' Eloise was puzzled. Desmond had inherited an ancient chalet in Switzerland from his parents' years ago and had given it to his son Lawrence, who was mad about skiing and mountains and now ran it as an expensive holiday let.

'A *chef.*' Desmond almost shouted as if her ears were defective. 'The one he had left unexpectedly... in a private plane with one of the guests. I warned Lawrence not to employ any attractive women, but he wouldn't listen. But I was right and he was wrong: she made a beeline for some rich tycoon and ran off with him, leaving poor Lawrence in the lurch at this crucial time.'

'I'm sorry, but...' Eloise began, but Desmond went on, his voice getting louder and more strident.

'And the last two chefs that arrived couldn't cook an egg, but you can: you're cordon bleu trained and you cook wonderfully and are reliable... aren't you?' he demanded.

She was shell-shocked: she hadn't seen Lawrence for years and hadn't much liked him then. Had Desmond told him she would cook for a chalet full of people without even asking her first... and assured him that she was not attractive enough to lure away any passing zillionaires?

It was years since she'd done the cordon bleu course and it was only a Foundation one, which in no way qualified her as a chef. She tried to explain this to Desmond, but he stopped her mid-flow, his voice calm as if he were soothing a wild animal.

'My dear, I've no doubt you've been through a terrible time with your no-good husband, but you need to keep your wits about you, not waste away picking over every painful detail. Lawrence is frantic, he needs a chef at Jacaranda from now until early January and you've just said you're free and you can cook. He'll send you the fare and you'll have a wage, board and lodging and even time to ski. Surely you'd jump at the chance?' He sounded peevish.

'You've sprung this on me, Desmond, let me think about it.' She was stung by his remark about wasting life while she agonized over Harvey's departure. It was true that she had lost much of her confidence over her divorce and no longer having the twins at home, and so making the two main points to her life – being a wife and mother – redundant almost simultaneously.

'But what *are* you doing for Christmas, Eloise. You sound as if you haven't got anything planned,' Desmond went on.

'I'm not sure, I've just moved house and...' She was not going to say curl up with box sets and books and eat chocolate, which suddenly seemed very tempting, hiding away to nurse her wounds.

'There you are then, problem solved. I'll tell Lawrence to ring you at once. Jacaranda's a lovely chalet... of course you know, having stayed there with me and dear Maddy and your parents... and didn't you all come one Christmas when you and Joanna were children? Oh, what good times they were. I wish I wasn't so old and infirm and could ski those slopes again.' He sounded wistful. He went on, 'You'll love it, you know you will, all those stunning mountains and powdery snow.'

'Oh, Desmond, it's just that...' but he cut her off once more.

'You can do it, Eloise, I know you can. Goodbye, my dear, and thank you.' He rang off, leaving her reeling.

She couldn't possibly cook for a chalet full of rich, discerning guests, no doubt plagued with food fads. She must contact Lawrence at once and tell him that his father was mistaken. But she didn't know his number, unless by some fluke she could find it from the times she'd stayed there years ago. She remembered the one Christmas she'd spent there as a child, with her family when she was about ten. A truly white Christmas with lashings of snow and she and Joanna making snowmen that lasted the whole time they were there. They'd given them names and been quite sad to leave them behind when they went home. She'd loved it, it was a truly wonderful place, but she hadn't had to cook for difficult millionaires used to the very best.

And yet it would be something different to focus on. Hadn't she promised herself that after the divorce, when she was an independent woman again, she'd take on new challenges? Change the rhythm of her life so she wouldn't feel so bereft.

This last year had passed in a mist of pain and confusion with Harvey – who, she admitted, had been making for the exit for some time – finally leaving her, escaping the confines of marriage to 'find himself' as he put it, lured away by a large-breasted 'sex toy', as she thought her. Then, almost harder to bear, her beloved twins, Kit and Lizzie, set off on their gap year to the other side of the world, relieved, she couldn't help thinking but not blaming them, to escape their parents' explosive break-up.

It had been a strange sort of marriage, she admitted now, watching yet more boxes being trundled across to number twenty-seven. However many people were they going to entertain? Certainly more than her if she stayed home alone as she'd planned. Against all the odds their marriage had lasted just over twenty years, though early on, when the twins were babies, to keep her sanity, Eloise had forced herself to turn a blind eye or, rather, not delve too deeply into what Harvey got up to when he went away on his business trips. He worked in the travel industry, which mostly involved beaches and the occasional ski resort, and these, with their skimpy clothing at one, and ski bunnies at the other, provided many opportunities for bedroom sports that she suspected Harvey indulged in. He adored the children and always came home to them, until they grew up and were bitten by the travel bug, and soon after their father left they set out into a wider world, leaving their nest empty.

She soon realized, or perhaps more likely accepted, that she was not enough for her husband. In fact since he had put on weight and his beautiful features were sinking into flabbiness he seemed to be more determined than ever to prove that he had not lost his power of seduction. The pain tugged tighter as she replayed the scene when he'd told her that he'd always love her, but he felt it was time – he made it sound like a supreme sacrifice on his part – for *both* of them to move on, breaking her heart.

She was twenty-one when they married. It seemed a long time ago. Harvey was twenty-eight. His parents had died in the same year, she remembered, and Harvey, their only child, had been born late in their marriage and no doubt spoilt rotten. He probably needed a home and someone to care for him, which she probably overdid, loving him so much... too much. When the twins were born two years later, and she had to spread her care for him more thinly, he could get quite grumpy if she couldn't give him her full attention when he expected it, though he did adore his children.

When she first met him, Harvey, encouraged by his friends, wanted to be an actor. With his dark smouldering eyes and manly torso, everyone said... well anyway his friends, he'd surely make a perfect romantic lead and even be a contender to play James Bond. But though he was animated in normal life, he became as wooden as a puppet in front of a camera or on stage.

He tried modelling and Eloise still recalled, with a lurch of sick embarrassment, the time she'd gone to a smart lunch given by one of her girl friends from school. The women boasted about their husbands who were bankers, lawyers, politicians or doctors. When it came to her turn, she sort of panicked and bleated out that her husband was a *lingerie* model, causing shrieks and gasps of incredulity. She hadn't meant to say it but explain he was modelling at the moment – in between acting jobs – true, his speciality seemed to be swimming trunks, but he had also modelled an occasional suit. Regardless, this profession hardly featured in the same class as medicine or law. But in time – after he'd swapped the acting world for the travel world – when she'd met these other women's husbands, she saw Harvey was by far the best-looking and far more exciting, and when some of their marriages broke down it was Harvey the women sought out to console them.

She should have faced up to the signs back then, but somehow she never thought that Harvey would actually leave her, until the divorce had gone through. She kept his name, Brandon, it had been her name longer than the one she was born with and she didn't want to change everything.

They had to sell their family house and she'd been so busy finding and settling into this one and getting the twins off on their travels that Christmas had crept up on her almost without her noticing. She need not be alone for Christmas. She could go and stay with Joanna, her older sister, and her family in Scotland, and various friends had invited her to spend it with them, but touched though she was by their kindness, she couldn't tell them that just now she couldn't bear to be among happy families when hers had self-destructed. She found it painful to be with couples chatting about their plans, just as she and Harvey used to do: '*We* are planning a holiday,' '*We* need to buy a new car.' Ordinary everyday things that she'd never noticed before she was alone.

No, she would spend Christmas alone. It was only one day after all and she'd be perfectly happy with her box sets, books, wine and chocolate.

The telephone rang again, setting her nerves on edge. Perhaps she'd let it go to the answer phone, but it *could* be the twins ringing from Tibet, so she answered it.

'Eloise? Lawrence here, Desmond' – he'd always called his father by his first name – 'said you are a cordon bleu chef and free to come out here and cook for the Christmas guests.' His voice was brisk with impatience as if he suspected he was wasting his time.

Her confidence had already been smashed by the divorce and his tone of voice now smashed it further. 'Oh... Lawrence, he did ring, I am cordon bleu... but hardly a...'

'Look, Eloise, can you do it or not? I need you here by the weekend and to stay until the second week in January. The guests are sophisticated and used to the best. I want someone reliable and who's not going to flirt with the guests, worse still run off with them,' he added sourly. 'Desmond is convinced you'll be able to do it, so can you?'

'Did he say I was nothing to look at, not one to tempt away your paying guests?' Despite her nerves she couldn't resist teasing him.

'You can look like the backside of a bus for all I care as long as you can cook,' he retorted impatiently.

His tone annoyed her now. 'I think Desmond could have exaggerated my skills. I can cook, but I'm not a chef as such, and I'm not keen on those fussy little messes arranged in the middle of a plate, they're too fiddly and far too time-consuming.'

'I quite agree,' he sounded friendlier. 'Look, I need roasts, fish dishes, duck, those sorts of things, good vegetables and puddings. People are hungry out here with all the mountain air, but they don't want school dinners. Can you do it or not?'

She couldn't, surely couldn't please a man who sounded so particular? Or please his even more particular guests? But something deep inside her, long squashed by the break-up of her marriage, struggled to assert itself. Hadn't she wanted to start afresh, change her life? Well, here was her chance.

'I'll give it a go,' she said, feeling rather weak at the challenge.

'Good,' Lawrence said, 'let's hope it works out. Over Christmas I've some very important people booked in and it must not go wrong. I'll email your ticket, give me your details, you'll fly out to Geneva on Friday and I'll send Theo, my son, to pick you up and drive you up here.'

'Will he hold up a sign with my name on or something so I can recognize him?'

'Of course. OK, Eloise, see you then, and please, I'm depending on you, don't let me down'. He made it sound as if it was life or death, which perhaps it was, and he rang off.

His son... he must be old enough to drive, did Lawrence have a wife there too and why couldn't *she* cook, or was she too glamorous, floating about as the perfect hostess?

Panic hit again, what on earth did she think she was doing, agreeing to cook for a chalet full of rich – and probably spoilt – people? She didn't want to go, she wanted to hide away, to lick her wounds, hibernate from the world and emerge feeling stronger in the spring. She picked up the telephone and dialled ring back and wrote down Lawrence's number. It was late now and she was exhausted, she'd call him in the morning and tell him she would not be able to come to Jacaranda after all.

2

Eloise came through to the arrivals, her stomach churning with anxiety. She didn't want to be here. She had intended to ring Lawrence and refuse his offer but two of her best friends happened to ring her that evening and when she'd told them of this 'mad' offer she'd had, they'd encouraged her to take it. What fun to have an adventure in such a lovely resort while they'd be putting up with difficult in-laws in a dark and probably rainy climate where the only mountains would be the washing up. But now here without them, she wanted to go home.

There was still time to escape, she could go to an airline desk and ask for a return ticket. Overcome with sudden panic, she almost turned to do so when she caught sight of a man, his face bronzed and eager, holding up a placard with her name on it. He looked so young, just like Kit, and tears rose in her, wishing it were him with Lizzie beside him, searching for her in the crowd. She'd told them she was coming out here for Christmas but kept from them her loss of confidence since the break-up of her marriage, not wanting them to worry and feel guilty at leaving her.

'Lucky you, shall we come and be kitchen maids, get in some skiing?' Kit had said.

'You'd be a hopeless kitchen maid,' she'd heard Lizzie

say, 'you'd be at the wine bottles, too pissed to be any help to anyone.'

'Speak for yourself,' Kit had answered and she had imagined them ragging each other, pushing and shoving like two overexcited puppies, and how she yearned to be with them now instead of being here trying to pretend she was something she most definitely was not.

But then she saw Theo, with his mop of blond curls, searching anxiously through the jostling crowd, thrusting up the placard with her name, Eloise Brandon, written in black felt-tip pen. She hovered uncertainly for a moment, struggling to resist an urge to turn and run. She glanced back at him and saw a small brown dog sitting by his feet looking hopefully at the people passing by. How could she be so selfish as to run away? She went over and said, 'Theo, it's me, Eloise.'

'Oh, great,' he looked relieved and the little dog got up and sniffed her, wagging its tail. 'This is Bert, hope you like dogs.' Theo watched her warily.

'Yes, I do.' She patted Bert, who rolled over on his back before jumping up and chasing his tail with excitement.

'Bert, stop showing off,' Theo said affectionately. 'Sorry he gets a bit hypo if he likes someone.' He smiled, making her feel better. Perhaps it would be all right after all. 'Let me take your case. Good flight?' He took it from her and she guessed he was used to dealing with the guests who graced the chalet.

'Yes thanks. Have you guests at Jacaranda now?' She wondered what they were eating if all the cooks had eloped with clients or been fired.

'They arrive tomorrow, we only had four people this week, I've just dropped them off here, and Dad... Lawrence,' he grinned, 'he is my dad but he thinks it more professional if we don't broadcast it about too much – he managed breakfast, but he had to buy in the dinner,' he explained as she followed him and a bouncing Bert out into the car park and over to a midnight-blue mini coach with *Chic Chalet Parties* written in white along the side, the description refuelling her fears that she would not match up to Lawrence's standards or those of his guests. Surely in her chain-store jeans, rose pink jersey and blue ski jacket she was not *chic* enough?

Theo, seeing her expression, laughed, 'Maddy, Desmond's girlfriend, thought it up, but sadly she died before they could get the business going.'

'I remember her.' Eloise thought back to the times when she and her parents and sister had come out here to stay at Jacaranda and Maddy had been there. She was such a warm and caring person, who lit up everywhere she went. Later, after her marriage, Eloise had come a few times with Harvey and the twins. The first time the children were barely on their feet, though Harvey insisted on putting them on tiny skis, which they loved, finding it easier to slide down a small slope than to walk. Jacaranda was full of memories of happy times. She hadn't been back for about ten years and she wondered what it would be like now.

Theo put her case in the boot and got into the driver's seat, she got in beside him and they started the journey towards Verbier, Bert supervising the route from behind them, growling or barking at any other dog or cat he felt should not be wandering around.

Chatting to Theo as they drove, Eloise learnt that Verbier had grown ever larger and become one of the places to be, so Jacaranda – the chalet built by Desmond's father with its large rooms and elegant balconies, the wood mellowed to a rich brown, weathered by the snow and the sun – could now bring in a good income by having paying guests to stay. Guests she was going to cook for.

'The chalet and the land around it is worth a lot, but it's expensive to keep up, so Lawrence took up Maddy's idea and has turned what used to be my grandfather's home into a business,' Theo explained as they drove. 'We live there too, but there's plenty of room for guests to come and ski in the winter and to walk in the summer. There's a sort of plan that hasn't happened yet, to have painting or photo weeks, with experts teaching.'

'That sounds good, I remember it as such a beautiful place, but it's years since I've been here.'

Eloise looked out of the window at the rather plain houses, most of which had magnolia trees in their gardens, she remembered the beauty of them when they flowered, sumptuous against the plain bark of the tree. Ahead she saw the white peaks of the mountains, sparkling in the sun under the intense blue sky. There were thick blankets of snow on the ground, on the roofs of the houses and in the gardens, but the roads were clear, piles of snow lining the edges.

They reached the start of the mountain road and wound their way up towards the resort. She remembered the road, the frisson of fear as they rounded each corner, blind to what could be coming the opposite way, and the sheer drop beside them.

Theo didn't seem at all fazed by it, he chatted away, turning to her every so often to emphasize a point, sometimes lifting his hand from the wheel, and her nerves stretched tighter.

'Do keep your eyes on the road,' she said once and he laughed.

'It's OK, you're quite safe, I wouldn't dare return without you; Lawrence would kill me.'

'If we're not both killed before we get there,' she muttered under her breath, imagining Kit and probably Lizzie being just as confident as Theo, thinking they were immortal.

They reached the resort in one piece and Theo took a side road and drove on up the hill. It was lined with fir trees, their dark branches laden with snow. Below them, other chalets were scattered down the mountainside as if a huge hand had flung them there. Some were in clumps, others alone, many were decked with Christmas lights, and here and there wild fir trees were wearing strings of lights and shining baubles. Jacaranda was somewhere ahead, but she didn't recognize the place now with so many new buildings around.

'I don't remember so many chalets when I was last here,' she said.

'There's been a lot of building, it's getting far too big, it's a town really, lots of celebs come here, some even take helicopters to the slopes as they won't go in the ski lifts like everyone else,' Theo said, laughing.

'So is Jacaranda swamped by other chalets,' Eloise asked, wondering how far the town had spread out, climbing the mountain and invading its open spaces.

'No, not yet anyway. Fortunately no one can build on the land around Jacaranda unless we sell it, so we are still quite enclosed and private.'

The Verbier she remembered was a charming village, still inhabited by local people, farmers who grazed their cows on the grassy slopes in the summer and even tucked them into their chalets in the winter as they'd always done. Time moved on and there were bound to be changes, but she hoped the place had not lost its charm.

It was early afternoon and the winter light would soon be fading. They drove on a little further and then turned onto a track and ahead she saw a line of fir trees strung with garlands of silver lights, picking out the dark, rich wood of Jacaranda, surrounded by pure white snow. It looked comfortable and stalwart in its place, old and distinguished among the more orange wood of the newer chalets.

'Here we are.' Theo pulled up and jumped out, Bert followed quickly behind, disappearing into the trees. 'Welcome, Eloise,' Theo grinned at her. 'Welcome back.'

He unloaded her suitcase and she followed him up to the door of the chalet, her memories of the few times she'd been here before jostling in her mind, first as a child herself, then later as a married woman and mother of small children.

Theo opened the door and ushered her to the hall, where coats and jackets huddled together on the wall and the old cuckoo clock that had amused her as a child was still ticking beside the staircase. Alerted by the cold blast as the door opened, a man came out of one of the rooms to greet them, he was tall, his auburn hair gilded by the sun, his face lean and tanned. For a long moment he studied her, his grey eyes searing into her, as if judging whether she were indeed unattractive enough to be invisible to his randy guests.

He said briskly with the semblance of a smile, 'Eloise, good to see you. I hope you had an easy journey. Theo will show you to your room and then we'll discuss menus. Sorry to rush you, but we've a party of six arriving tomorrow and we need to get in the shopping. My office is downstairs; Theo can show you if you can't find it yourself. The place has probably changed quite a bit since you were last here.'

'It has.' The outside and the hall was much as she remembered but there was a different feeling to the place.

Looking over Lawrence's shoulder, she saw the room behind him had been enlarged and was smartly decorated and gone were the mishmash of pictures and old but comfortable chairs and sofas. She remembered the fun and laughter when Desmond and Maddy were here. When every day had been magic, surrounded by mountains, and skiing and warm, informal supper parties with games and music among friends and family, but then it was a home and now, she must realize, it was a business.

Perhaps guessing her thoughts, Lawrence shrugged with a small, regretful smile as if to say, that's how it was, life moves on.

She felt way out of her comfort zone. Lawrence, she guessed, had thoughts only for his business; he'd give her no time to settle in, take things slowly.

Her fears were confirmed when halfway down the stairs to the lower floor, he turned back, 'I've invited some friends for dinner tonight, so if you can have everything ready for eight. He disappeared from sight before she could protest.

3

Theo led the way upstairs to the first floor, carrying her case. The last time Eloise had been up here, she remembered, the landing had been a jumble of people's possessions lurching out of their bedrooms. The doors to their rooms often left open as they scrambled to get ready for ski school or the slopes before the crowds descended, or into the bathroom before anyone else hogged it. Now, with no one here, it was an empty space, with all the doors closed, and a solitary beautiful blue and pale green rug lay in the centre of the landing.

On the wall in front of her, by the staircase leading to the upper floor, hung a collection of stunning photographs of sculptures made by nature, drifts of snow blown into shapes by the wind, under a bright or stormy sky.

'These are awesome,' she said to Theo, lingering by them.

'Yes, they're Lawrence's,' he said, 'one of his passions.' He laughed, and she wondered how many other passions he had and what they were.

She followed Theo up the staircase tucked into the corner, which she remembered led to the attics under the eaves, and she supposed that was where she was going to sleep. The space had been crammed with all sorts of things when she'd last been here: odd bits of furniture, forgotten toys, old framed photographs, heavy leather ski boots long replaced by the lighter plastic ones. Was she to bed down among all these things? Crammed in among once loved possessions now forgotten, she almost joked to Theo, but he was gesturing towards another door.

'There's a shower room there, we don't tell the guests or they keep using it. We have three bathrooms on the first floor and a tiny shower and loo on the ground, but if everyone's in a hurry to get out, some get annoyed at having to wait so they sneak up here.'

'There weren't so many bathrooms the last time I was here,' Eloise said, remembering the scramble to get dressed, washed and out.

'I know, but when we turned this into a business we had to put them in, people hate sharing bathrooms now, even with their own family. Some of the best chalets are all en suite but we can't fit them in without spoiling Jacaranda's shape by building on another wing, not yet anyway.' Theo grinned, opening one of the attic doors. 'Here you are, used to be full of stuff, but we've cleared it out, hope it's OK. My room is there.' He pointed across the way and she could see a muddle of clothes through the half-open door. 'I'll try not to wake you if I come in late,' he added with a grin.

'Thanks,' she smiled, thinking of Kit and Lizzie who often made more noise trying to sneak into the house than just coming in normally.

She went into the room, curious to see what past treasures might have been left as her roommates, but everything had long gone, she couldn't recognize it now. They used to try and hide up here when they played sardines. Then you could barely get one person concealed in the room among the junk, let alone any more who discovered the hiding space. She was surprised that the room was quite large with its old-fashioned double bed and its carved wooden headboard painted dark green with a posy of alpine flowers in the centre. She hoped the mattress was younger.

Theo guessed her thoughts for he said, 'Lawrence bought the bed in a sale, it's an original one, but don't worry, the mattress is new.'

'That's a relief,' she said, dropping her coat and handbag on the cream bedcover.

An ancient built-in cupboard took up much of one wall and a faded but comfy-looking armchair and a desk in the corner lined the other. Peering out of the small window, she saw the peaks of the mountains in the distance and the roofs of other chalets scattered over the steep slope beneath them down to the village.

'It's fine, thank you.' She turned to Theo, who having dumped her case on the bed now hovered in the doorway. 'I'll be down in a moment, I'll unpack later.' Perhaps she wouldn't unpack completely in case Lawrence, who, at first glance, she felt, did not take prisoners, decided to send her home once he realized she was not the master chef his father had led him to believe.

'See you in a minute then, I have to take you to the shops when Lawrence has told you what he wants,' Theo said, increasing her anxiety. He grinned and left her and she heard him running down stairs. She liked Theo, he reminded her of her own children, full of life and so eager to please. She stared out of the window thinking of them, wishing they were here, her confidence, so brittle since Harvey had upped and left her, waning even more. But it was no good, she had a job to do and she must go down and speak with Lawrence.

Should she take some of the cookbooks she'd brought with

her to suggest menus or would that appear too amateur? How did *real* chefs behave?

She caught sight of the savage beauty of the mountains like a snapshot in the small window – she was here and she had to get on with it.

She had a quick wash and brush up and, taking one of her files containing home recipes, she went down to the next floor, taking a moment or two more to admire Lawrence's photographs before going on down to the ground floor.

She paused when she reached the hall. The door to the living room was open so she went in to see it properly. She remembered there had been two rooms here before, but now they had been knocked into one she had to agree it created a sumptuous space with the huge window framing a stunning view. The room opened out to a veranda, which ran the length of it, so there was space to sit out, even eat out, in the summer, with a breathtaking view over the valley. The living room had a large wood fire and comfortable sofas and chairs, with well-stocked bookcases and lamps on small tables. On one side, by the huge window, was a dining table and chairs, enough to seat ten.

But Lawrence was waiting, no doubt impatiently, for her and she mustn't start out on a bad note. She put her memories of the times she was last here on hold and went down the stairs to the basement floor. Theo was nowhere to be seen, but one of the doors was open and she could see Lawrence sitting at a desk, so she went in.

He was on the phone, he glanced up and gestured to a chair by the window and she pulled it round to face him and sat down. This side of the chalet had been dug out so there was plenty of daylight and it seemed not to have changed much since she was last here. She remembered there used to be a snooker table somewhere down here beside the washing machines, wine cellar and some storage space.

She was rather miffed that Lawrence was continuing with his telephone call when he expected her to find a menu for tonight, go down to the village to do the shopping and cook it all within a matter of hours.

'Lovely, Aurelia,' he purred, 'they sound delicious; I'll let you know how we get on. See you very soon.' He rang off finally.

Aurelia. She remembered Theo telling her on the way up here about Aurelia who had a business that produced ready-made dishes. She was, by the sound of Lawrence's voice and the gleam in his eyes, someone he had a close relationship with. Perhaps she was hoping to provide more of her dishes, and even much more besides. Was Aurelia standing by ready to snatch her place if Eloise failed? Though why hadn't he used her in the first place and saved himself the price of a plane ticket?

Lawrence smiled at her, a kind sort of smile often bestowed on lesser mortals, who, through no fault of their own, were deemed to be inferior beings. Eloise remembered meeting him with Desmond years ago, before she was married. He was far better looking and more together than the other boys she knew, though then she'd thought him arrogant, but obviously other girls did not for he always seemed to have a stunning woman about his person.

She studied him covetously. No doubt having glowing skin and an agile body from spending so much time on the slopes enhanced his good looks.

'I'm so relieved you've been able to come, Eloise,' he said, barely looking up from the papers on his desk. 'Christmas is the most difficult and the most important time of the year to have a good chef and we had a disaster here.' He faced her now, frowning as if warning her not to cause any disasters herself.

'I'm sure Desmond filled you in with the details, so we needn't go into them again. All the best chefs are booked up, have been for months for Christmas, but he says you are just what we want, so…'

'I feel I should say,' Eloise interrupted him, butterflies fluttering a war dance inside her, 'that I only did a short cordon bleu course, a Foundation course just after I left school.'

Lawrence's frown grew deeper; lines folding in round his eyes. 'But you must have cooked since then,' his voice held a hint of desperation.

'Yes, I cooked for my family and friends, but I chose to work in picture restoration instead of…' she was about to say slaving over a hot stove all day, but changed it to, 'well I thought cooking both for a job and for my family was too much. I like to cook, believe in feeding my family well, but that's different to doing it professionally.' She was tying herself in knots in her effort to explain. She didn't want to let him down and yet she felt she had to fess up now that she had never even cooked *one* dish professionally.

Lawrence sighed, 'I don't want a picture restorer,' he said darkly, 'I suppose my father was trying to be helpful, but it looks like he's dumped me… both of us in it. Look, Eloise, we have some very tricky clients coming for Christmas. They were determined to come to Verbier but left it too late to have one of the modern, luxurious chalets further down in the village, so we start off with them not wanting to be here anyway and if the food…' he tailed off.

The tone of his voice infuriated her. 'Just because I chose

not to cook professionally doesn't mean I can't cook,' she said firmly. 'I've given dinner parties, fed my family and no one's died of food poisoning. I can do the same here, but I'm not the sort of chef you see on *MasterChef*. You know, sort of work of art on a plate with lots of clever little bits and pieces scattered about, covered with some complicated *jus* that probably took longer to cook than the rest of it.'

A ghost of a smile hovered on Lawrence's lips. 'No, I don't expect that, but you'll have to produce good food, these guests are used to dining in the top restaurants in the world and can't be fobbed off with shepherd's pie and chips.' He eyed the phone slightly desperately, no doubt itching to contact this Aurelia person and beg her to come round with her upmarket takeaways. But Eloise, who had minutes before yearned for home, safe and cosy with her box sets, wine and chocolate, was now desperate to stay here, surrounded by the massive beauty of the mountains, the snow sparkling in the sun, the air so crisp you could cut it. Though perhaps she'd see none of it, be confined – like Cinderella – to the kitchen, without a moment off. But she wanted to give it a go.

'I understand,' Eloise said with more confidence than she felt. 'Tell me what meals I'm to cook and I'll make out a few menus and you can decide, and sometimes,' she remembered some of Harvey's business colleagues she'd entertained for dinner over the years, 'people who dine out in top restaurants all the time just want something more simple – well cooked food made with good ingredients.'

'I suppose I must give you a chance.' Lawrence reluctantly turned away from the phone. 'You'll be expected to cook breakfast – the guests usually like porridge as it gives them energy for a day's skiing, eggs and bacon, toast, and coffee. Strong coffee, none of that pale brown liquid that some people pass off as coffee. Then a cake or home-made biscuits to serve with drinks before dinner and a proper three-course evening meal. *I* will organize the wines,' he said fiercely as if that surely was something she was incapable of.

'Harvey… my ex-husband…' just saying his name hurt, 'we both did a Christie's wine course, so I know a bit about wine,' she said, determined to show him she was quite capable of choosing the right wines for a meal.

Lawrence looked dubious, 'You seem to have done a lot of courses, but none of these are professional, and we're talking *professional* here, Eloise. The people who come to this chalet expect the best; we rarely have families who are happy with anything warm and filling to eat. They can't afford the weekly rate.'

'Understood.' She didn't think she'd like the sorts of rich people who came here at all.

Lawrence must have guessed her feelings from her expression for he said, 'You're not here to like the guests but to cook for them. They arrive tomorrow evening for the week, then leave before Christmas. I want to see the menus for dinner and for the next week. You can cook us a sample dinner tonight; I've invited some friends to come round. Make a shopping list and Theo will take you to the shops shortly and tell you which ones we use, but you can take one of the jeeps and go yourself after that.' She remembered she'd seen a couple of sand-coloured jeeps parked outside.

'You just buy the food, not the drink, you'll have a credit card to pay for it and I want all the receipts given in to me every week, is that clear?' He was frowning again, a look of desperation in his eyes. 'Your salary will be paid into your bank account at the end of every week. You get a free ski pass and have one day off a week, the changeover day, which is usually Saturday, though I expect a dinner to be cooked for the new guests that evening. If you want to ski, you must fit it in around your work, do you understand?' He stared balefully at her as if he was certain she did not.

'Of course.' She stared him out; she may feel terrified inside but she was not going to give him the satisfaction of knowing it.

He went on. 'I'll give you the list of this week's guests. I always ask them if there are any foods they can't eat so that you can steer clear of those. Some people don't eat things for religious or health reasons,' his voice was edged with boredom as if she ought to know these things, which she did, but he seemed to think he must point them out. 'I assume you can produce good vegetarian and vegan dishes?' he finished.

Vegetarian wasn't difficult, she loved vegetables and often cooked a vegetable dish at home, but she wasn't sure exactly what vegan entailed and she wasn't going to ask Lawrence. 'And what happens if you don't like my cooking?' she eyed him firmly.

'Well then you'll have to go home and I'll have to buy in expensive food from a friend of mine which will cut my profit margin almost to the bone, which I can ill afford to do. I've lost enough money over this chef business as it is.' He handed her a list of the guests and told her to come back in half an hour with her menus for the week, 'And if we like the dinner you cook for us tonight you can do the same menu tomorrow as well.' He threw the remark out as if he was awarding her a prize as she escaped from the room.

4

The kitchen was another shock. It was more like an operating theatre. Eloise remembered the cluttered cosy room it used to be – the hub of the chalet – that drew them all in, with its ancient, temperamental cooker that demanded a high level of TLC, and a huge free-standing fridge that hummed and hawed to itself in the corner. An old wooden table had stood in the centre of the room where they congregated to eat, write postcards to their friends, or just chat and joke with each other or whoever was cooking, whilst the children would draw or build something out of Lego.

All that had gone and been replaced by a cruel-looking steel cooker with a long row of shiny knobs. Instead of the table a great cube stood in the middle of the room with various slots in it, housing baskets with other kitchen paraphernalia arranged in them like a display in a shop. Above was a high steel pole with pans and other cooking utensils hanging from it like instruments of torture. The walls once decked in posters, drawings, holiday photos and postcards now held severe-looking cupboards, which, she assumed, hid yet more kitchen appliances.

The room, with its aura of stark professionalism, seemed to mock her, as if deriding her cosy home cooking. Fighting down her panic, she sat on the window seat with her folder and began to go through it. Tonight's dinner was to be her test and, now she was here in the thick of it, she was determined to combat Lawrence's obvious fears of her incompetence. She checked through the list of guests arriving the following evening, worried about finding they all had impossible food intolerances.

There were six people on the list – four men and two women – and to her relief no one seemed to have any intolerances, or they weren't listed.

She took longer than half an hour to make up her menus. She would have liked to go to the shops first to see if they had all the ingredients she needed, but they were down in the village, and would take too much time to walk to. Before she had finished making a shopping list, Theo came in, with Bert skittering behind.

'Lawrence has had to go,' he said, 'but I'm to take you to the shops for the food. Here's your credit card.' He handed it to her; 'I'm ready when you are.' He looked wistfully out of the window at the mountains now disappearing in the dusk and she guessed he'd much rather be out there skiing on the last run down than trailing round a supermarket, but then so would she.

She'd been fortunate to learn to ski as a child and taken a skiing holiday most years in various resorts, though it was three years since she'd last been. Now back here, in a once familiar and loved place she yearned to go out again, to rediscover the places she used to know. But that was for later, now she must grapple with this cooking lark and produce a meal fit for Lawrence's discerning guests.

As he drove her back into the village, Theo told her the best shops to use. 'We always buy the cheese from the shop on the square and the meat from the butcher a little further down. Lawrence won't buy meat from the supermarket; he says it has no taste. But you can buy other stuff there,' he said. 'And if you need wine for cooking, ask Lawrence and he'll order it.'

She nodded to show she'd heard his instructions while deciding to forget that last one about the wine, not being prepared to wait until Lawrence was available for something she was more than qualified to do herself. He could choose what wines they drank but *not* the ones she wanted to use for the cooking. She was the cook, or rather the *chef*, and barring food intolerances, she'd put what she wanted into her dishes.

They arrived at the centre of the village and she looked eagerly out of the window to see how much it had changed, but to her relief, among some new and bright-looking shops, she saw some of the old, familiar ones.

'Do you live out here?' she asked Theo as he slowed down to park, thinking how much Kit and Lizzie would envy his life.

'Sort of,' he said, 'for the skiing season anyway, and then I go to Mum, who lives in Italy, for the summer.'

'Lucky you, so you have the best of both worlds.' She wondered who his mother was, but she didn't ask.

'Yup, but I want to be a skiing instructor, so I'm hoping to train for that next year, and study languages – French, German and Italian,' he said. 'I can do all that out here, fit it in while helping Dad.'

She was touched by his enthusiasm, her heart aching with missing Kit and Lizzie and their bright faces. She felt incomplete without them. Theo parked the car and they got out.

'Eloise... I don't believe it.' A female voice cut through

her thoughts like a clarion call. She spun round and saw Saskia Williams whom she'd last seen – some years ago – as a harassed mum at the primary school gates in London.

'Saskia, what a surprise.' She was enveloped in a bear hug.

'Are you out here for Christmas with Harvey and the twins?' Saskia released her. 'So good to see you.' She squeezed her arm, grinning with pleasure.

'And you.' Eloise stared at her. Saskia looked good, her face was tanned and her dark hair pushed back by a wide blue band covering her ears. Mixed feelings chased through her. This often happened when she met girl friends, especially ones she hadn't seen for ages, as she wondered if they'd slept with her ex-husband.

But all that was behind her and she must forget it. It was amazing to find Saskia here. It was ages since they'd last seen each other because Saskia and her family had moved to Norfolk when her children went to secondary school and they had lost touch.

'So you're here with Harvey, Kit and Lizzie?' Saskia repeated.

Eloise was aware that Theo was getting impatient. She said quickly, 'No, it's a long story and I haven't time to tell you now. Harvey and I are divorced, Kit and Lizzie are in Tibet on their gap year and I'm out here to cook in my godfather's chalet, Jacaranda. This is Theo…'

'Of course, I've seen you around,' Saskia exclaimed, smiling at Theo. 'Lawrence is your father, owns Jacaranda.'

'Yup, that's right,' Theo said, edging towards the shops.

Saskia regarded Eloise with sympathy. 'Really sorry about your divorce, love. Toby and I have been divorced for ages. I live with Quinn Pearson now… you know, the food writer, although he's lost his sense of taste.' She lowered her voice, 'He's much older than me but cosy and...' she leant in, dropping her voice still lower, 'he's fabulously rich and I got so tired of never having enough money with dear Tobes, always having to worry if the next bill would be paid or if there'd be bailiffs smashing down the door.' Noticing that Theo was getting impatient, Saskia said, 'Might see you tonight if you're staying at Jacaranda. We're coming to dinner to try out the new chef.'

5

Eloise could feel Lawrence's impatience smoking off him like dry ice as he explained how the gleaming oven worked. He was waiting for them, pacing like a prowling panther when she and Theo returned from shopping, and when Theo had lugged it all into the kitchen and scooted off with Bert to meet up with friends, she was left, much to her consternation, alone with Lawrence.

'Show me the menu for tonight so I can choose the right wines,' he demanded. 'I need to put the whites in the fridge, and bring up the reds from downstairs.'

She pulled her menu for dinner out of her bag; the paper was creased and tattered now – rather like she felt. She was still struggling to overcome her panic that Quinn Pearson, the renowned food writer – with or without working taste buds – was coming to dinner tonight. This really was a baptism of fire.

Lawrence took the menu from her, smoothing it down on top of the fearsome cube, the steel cooking utensils gleaming on the rail above his head. He frowned as he read the list, his mouth tight, as if trying to contain his displeasure. She was about to explain that she was going to copy it out more neatly when he pushed the crumpled menu back at her.

'So the canapés to have with the drinks are Parmesan

wafers, raw vegetables with a creamy dip, and spiced nuts, followed by the starter – a tomato sorbet garnished with avocado and chives – then lamb in red wine, and *Moroccan* oranges... whatever's that?'

He reminded her of a difficult child picking over the food on his plate. 'It's the pudding. A salad of fresh oranges with chopped dates and cinnamon,' she eyed him firmly, 'and to go with it, baby meringues made with brown sugar.'

'Quite sweet, perhaps a Sauvignon Blanc,' he murmured to himself.

She waited for him to ask her what wine she would use for cooking the lamb, but to her relief he did not. To distract him further, she said, 'I saw a friend of mine in the village who I haven't seen for ages, Saskia Williams... maybe she's not called that now as she's divorced. She said she was coming to dinner this evening.' Eloise wondered how well Lawrence knew her.

'Did she mention her partner Quinn Pearson...' he watched her carefully as if wondering whether to tell her Quinn was a famous food writer.

'The food writer, yes I know. Are they married?' she asked nonchalantly, determined to conceal from him how daunted she was by the prospect of feeding Quinn.

'I've no idea. I doubt it. Anyway, I'm deciding which wines to serve with the meal. And while we're on the subject, what wine will you use to cook the lamb in?' he frowned at her.

Her spirits fell – she had not got away with it after all. 'I bought one like I use at home, a heavy-bodied Burgundy. It's always been a success and I wanted to get all the ingredients I need for the dinner, so I could get on with it. I know you choose the wines to drink with the meals.' She smiled at him as if it were no big deal.

'Fair enough, if you are going to cook with it,' he said, skimming through the menu again, sighing heavily as he wondered aloud if he had the right wine to drink with the lamb or would have to go out and buy some.

He sighed even more when she asked him to run through the instructions again as to how the cooker worked. They sounded so complicated she hadn't taken them in the first time he'd told her. She'd have a dummy run when she was alone. She was relieved when the telephone rang and he left her to it.

She'd given many a dinner party over the years, so she decided she'd pretend this was just the same, she'd cook dishes she knew and hope for the best, and if her best weren't good enough... Better not go there.

To suit the part she wondered if she was supposed to dress as a 'chef' in a gleaming white uniform, not that she possessed anything like that, and anyway these auspicious guests would surely not expect to meet her, so she decided she would wear her apron, a present from the twins that she hadn't yet used. She pulled it out from its packet and saw that it had, 'Kiss the Cook' written in large letters over the front. It was hardly professional, but it would have to do, she didn't have another. It made her smile thinking of them, bringing them closer.

She turned on the oven and to her relief it began to heat up. Looking through the cupboards, she found a deep dish for the leg of lamb and settled it in with the wine and herbs and put it in the oven to cook.

Theo was the waiter for the evening and, judging by the amount of food he stole and nibbled, the chief food taster too. 'Great, wow these are great,' he said, sampling the Parmesan wafers, 'and those tiny meringue things,' he stole one, 'do hope there'll be leftovers.'

'Aren't you eating with the others?' she asked, while she sliced up the oranges and dates for the pudding. She was glad he was here, his enthusiasm for her cooking upping her confidence.

'No, I'm helping serve then I'm going out,' he said. 'We'll stack all the plates in the dishwasher and Vera will clean up – you've met her, haven't you?'

'No, who is she?' Eloise asked.

'She cleans. She comes every day, but perhaps you missed her today. Lawrence nicked her from someone else who treated her badly, wouldn't even let her have a glass of water without asking.' He exclaimed, 'Some people.'

'I look forward to meeting her, I'll try not to make too much mess.' She was relieved that she didn't have to do the clearing up as well. She was exhausted and she was only halfway through cooking the dinner. She cleared a place on the cube to set out the bits she needed for the starter, wishing that battered old table that had so much more space was still there in the middle of the room.

With its new role she accepted that the layout of the chalet was different to the time she was last here. These rich guests were far too important to eat in the kitchen, as she had done in the past, but at least it meant she could stay out of the way in here. Bert came bustling in, sniffing hopefully round the floor, when he didn't find anything he gave a long sniff of disapproval and left the room.

Half an hour later she heard the guests arrive, clumping into the hall in their boots, having had to walk through the snow from the car before changing into their shoes for inside.

Saskia crept into the kitchen. 'Wow, look at you, Kiss the Cook,' she giggled, 'is that an invitation to Lawrence?'

'No, of course not,' Eloise said hurriedly; she hadn't

34

thought of that. 'The twins gave it to me for my birthday, and it's the best one I have, my others are faded or stained. I pushed it in at the last minute without thinking. No one's going to see me anyway.'

'They might come in to congratulate you, well not Aurelia, she can't bear anyone to upstage her.' Saskia rolled her eyes.

'Aurelia?' Eloise's heart did an annoying little dip, remembering Lawrence's conversation with her on the phone making her think she was waiting for her to fail so she could rush to the rescue. 'The ready-made food person?'

'Yes, Quinn thinks it's disgusting; he believes food should be freshly cooked not frozen or cooled and put in some tarted-up box for someone to shove in their own oven.'

'I suppose,' Eloise said mournfully, dreading what he'd think of her cooking.

'Better go and join them, we'll catch up later; so glad you're here. Ohooo, baby meringues.' She stretched out her hand towards them.

'Oh, please don't. Theo has eaten some already and there won't be enough,' she begged her.

'OK,' Saskia smiled as she left the room. 'If there are any leftovers… which I doubt, maybe I can take them home in a doggy bag.'

Eloise laughed, 'I'll see to it, if Theo hasn't got there first.'

A little later, Theo, who'd been pouring out the drinks, came into the kitchen, announcing the guests were about to eat.

'Most of your canapés went,' he said, 'now I'll take in the starters.' He watched her putting the finishing touches to them. Individual tomato sorbets scattered with avocado and chives. 'Too pretty to eat, but they're not much more than a mouthful,' he said, picking up the tray.

'They are only the starters,' she wailed but he'd gone, leaving her feeling anxious that they'd complain the portions were too small.

The evening passed in a whirl, Eloise was so tired she felt like a robot. Each time Theo came back with the finished plates he told her their verdict.

'They liked the sorbets but Aurelia thought they were too cold,' he announced. 'Lawrence said the lamb was not very well carved.'

'I thought it easier to carve it in the kitchen,' Eloise said, wondering how many more criticisms there'd be.

At last the dinner was finished and when Theo had stacked the plates in the dishwasher and she'd left the pans soaking for Vera, she was about to slip up to bed when Theo, his jacket on ready to go out and Bert jumping impatiently round his feet, appeared saying; 'Lawrence said to go and meet the guests, they want to thank you for the dinner.'

'Oh, no,' she said, 'no doubt Lawrence will tell me every detail of what they said tomorrow.'

'No, you must go, it won't take long, they'll be gone soon.' He went out and she heard him open the door and felt the shaft of icy air come in before he closed it behind him.

Taking off her apron and pushing back her hair, she went down the passage to the large room that now took up most of the ground floor of the chalet. Struggling to calm her nerves, she entered the room and stood awkwardly just inside surveying them.

For a split second in her befuddled mind she thought a polar bear had got in until she saw it was a woman, her blonde hair smoothed back from her face by a sort of white fur halo with two little tufts like ears sticking up. She was dressed in a furry white jacket and white trousers too.

Saskia noticed Eloise. 'Eloise, what a scrummy dinner,' she exclaimed and then all of the other guests turned towards her, murmuring small platitudes with kind smiles, all except for the woman in white, who said dryly, 'Darling, just a few little tips. I had some ice shards in my sorbet, and the meringues were too sweet and...'

'It was all absolutely delicious,' Saskia said firmly. 'Didn't you think so, Quinn?' She nudged the rotund man with curly grey hair and a craggy, bronzed face sitting beside her.

Eloise held her breath waiting for the great man's verdict.

'Indeed... perhaps the presentation could have been a little sharper, but no, a good try.' He smiled in her direction.

'Thank you,' Eloise was encouraged by his smile. 'Good-night,' she said quickly and she left them, fighting back her tears of exhaustion, before Lawrence had time to add his own criticism of her failings.

6

The dazzling light cut through the gap in the curtains, waking her, and for a moment Eloise lay there trying to get her bearings, before springing up in alarm. She glanced at her clock, almost ten o'clock! If she hadn't failed the cooking test last night, she'd failed big time this morning by oversleeping and missing breakfast. By now it would be too late for the early risers who wanted to beat the queues to get up the mountain.

But this week's guests had not yet arrived, she reminded herself as she pulled on her clothes, there was only Theo and Lawrence; surely they could get their own breakfast? She'd make sure she'd be up bright and early tomorrow when the guests had arrived. Theo was very easy-going but Lawrence was not, after all he was responsible for running the chalet, and having had one of his chefs running off was perhaps wary of all of them. She hurried to get ready before running downstairs, gearing herself up for his disapproval. She dashed into the kitchen and a small wiry woman in a blue overall who was polishing up the monstrous cooker turned and smiled at her. 'Good morning.'

'Good morning... You must be Vera. I'm Eloise. I... I overslept, have they had breakfast?'

'Yes, Theo was up very early to go to the mountains and Lawrence has gone out. He said to remind you the new guests arrive this afternoon and please make a cake.' Vera gave the cooker one last sweep of her cloth before going over to the sink, her darting movements reminding Eloise of an eager bird.

'Was he angry?' she asked.

Vera looked round at her, frowning in surprise, 'No, why would he be angry?'

'Because I wasn't up in time to cook his breakfast.'

'He usually gets his own, or sometimes I do it for him,' Vera glowed as she spoke of him. Eloise remembered Theo had told her that Lawrence had rescued her from an unkind employer.

She was stressing too much about Lawrence's opinion of her. Surely if he'd wanted her to do breakfast he'd have thundered up the stairs to get her out of bed? Having been let down by so many chefs he was obviously worried she'd be a failure too, she would show him she wasn't, that he could rely on her.

'But *you* must have something,' Vera bustled round, her arms swinging like a windmill. 'Coffee machine is there, tea and coffee in the cupboard, eggs and milk in the fridge... porridge there.' Eloise guessed from her accent that Vera was from the Italian side of Switzerland.

'I'll just have coffee and toast, but if you're busy in here I don't want to get in your way.'

'I've finished in here, now I will do the big room, it's no trouble.'

Even though Theo had assured her that Vera would cope with the pans and dishes, Eloise felt guilty about all the dinner party stuff she'd left in the sink. She said, 'I'm sorry I left such a mess last night, I only arrived yesterday and I had to cook dinner for Lawrence's friends as a sort of test to see if I was up to cooking for his rich clients. I meant to clear things before you arrived this morning, I'm sorry I didn't.'

Vera laughed, 'You should see how some of these cooks – *chefs* they like to call themselves – leave the place. Don't you worry, now have your breakfast and then make your cake. What kind will it be?'

'Do you think they want a sort of sponge with layers of icing or something more substantial like a fruit or carrot cake, or chocolate?' Eloise went over to inspect the coffee machine – another gleaming appliance she felt was better suited to a coffee bar than a home.

Seeing her consternation, Vera came over and showed her how the coffee machine worked, saying she'd have coffee now too before starting on the main room. 'I think it's best to have more cake than icing,' she said, 'then when they arrive you can ask them what they like, some don't even want cake, though what about Christmas cake? Lawrence loves his Christmas cake.'

Christmas, why did she keep forgetting that it was only two weeks away? Probably because she couldn't bear to think about it, as she was now on her own instead of being surrounded, as she'd been in the past, by her family.

'I usually make mine some weeks before Christmas, so it can marinate in the brandy,' she explained to Vera.

'You could start it today, as you will have some time before the clients arrive.'

'I haven't got the ingredients,' Eloise said, 'I should have thought about it and bought them yesterday.'

'You can go to the shops. Lawrence left you the car keys, he said to use the jeep when you want.'

Eloise felt slightly queasy at the thought of driving down

the snow-covered roads to the village. 'When will Theo be back?' she asked.

Vera smiled, 'He's off skiing and will be back just in time to go to the airport to pick up the clients.' She frowned, 'Can you not drive?'

'Yes I can, I've just never driven in the snow, but I will. I'll just have some breakfast and make the cake for this afternoon. I think I'll do a lemon drizzle cake, most people like that, and perhaps some shortbread biscuits, and then I'll go to the shops for the dried fruit, nuts and brandy. Or should I wait to see if Lawrence has some brandy already?'

'He's got a special brandy, so I'd ask him if you can use it first, he keeps his eye on his cellar.' Vera's voice held a warning. Eloise wondered if other chefs had been driven to raid the cellar to gear themselves up for the job. 'The shops close over lunchtime, they open again in the late afternoon,' Vera reminded her, before saying she'd better see to the main room.

Left alone in the kitchen, Eloise spent the morning baking and prepared some of the dinner for the guests arriving later. While the cake was cooking, she went outside to get her bearings; the resort seemed to have changed so much since she was last here all those years ago.

The thick carpet of snow crunched under her feet. Tiny footprints left by the birds crisscrossed parts of it, along with Bert's paw prints. She hadn't seen him this morning and she wondered where he was.

The land that enclosed the chalet was edged on two sides by fir trees high enough to provide some privacy but not too high to overpower it. The front of the chalet was open to the mountain and the view down to the village, and the side coming from the road had fewer trees clumped on one side, leaving space enough to drive in. The blue minibus Theo had collected her in was parked beside a jeep, the second one had gone, the ridges of the tyre marks where it had stood still frozen from the night.

She walked along the road. Way down, she saw the stream cutting its path through the snow. She smiled, remembering how she'd got stuck in it once, when she was about ten. She and her sister, Joanna, would ski down to the bus stop and they and other children would race each other on sledges. It would be hazardous to ski or sledge down there now amongst all the new chalets.

She headed back towards Jacaranda; the air was pure and cold, the mountains rising in the distance ahead of her, stark white against the sky.

The stillness and the peace was suddenly shattered by the sound of a car shooting up the hill. She stood back and a dark red sports car whizzed past her and turned into Jacaranda, coming to a screeching halt. She hurried on up to see who it was and as she arrived she saw Aurelia getting out. She opened the boot and took out a box, then seeing her, she said, 'Lawrence has ordered a cake from me, he's worried that you won't have time to make one for the clients arriving this afternoon.' There was a smug look of defiance on her face, her cold blue eyes staring scornfully at Eloise.

She was *not* going to feel intimidated by her. 'Oh, thanks, but I've made one already, I've just come to take it out of the oven.' She eyed the pink box in Aurelia's hands.

'What kind is it?' Aurelia asked.

'Lemon drizzle.'

'Oh, a nursery cake, one for the children's tea, that's nice, though there won't be any children,' Aurelia said dismissively.

Before she could think of a retort, another car arrived –

the jeep – with Lawrence in it, and Eloise escaped, leaving Aurelia to him. Inside, she struggled with the anger rising in her. How dare Aurelia try to undermine her by turning up bearing cakes like this? Had Lawrence told her he was unhappy with last night's dinner and instructed Aurelia to bring it round, perhaps ordering even more food to feed his discerning guests? And why go behind her back? Couldn't he at least give her a chance – it was so rude and demeaning.

She hadn't time to worry now though or her cake would burn and that would be the last straw when Aurelia had probably bought round a perfect croquembouche. She hurried into the kitchen to take it out of the oven and put in the rounds of shortbread she'd prepared. The warm, sweet smell of baking went some way to soothe her. She would not put up with Aurelia trying to upstage her, she would make that clear with Lawrence the moment she saw him.

She heard footsteps clumping down the passage into the kitchen and she tensed herself for the fight. Even if Aurelia came with him she would say her piece. Her job was difficult enough without this though.

Lawrence entered alone, carrying the pink cardboard box she'd seen in Aurelia's hands. He put it down on the table. *Tempting Delights by Aurelia*, it proclaimed in black scrawly writing on the lid.

'Hello, Eloise,' he smiled, 'hope you slept well. I left you lying in this morning as the real work starts today.'

She waited for him to tell her that he'd decided that Aurelia would prepare most of the meals, but he seemed cheerful, asking if she had everything she wanted. Instead of making her feel at home this unnerved her, wondering why he had ordered a cake from Aurelia having left a message with Vera to ask her to make one too.

As he said nothing about it, she said firmly, 'I'll be up early tomorrow. Tell me what time the guests want breakfast and it will be all ready for them.'

'Good, we'll ask them when they arrive.' He eyed the lemon drizzle cake cooling on the rack. 'Mmm, you've been baking.'

'Yes, Vera told me you wanted me to make a cake for the guests this afternoon,' she said, Aurelia's sarcastic remark of it being a 'nursery cake' still rankling.

'I did, and Aurelia sent a cake too,' he gestured towards the box, 'in case you didn't have time to bake one before everyone arrived.'

'I know, I've just seen her. Is she going to appear at every meal with some dish she has cooked and bill you for it?' Her voice sounded sharper than she meant it too.

He looked horrified, 'No, why ever would you think that? She just thought you might find it difficult on your first day to get everything done – she did it to be kind.' He regarded her with disapproval as if *she* was the one in the wrong, misinterpreting a good deed for a bad one.

He left the room before she could explain that Aurelia had told her that *he* had ordered it. Was that true and was Lawrence trying to avoid telling her that he had Aurelia on back-up? Or had Aurelia lied about Lawrence ordering the cake, and if so why? What was she trying to achieve?

Eloise opened the box containing Aurelia's creation and inside was a beautifully iced chocolate cake with *Welcome to Verbier* written in white icing, making her lemon drizzle cake look decidedly underdressed.

Who was the welcome to Verbier for? She didn't feel it was for her. It was more like a warning from Aurelia to keep off her turf.

She struggled with a sudden wave of homesickness but, what was worse, Aurelia had succeeded in making Lawrence think she was a bitch to undermine her generous gesture when in fact Aurelia was throwing down a challenge.

It looked as if she had a fight on her hands and she must do all that she could to win it.

7

It was bitterly cold but the sheer beauty of the sun touching the tops of the mountains and the crisp snow beneath his skis filled him with exhilaration. Lawrence pushed off down the slope, it was still icy so he must take care, by the time it had softened up he'd be back in the chalet seeing to the guests. He needed this hour to himself, just him and the mountains – though he wasn't the only skier here, but these first few were the fanatics, the real lovers of the sport and the majesty of nature. Very soon the slopes would be jostling with all the holidaymakers, swarming over the snow like multicoloured ants.

Here in his own space, the white peaks reaching on into infinity, he felt calmer, more able to assess his thoughts. The guests had arrived last night, quite late as their flight had been delayed. Eloise had made a delicious cake, and the home-made shortbread biscuits were perfect, so different to the bought variety. She'd laid them out on the dining table in the living room, alongside a rather sickly-looking cake Aurelia had given him for the guests' tea, only they hadn't arrived in time to eat them, so Eloise had put them away to bring out again today.

He had been surprised at Eloise's reaction to Aurelia's gift. He hadn't thought she'd take offence. Perhaps she felt intimidated by her, she was after all still settling in, but she should have taken Aurelia's gesture in good grace. Aurelia meant well, in fact she was a great support to him and the running of Jacaranda.

It was a difficult job being the host to strangers in his own home, for he saw Jacaranda as his home and business now. Having worked in hospitality in a well-known vineyard in France it had been good training, though nothing like what he experienced day to day at Jacaranda.

Some of the guests were lovely and had become friends, but he was dreading the people coming for Christmas who were mega-rich, and most likely spoilt, and were very disappointed that they had not been able to stay in one of the new, eye-wateringly expensive chalets down in the village, as they'd been booked up for months in advance, so they must 'make do' with Jacaranda. He suspected they would be very challenging.

Amongst the Christmas guests was a mother-in-law in her early sixties who didn't ski, which meant she would probably stay in for much of the time and expect lunch, which would add extra work for Eloise. He'd confided his fear to Aurelia, who said she'd be more than happy to provide lunch, but that would be an added expense and he needed to conserve his money to pay for the intensive repairs Jacaranda urgently needed.

Jacaranda needed to be rewired and to have new plumbing, he could not put it off any longer. These old chalets needed to be able to work with modern devices and he would like to put in another shower room and revamp one or two of the other bathrooms. All this had to be done well and not spoil the overall look of Jacaranda – and all of it needed money. He might have to close the chalet during the summer season while the refurbishments were being done, which would mean losing vital income. There was a lot to consider.

He did not want to burden his father with his worries, he knew how much he loved Jacaranda, it held so many of his precious memories of his beloved partner, Maddy. Desmond had tried to stay on here without her after she'd died, but it had been too hard and he had moved to Antigua to escape the constant reminders of her loss. He understood, and one of the many reasons he was determined to keep Jacaranda going was because it had been Maddy's idea to open the chalet for holiday guests to help pay for its upkeep, so Desmond and Lawrence could keep it. He remembered her enthusiasm and how planning the business had lifted her up through her months of illness. Her courage kept him focused on making a success of it in her memory. One day he hoped his father would come back and see just how Maddy's dream had been realized. But he would not push him; he must come when he felt ready.

His face was tingling with cold now as he increased his speed, his body agile, taking quick turns, slicing down the mountain, and when he reached the end of the slope he was surging with life and energy. There were only gentle slopes now down to the gondola, and sadly there was no time for him to go up again. He'd ski down to the chalet through the trees and get back to work. There were a few maintenance jobs to be done, and he must get in the drinks and ensure that the tree and a wreath for the front door were in place in time to greet the guests who would be arriving at Jacaranda for Christmas next week.

He went slower now, eking out the time before he had to go back. He was still annoyed with Denise – the chef he'd employed for the whole season – flying off with that paunchy grey-haired banker in his private helicopter, leaving him in the lurch. She was a brilliant chef, she'd worked for him before and he'd paid over the odds for her. He hadn't been impressed when he'd discovered she'd just upped and gone, leaving only a scrappy note in her room by way of explanation, 'Sorry gone with Mike,' and he'd had to ask Aurelia to produce some of her wildly expensive meals, which had been a help, but he couldn't afford to splash out so much for long, and though she talked about 'mates rates' for things she wanted, she wasn't prepared to offer them to her 'mates' herself. The last two chefs he'd hired were worse than useless, aged chalet girls who thought producing something hot with plenty of ketchup for dinner and bought ice cream with melted chocolate as a pudding was all they needed to do to please the guests, leaving them plenty of time to hit the slopes and the bars.

Faced with having to shell out for yet more of Aurelia's 'Tempting Delights' (and she put her prices up for Christmas fare), he had taken his father's advice to contact Eloise, his father's goddaughter, who he couldn't remember meeting. She was – according to Desmond – a cordon bleu chef, though in fact she wasn't, but he didn't hold his exaggeration of her skills against his father, he always saw the best in people.

Eloise was doing her best, both dinners she'd produced so far had been good but not spectacular, and he now worried that her best might not be enough, or she'd panic and not be able to cope with the Christmas guests coming next week. He knew this was unfair, she had been honest about her cooking qualifications and his father had no idea of the quality needed today and had recommended her in good faith, but what made it worse was that he was banking on these Christmas guests to bring him continued success. They were his first clients from one of the top letting agencies, where he'd only recently been accepted. If their visit were a success the agency would send other rich clients his way, which would solve the problem of keeping Jacaranda safe.

Switzerland was expensive, and now there were so many chalets and hotels to stay in and cheaper resorts in France and Italy, it was getting increasingly difficult to keep the place filled with the sort of clientele he wanted… he needed well-paid adults who loved skiing and were out on the mountains most of the day, expecting only breakfast and dinner and sometimes a cake for tea.

He didn't encourage families with young children, he had nothing against small children, but there were too many hazards around the chalet, and if they were not kept a strict eye on they could wander out on the road, which seemed to have more cars each year, or through the trees and even down to the stream. There were always stories, mostly true, of adults as well as children wandering off in the dusk and getting lost; some were not found before it was too late.

'Lawrence, you're out early,' Aurelia called to him, disturbing his thoughts. She was standing by the entrance to the gondola. One came up from Medran and stopped here. There was another one that took skiers higher up to the top of the mountain. Aurelia was dressed in baby blue with a pink, no doubt cashmere, hat pulled over her ears.

He was about to answer when an Adonis of a ski guide carrying her skis joined her.

'How's your little cook?' she asked.

'Fine, thank you,' he said, wanting to be on his way as he had things to do before Theo brought this week's guests back to Jacaranda.

'Well you know where to come if she can't cope, let me

know if you want anything she can't manage.' There was a touch of mockery in her smile.

'I'm sure we'll be fine, Eloise knows what's she's doing,' he said, surprising himself by feeling protective towards her. 'Have a good day.' He turned and left.

He made his way through the other skiers, some having just come up from the village, hanging around waiting for friends, others coming out of the restaurant, or about to go up again, and a few, like him, skiing down to the bottom. It amused him that Aurelia, who could ski far better than most people, usually skied with a private guide. They were always good-looking men, and he wondered what else she expected from them.

Aurelia was a complicated woman, a beautiful one, but now he thought of it she reminded him of a spoilt little rich girl. She never seemed satisfied with anything or anyone, a misfortune he guessed that came from a deep insecurity. She'd come out here a year ago with Malcolm, an older man, who, rumour had it, was a rich lover helping her start up her business, providing sophisticated takeaways. These were aimed at people who didn't do their own cooking or were giving parties or just staying in and wanting to enjoy a delicious supper they hadn't had to cook themselves. They could pick up a meal from her shop, or if they ordered a meal in advance it would be delivered to their chalet. It was expensive but she used the best ingredients and all they needed to do was to put it in the oven. There was no mess and preparing to do, but still, he thought, she charged too much, but then if people were prepared to pay for it, bully for her.

Malcolm was not here that often, though she often spoke of him, and although she showed an interest in Lawrence and especially Jacaranda, he had steered clear of any romantic entanglements since a relationship he'd had with a French woman had drifted to a close last year.

Lawrence skied through the dark trees with quick, tight turns. High above him glided the gondolas. There was no one else about now as he was off-piste and he felt the joy of skiing, the silence in this part of the mountain away from the main runs and above the bustle of the village. He wished he could spend the day outside, go up higher and do one of the longer routes up to Mort Fort or down Tortin, but if he was to keep Jacaranda as his home he had to give the business his time and attention and just snatch days off when it was empty. Theo did a lot, but he needed to be around himself when they had guests, in case there was a drama: a plane ticket lost, a complaint, or an accident. There'd been quite a few of those over the years, and it wasn't the highlight of the job, trying to deal with fractious guests often fuelled by tiredness or alcohol.

He'd reached the bottom of the run now; it opened out to an easier slope used by the ski school for beginners. As he traversed across the well-used snow, the ridges from previous skiers softening in the sun, he thought fondly of his father. Now some time had passed, he might feel comforted to be back where he and Maddy had been so happy. He remembered his father explaining to him after his parents' divorce how he'd met the love of his life, though he added quickly that he had loved Agnes, his mother, but it had been a young love, full of passion and torment, and they were really so unsuited to settling down, and though they both loved him, they couldn't stay together without one of them destroying the other.

Not until he was older had he really understood. He adored his mother but she'd always felt distant, in a world of her own, and when Desmond met Maddy, such a warm and loving person, Lawrence found himself gravitating more towards her, which filled him with guilt, but whenever he was with his mother there were such dramas. Men were always falling in love with her and she, like a child with her toys, picked them up, played with them a little, before becoming bored and discarding them. She'd had two more children, his half-brother Nathan and half-sister Tia, with whom he got on well when he saw them. They lived in the US now, where their fathers – both different – lived. Both his mother and Maddy were dead and, he admitted with a touch of guilt, he missed Maddy far more than he did his own mother.

Yes, he thought as he came to the path that led to the chalet, he'd encourage Desmond to come here in the summer. He hadn't seen him since the summer before last when he'd visited him in Antigua. He knew Desmond hated not being able to ski as he used to any more, but surely he could walk on his beloved mountains among the alpine flowers? Perhaps it would not be too difficult to persuade him to visit, especially as it would give him a chance to see Theo again.

Thinking of Theo made him think of Georgia. They too had been badly matched. They'd met at university and had a brief but passionate affair that had led to Theo's arrival. Despite their love for him, they both agreed it wasn't enough to sustain a marriage.

Georgia now lived in Italy and she and Lawrence kept in touch about Theo and were always pleased to meet up with each other, though now that Theo was old enough to travel on his own they hadn't seen each other for over two years. Georgia was happily married with two little daughters, Theo's half-sisters, who adored their older brother. He liked

Fabien, Georgia's husband, and when they were all together they got on well; such was the mix of modern families.

He skied across to the chalet as far as he could, then took off his skies, clanking them together to shake off the snow before hoisting them onto his shoulder and walking the last bit. Knowing he wouldn't be skiing again that day, he put his skis in the shed outside before going in and taking off his boots in the hall. A warm, sweet aroma wrapped itself around him, a scent of fresh baking, oranges and brandy filling him with a feeling of well-being and, absurdly, of being at home.

8

It was not the Cordon Bleu Foundation course but her grandmother who'd taught Eloise how to cook Christmas pudding. In Granny's day it would have been thought a disgrace to buy such things ready-made, if you could buy them at all. In contrast, her mother always bought the Christmas puddings as, she said, she had better things to do than boil up a pudding for eight hours.

Eloise had no idea what the Christmas puddings would be like here, or even if they sold them as they were a British, not European, tradition. After the cake episode she did not want Aurelia turning up with one of hers, which she suspected would probably come in a gold pudding basin stamped with her name and proclaiming *Tempting Delight*, which sounded more like an aphrodisiac than a homely pudding.

The guests who'd arrived late last night had finally left the chalet with Theo to go down to the ski shop and get kitted out. The men of the party were up early, prowling around like hungry lions impatient to be off, while the women seemed more relaxed and said as it was their first day they'd rather get up there for lunch and ski afterwards. Theo also prowled about, longing to be free of his duties of settling in these guests, keen to get on the slopes himself. Bert too was restless and kept barking to go out.

'Lawrence promised I could go when they have got everything, but it looks like I won't get there until it's dark,' Theo moaned, picking at the raisins and candied fruit marinating in brandy for the mince pies.

'I expect they are tired after their journey. There's nothing worse than sitting around for hours waiting for a plane to arrive. Travel stress is exhausting,' Eloise said, 'and this lovely air is apt to make one feel soporific as well.' She wondered how it must feel for Theo, always having to share his home with strangers, new people arriving every week or so.

'S'pose.' Theo dug his fingers in the mixture again, so she had to move the bowl out of his way. He was just like Kit and Lizzie, hovering round her in the kitchen, sampling her food before it was even ready. Kit said he preferred uncooked cake mixture to cooked so she needn't bother with putting it in the oven. She thought about them now and hoped they were all right out in the wide world. She realized that she was grateful to be here with lots to occupy her, to take her mind off worrying about her children.

After a bit of urging the women to hurry up from the men, the party finally left with Theo. They had all skied before so they knew the form, and with luck, Theo said, he hoped he could leave them to it, though he had to hang about until they were all kitted out and ready to go.

'I do remind them, but they often leave their passports or even money behind, or once,' Theo raised his eyes, 'a woman forgot to change into her ski boots and had to come back here and fetch them, holding everyone up even more.'

There seemed to be no such dramas today and at last Eloise and Vera were left in peace in the chalet and sat down to a cup of coffee and a slice of lemon drizzle cake. Aurelia's show-off chocolate cake would do for tea. Just the sight of the box upset her, not because of the cake but because Lawrence thought she'd been ungrateful for Aurelia's 'kind' deed and slighted this woman, whom she suspected was trying to take her place.

'You good cook.' Vera took another biscuit. 'Proper home cooking, not fancy stuff.'

'Thank you,' Eloise said, 'it's what I like best.' She got up to go and check on the Christmas puddings. She hoped she'd have time to go down to the village and get her boots and skis sorted out and find time to ski tomorrow. She didn't dare leave the Christmas puddings cooking to go skiing today – though it was so bright and beautiful – she couldn't risk them boiling dry if she got held up on the mountain. No, she would wait at the chalet with Vera. She didn't want to give Lawrence or Aurelia any more reasons to criticize her.

She wondered how old Vera was. She could be anything from fifty to seventy, or even older. Despite her small stature, she possessed great strength, she'd seen her heave the heavy furniture away from the wall to sweep behind it, and when she'd offered to help, Vera had waved her away, saying she could manage.

'So how long have you worked for Lawrence?' Eloise asked with a smile, not wanting to seem too inquisitive but longing to know.

'Four years,' Vera said, getting up from the table and collecting up their mugs and taking them to the sink to rinse them out. 'He is a good man,' she said, 'I would die for him, in fact I might have died without him.'

Before Eloise could question her further they heard the back door open and the sound of someone clumping in.

Lawrence came into the kitchen, his face flushed by the cold, his hair standing up like burnished feathers on his head. 'I can't resist the smell of your baking, Eloise,' he said, 'hope there is some I can eat. I'm starving.'

'Of course, help yourself.' Eloise wondered if he was trying to be friendly after their contretemps over Aurelia yesterday.

'I will make you a coffee. Was the skiing good?' Vera said, drying her hands before grappling with the coffee machine to make more coffee. Eloise pushed the biscuits towards him. Perhaps he'd rather have a slice of Aurelia's cake, though she wouldn't draw attention to it and remind him of his reprimand of her ingratitude.

'What else is cooking, smells like Christmas pudding?' he asked her.

'Yes, I thought I better make them as I didn't know what kind they sell in the village, or if they sell them at all.'

'Aurelia sells them, she makes all the things the Brits don't seem to be able to live without,' he said, smiling at Vera as she handed him his coffee.

She would, Eloise thought, wondering if she'd appear with a whole hamper of festive goodies.

'We Brits are an odd race,' Lawrence went on, 'we love to travel, but we don't like so-called foreign food and prefer to take our own. You should see the laden cars of some of the Brits coming here who self-cater, bringing marmite, cereals, even Cadbury's chocolate when Switzerland is the home of chocolate.'

'And yet your guests seem to expect the highest quality of food, not just spag bol and sausages,' she said.

'But they are different. They have money to spare and are used to eating in all the top restaurants throughout the world.' Lawrence took another biscuit before making for the door. 'See you later.' He lifted his mug to them in a salute and both women listened to him going along the passage and down the stairs to his office.

Half an hour later Saskia rang. 'Can we meet up, Eloise? I'm not skiing today and Quinn is playing bridge with his mates and I want to catch up with all your news.'

'I'd love it, but I've got the Christmas puddings cooking,' Eloise explained.

Saskia laughed, 'But surely you buy them? They take forever, don't they?'

'Yes, but I think they're worth it. I suppose I could leave them for a little while, if I don't go too far away. I'd love to see you.' Eloise felt a sudden fondness towards her, longing to see someone familiar even though they hadn't seen each other for years.

'Let's meet at Carrefour, have a drink and a quick lunch, or do you have to make lunch for everyone?' Saskia asked.

'No, I just cook the dinner.'

'Great. Meet you there in about half an hour, then,' Saskia said.

Making sure the puddings had enough water to stop them drying out for a few more hours and asking Vera if she could check on them, Eloise put on her snow boots and ski jacket and set off. She said nothing to Lawrence, not wanting to disturb him in his office, and after all she was free to make her own decisions over planning her cooking and going out.

Carrefour was a restaurant perched at the top of the Rouge, a slope for beginners, and a welcome stop for skiers coming down from some of the main runs after a day's skiing. Saskia was already there when Eloise arrived. They ordered a croque monsieur and a glass of wine and Saskia began at once to quiz her about how her life had panned out since they'd last seen each other.

'You and Harvey always seemed so happy together,' she said. 'I'm so sorry it ended in divorce.'

Eloise wanted to put their divorce behind her and not keep resurrecting the pain, prodding the wound by retelling the story, but it would sit between them, so it was better to tell Saskia and hope that would be the end of it.

'I suppose everyone but me knew he was sleeping around. I guessed it, especially when he was away on business, but I loved him and he was always loving to me and, more importantly, I wanted to give the twins a secure upbringing.'

'Did he go off with someone else then?' Saskia asked.

'He said he had someone, but now I can think more rationally about it, I suspect he couldn't bear to be stuck with me in the "empty nest" once the twins left.' Her eyes glazed with tears.

That day would remain with her forever, Harvey, recently back from a trip, explaining that he felt trapped, wanted to fly free, his face taut with injustice, making her feel she had imprisoned him against his will.

She must fly free herself but talking about it pulled her back into the misery of it instead of propelling her forward into a new life.

Saskia squeezed her hand. 'Going through a divorce is hell, even if you hate your partner,' she said, 'you sort of hope you can somehow switch on the magic the relationship once had, all that love gone in a puff of smoke.' She clicked her fingers.

'It's true. I was so shattered by his announcement. I knew he was unfaithful, played around when he went on his trips to holiday resorts, but somehow I never thought he'd leave. He went almost at once, as if he had a taxi ticking by outside.' She tried to joke. 'Then the divorce papers arrived and I came to my senses. Although I still loved him, I accepted that the marriage was over and I must let him go. We met up to discuss selling the house but we were like two strangers,' she shrugged, 'who didn't even speak the same language. We never really said goodbye, just packed up our marriage and walked away. Perhaps if we had talked it through, it would be easier to come to terms with now.' She stared out of the window at the slope beside her, watching a class of children struggling down.

'And horrid for you losing the twins as well, not that you really have *lost* them of course, but them going off on their gap year is hard, especially over Christmas,' Saskia said.

'They'd been planning it for ages and everything was set up. They're going to uni next year, so they couldn't put it off, though they did suggest they would if I needed them to stay with me.' Eloise remembered their crestfallen faces at the thought of cancelling their plans, and yet they were decent enough to suggest that they would stay behind with her, and she knew that if she'd wanted them to, they would have done so, but she wouldn't ask it of them. Hard though it was, she'd get on without them, without Harvey.

'Well, you're here now, and if they were still at home and you were still married you couldn't do this job,' Saskia said cheerfully. 'Are you happy here? Not that you've been out here for long.' She studied Eloise's face intently as if to winkle out any distress.

'It was all a bit sudden and I worry that Lawrence will not think me a good enough cook, or rather *chef*,' she emphasized the word with an ironic grin, 'for his discerning guests. I'm here under false pretences, you see.' Eloise told her about Desmond's misplaced pride in her cordon bleu credentials. 'I'm cooking the sort of food I do when friends come to dinner and I had no complaints from them, but then they weren't paying for it. Lawrence is running a business.'

'I'm sure he'd tell you if he wants any changes. That dinner you cooked the other night was delicious,' Saskia said. 'You'll be fine and if you weren't he'd have packed you off already and raided Aurelia's dreadful delights,' she laughed. 'It was jolly mean of Denise, letting him down like that. She was nice though; we skied together sometimes. She told me she was getting tired of cooking, so I suppose she saw her chance and grabbed it. Tough luck if she finds he's one of those mega-rich men who have miserly habits.'

'Tell me about you and Quinn.' Apart from being curious Eloise wanted to steer Saskia away from her problems. 'I've sometimes read his articles, though it was a bit scary cooking for such a prestigious food expert,' she finished.

'I wouldn't worry, he has to eat my cooking and he doesn't grumble, not often anyway. It's restaurants he writes about and some of those chefs can be so bumptious he can't resist putting them down.' Saskia smiled, pouring them more wine. 'Well, my marriage didn't work out either. I suppose Toby and I did fall in love, but when you're young you confuse sexual desire with true, lasting love. We had the children and life was busy, but we somehow didn't fit together. I found Toby lazy – no, not exactly lazy that's unfair, but apathetic, too laid-back. He had a job in a mediocre firm and just trundled along with no ambition, and though he wasn't unkind or anything like that, he treated me as just someone who was always there, like a piece of familiar furniture. So I had an affair.' She looked ashamed of herself and Eloise felt a grab of pain in her stomach. Had she had an affair with Harvey?

There was a silence between them a moment. Eloise

fidgeted on the edge of her chair waiting for Saskia to confess that she'd slept with Harvey, before deciding it better to know the worst and get it out of the way.

'Who did you have an affair with, was it Harvey?'

Saskia started as if she'd been stung, 'Oh no... whatever made you say that?' She fiddled with the stem of her wine glass as if she was moulding it into something. 'No, it was someone else, someone I met on holiday. It didn't last long, a few months, and our marriage limped on a bit, but then Toby met someone and we divorced, an amicable divorce,' she shrugged. 'I've always thought that a silly description, if it's amicable you can surely keep going, at least until the children grow up.'

Eloise wondered if she believed Saskia's denial or not. Once she and Harvey had divorced, various 'kind' friends had told her he'd slept with several women they knew. None of them confessed to being one of them themselves, but she found it difficult to trust them. She didn't want to feel the same way about Saskia, she was her only friend out here and she was glad they had met up again; they'd always got on well before.

Harvey was like a butterfly, she'd realized after the divorce, alighting for a moment on a flower and then, having had his fill, flying away to the next one. Life was all about him, and any woman who expected his full commitment would be disappointed. Thinking like this wasn't helping her to move on, Eloise told herself, she should try and remember the good times. And of course, she had her children and that was the greatest gift of all. She became aware that Saskia was scrutinizing her.

'You think I went to bed with Harvey, don't you?'

'No... well, not really,' she admitted, 'but I do wonder

about all the attractive women we knew, after all he was so good-looking and made women feel so desirable. I would have probably succumbed to him myself if I hadn't married him,' she said in a rush.

'Well I didn't. He did try it on once, but I told him off and walked away, though I was tempted,' she blushed. 'Perhaps it was a good thing we moved to the country, kept out of harm's way. Anyway I've made it a rule that I've never broken – never to sleep with a friend's man. Good friends are far more important than a quick fling.' She smiled.

'That's true.' Eloise felt relieved. 'So how did you meet Quinn?'

'Through a job I had, working for his publisher. He'd just broken up with someone and was lonely. I know there's quite an age difference between us, but he's kind and dependable and nearly always at home, writing his reviews. He lives in lovely places; he has the chalet here, a villa in the South of France and a flat in London, so we move around, though we don't often go to London, and he can afford people to help in the house.' She smiled, 'Call me money-grabbing if you like, many people do, and I suppose I am but, like Denise, I saw my chance and took it. I love him in my way and we look after each other. I was tired of being alone, having affairs that meant nothing, and I felt so lonely when the children left.'

'I understand.' Eloise wondered if she would do the same if she met some kind older man who showed an interest in her.

'It's the loneliness that gets you in the end,' Saskia said, 'having no one to come home to, don't you find that?'

'Perhaps, but I haven't been alone that long. We divorced eight months ago and I was busy moving house and Kit and

Lizzie were still around, and now... I'm here,' Eloise said.

Saskia smiled, 'And you'll have a great time. I'll give a party, introduce you to people, quite a lot of fun people live out here, for the season anyway.'

'I've only been here a couple of days and I've already met quite a few people, you and Quinn of course, Theo, Lawrence, Vera, and not forgetting Bert... and Aurelia.' She was about to tell her about the cake scene when Saskia went on.

'Oh, Aurelia,' Saskia frowned, 'she's after Lawrence or Jacaranda, or both I suppose, for she won't get the chalet without him.'

9

The following day Eloise was free to go skiing. She'd cooked a hearty breakfast, got in enough food for dinner and now there was no more to do until the evening, although she needed to quickly drop in on Lawrence.

The previous day the guests had come back around teatime. They praised her lemon drizzle cake – though they ate it guiltily as if it were illegal, the women taking minuscule slices – 'because you've gone to so much trouble to make it,' Celia, one of the guests remarked, though not before helping herself to another sliver. They found Aurelia's cake too cloying, though one of the men enjoyed a hefty piece and would have gone back for more if his wife had not forbidden it, saying it would more than treble his sugar intake for the week.

'Don't worry about making cakes for us,' Celia had told her, 'we have a big lunch on the mountain and a good dinner here, we don't need cake, and it's far too tempting if it's there.' She eyed the lemon cake longingly.

'If you're sure,' Eloise had said, wondering if the men agreed, but whether they did or not, the women decided that no one needed it.

She wanted to mention the lack of a teatime cake to

Lawrence, in case he thought it was because she couldn't manage to bake any more, and if he told Aurelia she would think it gave her carte blanche to bombard them with her sugar-packed delights. Since Saskia had told her Aurelia was determined to get her hands on Lawrence and Jacaranda, she felt she needed to keep an eye out and guard Jacaranda – for Lawrence and Theo – though she was only here for a few weeks and when she'd gone home Aurelia could pounce.

She went downstairs to Lawrence's office where the door was always open, as if he could not bear to be confined when outside the mountains called to him with their savage beauty.

'No point in doing it if no one wants it,' he said when she told him what the women had said about not baking cakes for them. He was looking slightly harassed, with papers strewn across his desk.

'I want it.' Theo was lounging on a chair by the window, staring longingly out at the slopes. 'And you eat it, I've seen you, Dad,' he added, eyeing Lawrence accusingly.

Eloise had noticed too that if Lawrence were in the chalet at teatime he managed, on some pretext or another, to come into the kitchen and help himself to a slice of her lemon cake – or a shortbread biscuit.

'Yes, well we don't *need* it and Eloise has a lot of other things to do and must keep all her energy for when the guests arrive for Christmas,' Lawrence said.

She left them, thinking they were rather like chained beasts having to be inside when a wonderful outdoor world beckoned. It was sad that they couldn't enjoy Verbier and Jacaranda as it was when Maddy and Desmond were here.

'Don't worry, I'll see there is cake or biscuits in the tin for you,' she said to Theo when he followed her into the kitchen in search of a snack, reminding her of Kit who was always hungry. 'Next week's guests might want it, though there's the Christmas cake and I'll make mince pies.'

'I think they'll be a great pain, Dad's stressing about them already, and Bert has to sleep in the basement, he's not allowed upstairs in case they hate dogs,' Theo grumbled.

Lawrence, who'd come up from the basement and followed them into the kitchen, interjected, 'Nonsense, Theo. Go and bring in some logs, we're running low in the living room.' He put his empty coffee mug in the sink, saying he'd see them all later.

Theo slouched off to fetch the logs and Eloise waited until she heard the front door close behind Lawrence before going to put on her outdoor clothes, relieved to be going out.

She drove the jeep up to Medran, parked and went into the ski shop to hire her boots and skis. She was meeting Saskia, and possibly Quinn, to spend a couple of hours skiing. It was such a relief to be in the open air and not cooped up in the kitchen, cooking. She enjoyed cooking, but the beauty of the mountains and the snow were too good to miss and before she knew it she'd be back home.

She met up with Saskia and was relieved that Quinn did not come with them after all. She'd been dreading a lecture on how she could improve her culinary skills, though, to be fair, he might not have done that at all, just enjoyed his skiing.

'Does Aurelia do her own cooking?' she asked Saskia as they queued for the gondola, not able to imagine her slaving away over a clutch of pans.

'Goodness no. Rumour has it she keeps a group of poor immigrants and makes them cook, but I don't think that's true. Quinn is convinced she freezes masses of dishes and whips them out when they are needed,' Saskia joked as they moved forward to board the next gondola. It was quite full and reminded Eloise of being all squashed together in the Tube in rush hour, though here, of course, people were carrying skis and everyone was cheerful, looking forward to being on the slopes instead of at work.

Saskia insisted that they do a short run on Lac des Vaux – the lake covered now with a thick blanket of snow – for her to get her ski legs before going higher to Mort Fort.

It was a rather grey day, the sky heavy with more snow, and bitterly cold, but Eloise, who hadn't skied for a while, was thrilled to be back on the slopes. There was a special magic about feeling the snow, like crunchy silk under the skis, being among the beauty of nature, though much of the mountain was manicured to make more pistes for the thousands of skiers that came here each season.

At the end of one run they caught up with some of Saskia's friends, Paul and Katie Hammond, who also ran a chalet near the Rouge, though it was much lower key than Jacaranda, catering for families with young children. Katie had once been a chalet girl and she did the cooking, while Paul was a freelance ski instructor and wrote articles for various magazines.

'Oh, aren't you the cordon bleu chef that's come to Lawrence's rescue?' Katie exclaimed, her face obscured by goggles and a hat like a woolly visor round her face.

'Not exactly, but I'm hoping I'll do.' Lawrence had made a few remarks... suggestions he called them, about her cooking. Nothing too drastic, though she felt she was still on probation. But having remarked on it to Vera, she'd laughed, saying Christmas was so close now he'd find it impossible to find someone else at such short notice and if he hadn't liked her she'd be gone already. Eloise still didn't feel completely at ease, especially with Aurelia waiting in the wings.

'The story went viral – Denise leaving like that,' Katie said, 'though she wouldn't be the first one to chase after a millionaire. Many of us came here as chalet girls hoping to meet the right man, as I did,' she giggled and snuggled up to Paul, who didn't notice as he was busy talking to a man, incognito under his goggles like the rest of them. 'It's lucky you were able to drop everything and step in; I bet Lawrence is thrilled he found a new chef in time.'

'Cooking is not something I do professionally,' Eloise said and then wished she hadn't. If Lawrence's rich guests got wind of the fact, they might demand their money back. She went on hurriedly, 'I mean... I haven't cooked for a lot of people for a while.' But Paul, urging Katie to come on as they must get back, said goodbye and the pair carried on down the slope and were soon out of sight.

Saskia too said she must speed on as she had to meet Quinn and he fussed if she were late. Eloise, who wanted to take things carefully this first day, told her not to wait for her. She remembered the way down now, anyway it was marked and she could take the gondola down if she felt like it.

'If you're sure,' Saskia said. 'We're going to meet friends at La Chable and I've got to change and everything. I'll call you tomorrow and we'll meet up again. Oh I'm so glad you're here, Eloise, we'll have such fun together.' She squeezed her arm affectionately before turning and disappearing down the slope at speed.

Eloise followed more slowly. It had begun to ice up, her skis scraped against the icy surface; she must not fall, it would be terrible if she slipped and hurt herself and was not able to cook.

She reached a tight little slope full of moguls. The slope was crowded, skiers and snowboarders of all levels having to go down this way on their way home. Some skied badly, the terrain making them lurch off balance before hitting the next icy mound. Other, better skiers, danced between them.

Eloise had forgotten this short but potentially lethal run and she struggled on, remembering how she used to bash her way down in the past, but now her legs felt like cotton wool and she found it hard to push them.

Someone cut in front of her, catching the tip of her ski, and she stumbled. The person behind her couldn't get out of the way in time and came tumbling down with her. They lay there on the icy snow together while other skiers steered round them, their skis rasping through the ice, perilously close to them.

'Sorry,' the man who'd fallen on to her, said, 'you OK?' He helped her up and she felt a stab of pain in her shoulder. It wasn't bad enough for a break, she told herself firmly, she was just bruised.

'Thanks,' she said, as the man handed her one of her poles and with a nod he was gone. She hadn't even had a chance to apologize, and she was just grateful that he'd been so gracious, she wasn't sure that another skier would have looked so kindly on her getting in their way.

It was dangerous standing here with all the skiers rushing down around her and she started to move, her shoulder in agony as she pushed off. Just my luck, she thought as she cautiously navigated her way down to the flatter surface as the slope straightened out. She'd get some heat on it when she got back to Jacaranda and hopefully she'd be all right.

She neared the bottom of the mountain at last, hardly able to use her injured arm, just a few yards now until she reached the end. A woman wearing bright pink shot past her, almost knocking her over. Eloise swore at her as the pain flared in her shoulder, but she had to keep going as more and more skiers came down at the end of the day.

She reached the cheerful crowd congregating at the finish. Some had skied together or met up with others and were exchanging news, taking off their skis and going home to join friends or family. There was no one waiting for her and she struggled to banish her mournful feelings of self-pity. There'd be no one to commiserate with when she got back to the chalet. Vera would have gone home, and she couldn't mention it to Theo who'd tell Lawrence – he would be furious she'd hurt herself and might ban her from skiing altogether, or even worse, call in Aurelia. It was only because she had hurt herself and yearned for a word of comfort that she felt this way, she told herself firmly.

Stiffly she released her skis and bent down to pick them up to carry them to the jeep. Among the cheerful crowd jostling beside her she caught sight of the woman in pink and beside her a familiar face. It was Harvey.

10

Head down, Eloise hurried back to the jeep in the crowded car park. She was relieved she was wearing a hat, which she pulled down tight now and she kept her goggles on, hoping Harvey wouldn't catch sight of her, or if he did she'd be just another anonymous skier, or more likely, he'd be so wrapped up in the woman in pink he would not even notice her.

She had not seen her ex-husband since that painful day in court eight months ago where they'd gone to sort out the division of their assets. The soulless rooms of the divorce court were a stark contrast to the pretty old church and banks of scented flowers of their wedding day. It had felt so right, a perfect backdrop for starting their life together. The beginning of their marriage clothed in such beauty and hope, and then ended in such pain and despair, conducted in a place that held lost dreams and broken hearts.

It was sod's law that Harvey was here at the same time as she was. He loved skiing and Verbier was one of the best resorts, so it made sense that he was here. Was he here for Christmas, or just this week and, more importantly, who was he with?

She forgot the pain in her shoulder, the pain in her heart was far worse. She thought she'd got over him, or was at least well on the way to accepting the end of their marriage. But seeing him here caused a fresh stab of sadness and anxiety.

She wondered if Saskia knew Harvey was here, though why should she? Verbier was now enormous, with chalets and hotels dotted all over the place, and people came in from other nearby resorts to ski the vast slopes. It was possible to spend time here and not even glimpse friends and acquaintances. He might not even be staying here but be in Nendaz or some other resort.

She drove slowly back to Jacaranda. The joy that had filled her while she'd skied in the open spaces, the sharp, clean air and the beauty of the mountains, even on a grey day, evaporated. Seeing Harvey had spoilt it, though surely he didn't know she was here, unless the children had told him? She'd asked them not to say anything about it in case she was mortifyingly sent home before Christmas, but perhaps it had slipped out when the twins were talking to him. It was so hard to change the way you'd always behaved with someone close, especially a beloved parent; she couldn't blame them. On the other hand, it could just be a dreadful coincidence. She could hole up in the chalet, which was thankfully not in the centre of everything, and keep out of his way. But why should she? She wanted to enjoy the mountains and skiing too while she was here. And if the children *had* told him she was here, he knew the way to Jacaranda in the unlikely event that he'd come to find her.

She reached the chalet and parked the jeep. Her shoulder was hurting more now; she must soak it under a hot shower, or better still she could soak in the bath in one of the rooms on the first floor, if everyone was out.

She put her skis away in the shed and saw there were two other pairs there, still damp from the snow. The skis were not Theo's or Lawrence's; they must belong to two of the guests. She sighed; she wouldn't be able to use the bath now. She went inside, taking off her boots and hanging up her ski jacket. There was a scuffling sound from the floor above where the bedrooms were. She hoped the guests hadn't taken all the hot water or that they would now want tea before she had time to soothe her shoulder under the shower.

She went upstairs quietly in her stockinged feet and saw Celia coming out of a bedroom which was not Celia's bedroom. She and her husband Derek slept on the other side of the landing, Eloise remembered: Celia had come out of Susie and Neil's room. Perhaps both women had returned early and were just gossiping, though by the guilty look on Celia's face, Eloise doubted it.

'Oh, it's you,' Celia said, her face flushing, her eyes defiant, 'good day?'

'Yes thanks and you?' Eloise replied.

Celia's shirt was hanging out of the back of her jeans, her hair was all mussed and she had a sort of glow tinged with guilt that gave her away.

'Great,' Celia said, not looking at her.

Eloise crossed the landing to the small staircase in the corner that led to the upper floor, and Celia darted into her own bedroom and shut the door. Upstairs, in her room, Eloise lay down on the bed, her heart full. Was everyone at it, cheating on their partners? she wondered in despair. Was Derek somewhere with Susie, and what about Harvey, who was he with, his large-bosomed sex toy or someone else? Painful jealousy curled into her like a snake. She knew now that Harvey was incapable of loving anyone but himself but still it hurt. And Lawrence, was he with Aurelia? Everyone but her paired up?

She was reminded of Saskia's comment about Aurelia wanting Jacaranda; she supposed combining the two together – Aurelia's food and Lawrence's lovely, old chalet – could make them a fortune. There were quite a few super luxury chalets out here now, all spruced up with gyms, Jacuzzis and cinemas, but Jacaranda had genuine old-fashioned charm, class you could call it, something the new-builds often didn't achieve. If Aurelia got her teeth into Jacaranda she might be able to make it *the* place the super rich wanted to rent, but she feared she'd change it for the worse, take away its unique atmosphere. She'd probably build on the garden: there was space enough for another chalet, perhaps a small pool and gym, even a cinema, so no one need go out after a day on the mountains, or mix with other people in the village. But it was pointless thinking of it, or caring who was in bed with whom. It was nothing whatever to do with her; she was only the cook, and only here for a short time.

It was seeing Harvey here that had upset her, churned up the painful emotions again, making her feel out of it, unloved and unwanted.

But she must stop feeling sorry for herself, have her shower – in fact she'd have a bath in one of the rooms on the floor below, she decided firmly, and hang what Celia and Neil thought, they could hardly tell her what was right and wrong. She undressed painfully, put on her towelling gown and went down the stairs and into the bathroom, locking the door.

The bath took some time to fill, the water juddering in from the old brass taps and when she sank down into the warmth, she tried to keep her shoulder under the water to ease it. It worked a little but it was still sore when she was dressed, but she must prepare the dinner.

'Good day?' Lawrence said later, coming into the kitchen

76

to get the wine ready for the evening meal.

'Yes, and you?' She winced as she lifted the pan from the stove as the pain from her shoulder bit, turning from him so he wouldn't notice the anguish in her expression.

'Yes, I skied down to Nendaz,' he said. 'Where did you go?'

'Mont Fort. I skied with Saskia, I'm so glad she's here, a friend from the past.' She wasn't going to say she'd spied her ex-husband, she might cry, cause Lawrence to panic, think that she'd be too emotional to cook. She wondered if Lawrence knew him, she couldn't remember if they'd ever met here in Jacaranda all those years ago.

'Nice for you. Now what's the menu, red or white, or probably both?' He smiled at her and caught her grimace of pain as she turned to face him. 'What's wrong?' His smile changed into a frown, a worried look in his eyes. 'Don't tell me you've hurt yourself...'

'No, I'm just stiff, haven't skied for a few years,' she said hurriedly, bending down to look in the oven on the pretext of seeing how the slow roast duck was progressing.

'Please be careful, Eloise.' He watched her with concern as she stood up, studying her for a moment, making her feel he was worried about her, soothing her pain before going on, 'You've got a lot of cooking to do over the Christmas week.'

'I know,' she muttered, now feeling near tears. She'd told herself that taking this job would be an escape from her pain and loneliness as she adjusted to her new life as a single woman again. But it was out of the fat into the fire, with Harvey being here with goodness knew who and now Lawrence worried that she would not be able to cook for his blessed clients.

Perhaps feeling he'd upset her, Lawrence said with a roguish smile, 'Like the apron.'

She'd forgotten the words 'Kiss the Cook' were blazoned across the front.

11

The guests, especially Celia and Neil, who were obviously nursing guilty consciences, were especially glowing in their praise of the dinner when Eloise came in to clear the plates. Theo had disappeared on a night out and Vera had the evening off.

'That duck was delicious, do tell me what was in the recipe,' Celia said, her staring doll-like eyes homing in on Eloise.

'Oh, it was just roasted slowly with honey and orange and a bit of basil and fresh ginger, glad you liked it,' she said, not looking at her. She put the pudding, a chocolate roulade, and a plate of tuile biscuits on the table in the space Neil quickly cleared for her.

'And the stuffing balls, rather like people do with the turkey at Christmas,' Celia went on, slightly frantically. Eloise wondered if Celia was afraid she'd suddenly announce to them all that she'd caught her bed-hopping when she'd come back to the chalet earlier in the day.

Lawrence helped stack the dirty plates and serving dishes on to the tray before going round again with the wine. Worried she might drop the tray with her sore shoulder, Eloise was relieved when Neil jumped up to take it from her and then insisted – despite Lawrence's protests that he'd just finish replenishing the wine glasses before carrying it to the kitchen himself – on ferrying the rest of the used dishes to the kitchen. Eloise thanked him but stayed by the table, handing out clean plates, determined not to be alone with Neil in the kitchen and have to listen to his explanation of his bedroom antics. By their covert looks at each other she guessed they were frantic to explain, but she didn't want to know. Their sex life was their own business, though it triggered painful memories of Harvey's infidelities. Perhaps many people were like that if they could get away with it. Though Eloise was not going to embark on any new love affairs if one should come her way for a very long time, if ever again.

Neil came meekly back, throwing her a petulant glance, which she ignored, and she left them, returning to the kitchen to stack the plates in the dishwasher. She was grateful that she wouldn't have to see them tomorrow evening; they were all out to supper. Initially she had planned to spend the whole day on the slopes, but after injuring herself today, she didn't want to make her shoulder worse, she told herself, not wanting to admit the real reason for staying at the chalet was that she didn't want to come across Harvey with his pink-clad sexpot. She could imagine their meeting. Harvey would hide his consternation under his charming, boyish smile – the naughty boy who loved her really, only she saw through it now and his charm appeared fake and foolish.

There was plenty to do here anyway, not least the menus for Christmas. She didn't know if the guests would be skiing on Christmas Day itself and how many other meals there'd be to cater for. Perhaps the Christmas guests would have a party, invite people in. She must check it all with Lawrence, but he beat her to it.

He came into the kitchen at the end of dinner and said,

'That was delicious; everyone enjoyed it, well done, Eloise. Now have you thought about your menus over Christmas? I think we should meet tomorrow to discuss them.'

'Exactly what I thought,' she agreed, warmed by his praise, though she wondered if the compliments had come from Neil and Celia, intended as a sort of bribe to keep Eloise quiet about their sexy interlude. 'I'll start buying the things – chestnuts, butter and stuff that will keep. Do the food stores stay open?'

'Some,' he said. 'You may have to provide lunch sometimes,' he paused, regarding her carefully as though she might refuse. 'Do you mind doing that?'

'No,' she said, though she meant yes and she guessed Lawrence knew it too for he smiled at her, lifting the frown lines on his face, suddenly making her feel drawn to him and almost as if she wanted to confide that she'd seen her ex-husband on the slopes and it had thrown her. But she kept quiet. The last thing Lawrence wanted – or needed – was his latest cook to be suffering from a broken heart.

'Don't worry,' Lawrence said. 'We'll make sure you escape to the slopes occasionally.'

'Let's wait and see,' Eloise said, realizing that she would be going home not long after the guests left. Second week in January, he'd said on the telephone, though he hadn't mentioned it again. What about New Year? Would there be an extravagant party she would have to cater for, or would the millionaire guests have left to party somewhere ritzy with a real chef? She didn't want to ask him now, put a time limit on her stay, though she'd always known it would not be for the rest of the season. He'd wanted someone to cook for Christmas and once that was over he had no more need of her. A proper *chef* was coming and perhaps he had friends to stay instead of clients, or Aurelia would keep him going with her 'Tempting Delights'. She was hit with a sudden sadness that it would all be over so quickly and she'd be back home, coming to terms with her new life as an independent woman again.

*

Her shoulder was worse the next morning when her alarm went off, calling her to the kitchen. As she struggled to get dressed, she told herself it was just because she'd slept on it and it would loosen up during the day. She cooked and served breakfast, saying nothing about it, biting her lips against the pain, but Lawrence came into the kitchen and said, grimly, 'You are injured, aren't you? How did it happen, did you fall skiing?'

She had to confess. 'Yes, I was skiing on that moguly slope down to the gondola and someone knocked me down. It will be fine though.'

'You better go and see Pascal, the physio we use, he'll deal with it, strap it up or something, and if he can't...' he sighed.

'It will be fine,' she repeated without much conviction.

'I'll ring him now, get you an appointment, he's near the swimming pool, Sports Aid, you'll see the sign flashing on and off. You can park there.' He frowned. 'Can you drive with it?'

'Yes,' she said, wondering how much the appointment would cost.

As if he could read her mind, he said, 'Tell him to put it down on the Jacaranda account. I'll ring him now.' And he swept out of the kitchen.

The appointment was made for mid-afternoon so she

spent the morning poring through her recipe books. Bert lay under the table, his head on her foot, every so often sighing mournfully. He often went skiing with Theo, who carried him on his back in a rucksack, but after letting him out for a short run this morning, Theo had gone back to bed and Bert no doubt guessed that he'd be confined to the basement when the new guests arrived.

'Don't be sad, Bert.' She fondled his ears and he snuffled his nose into her hand. 'We'll go out for a walk later.'

She planned to buy the non-perishable items now, then at least the bulk of the shopping would be done. The turkey and the meat for the stuffing had been ordered and she could send Theo down for those. She wished he were free today to help her, but he'd come back at dawn and she wouldn't disturb him. She'd done the same with Kit and Lizzie. There was such a hole in her heart without them now, but she had to set them free and they would come back, she remembered a friend telling her. In her friend's case, holding a grandchild that had landed her daughter back home.

Eloise drove the jeep down to the village and found Pascal's practice. The waiting room was small and rather dark, lit by a pinkish glow from a lava lamp with its mesmerizing blobs of oil gently belching shapes. A young woman sitting at a desk confirmed her appointment, telling her Pascal was running a little late but would see her as soon as he could.

If she wasn't in so much pain she'd leave it and come back another time, but she sat down on one of the straight-backed chairs that discouraged slouching and leafed through some old magazines.

Pascal obviously wasn't the only practitioner here for there were two other women waiting who were soon called into other rooms. The time ticked past, the outside door opening to let in other people, and just when Eloise thought she really couldn't wait any longer Pascal's door opened and a woman dressed in a blue tracksuit came out.

'Thank you, Pascal,' she drawled, bending back to kiss him, 'much better now, I'll come back for another session soon.'

At the same moment the outside door opened and she heard Harvey's voice, 'See you later.' The door closed and a woman in a shocking pink ski jacket came in. Eloise was rooted to her chair, her feelings in turmoil. Pascal had come out of his room and now leant over her, speaking quietly, apologizing for keeping her waiting, asking if she needed help getting up.

She shook her head and struggled up, following him into his consulting room. His voice was soothing in her ear, saying that Lawrence had sent her to him and what bad luck it was to be injured on her first day out. He ushered her into a light peaceful room scented by a large candle that glowed on a table, and she sat down where he showed her, opposite his desk. He shut the door, cutting off the scene outside, of Harvey's woman.

She realized he was watching her intently and she pulled herself together. He began to question her on her injury and she forced herself to focus on the matter in hand, her injured shoulder that must be cured so that she could cook over Christmas. Harvey and his sexpots were not her concern any more. She concentrated on Pascal.

She imagined he was much older than he appeared; he was lean with a healthy look about him, his face baby smooth without a line anywhere.

The pain from his manipulation was agony, but it took her mind off the pain in her heart. After a while her shoulder felt looser, and he strapped it up to give her more comfort whilst still ensuring she could use her arm.

He suggested she came to see him again. 'It's not so bad, but I'll give you some painkillers,' he said, writing a prescription, 'it shouldn't keep you off the slopes for long.'

'That's a relief.' She didn't say that Lawrence was more concerned about her being able to wield heavy pans than skis.

As she left his room, she walked tall, determined to inspect Harvey's woman, but she was not there. She went out into the street, afraid now of bumping into Harvey. How could he be here just when she was getting over him, doing something different with her life?

She struggled round the shops, wishing she had Theo to carry and heave things for her but relieved she hadn't bumped into Harvey or his pink lady. At last, with everything in the jeep and feeling slightly woozy from Pascal's wrestling and the painkillers, she drove back up to Jacaranda.

To her relief she caught Theo, who was on his way out. He told Bert to wait and carried everything inside for her, dumping the boxes on the island in the middle of the kitchen. She took off her boots and headed into the kitchen.

Aurelia was sitting in the window seat, drinking coffee with Lawrence. There was a shiny brochure on the table between them.

'Why, hello, if it's not your little cook,' Aurelia greeted her. 'Been shopping, what have you bought?'

Her heart fell – first Harvey and now Aurelia. She was looking so... smug, at home, whatever. Saskia's words – 'it's Jacaranda she's after' – buzzed in her brain.

'Just stuff for Christmas,' she muttered.

'I hope Pascal sorted you out.' Lawrence eyed her intently

as if he were worried she'd tell him she'd been forbidden to cook.

'Why, what's wrong?' Aurelia perked up as if she hoped that something serious had happened to prevent Eloise cooking so Lawrence could order his whole Christmas banquet from her.

'I'm fine now, thank you so much for suggesting the appointment,' Eloise smiled at him.

'Good, now don't get knocked down again,' Lawrence sounded relieved, 'we need you here and next week will be a hard one.'

'Do you really think you can manage?' Aurelia's tone of voice suggested that she thought she could not and that she was surely the better choice to ensure these exclusive guests were served the kind of food they were accustomed to. She leant closer to Lawrence, her hair brushing his face as she pushed the shiny brochure towards him. Eloise had a glimpse of luscious photographs of succulent meats and colourful vegetables all beautifully arranged on silver dishes.

'Of course I can,' Eloise said, not looking at her. She had hoped to have a lie-down before she tidied her shopping away but she didn't dare leave now. Left alone with Lawrence, Aurelia would no doubt try and persuade him that it would be wiser to count on her, if she hadn't been trying already, coming here with her shiny brochure to tempt him. She started to unpack the shopping, picking up two tins of sweet chestnut puree that she'd bought as a filling for a meringue vacherin.

'Oh, tinned, they really have no flavour compared with cooking them from scratch. Anyone who's a serious cook on the continent makes their own,' Aurelia said disdainfully, shoving her brochure into Lawrence's lap before springing up and coming over to the boxes and picking through the contents. 'And this chocolate.' She held up the bar by the tips of her fingers. 'I wish you'd asked me. It doesn't have nearly as much flavour as the eighty per cent one, and this butter's not the best. I suppose you can just get away with it if you use it for cakes or pastry, but it burns too quickly to fry with.'

'I'll take you with me next time and you can point out the best things,' Eloise said sharply. She didn't want her here in her kitchen and she didn't want her to have anything to do with Jacaranda. She thought back to the good times when she, her parents and Desmond and Maddy were here. Then later Harvey, Kit and Lizzie. It had always been a noisy, chaotic, happy place and now with this cold, designer kitchen and Aurelia hovering like a bird of prey waiting to pounce, she felt that something was missing.

Aurelia sat down again on the window seat close to Lawrence. She picked up the brochure which lay untouched on his lap. 'You can buy chestnut puree from me, you know,' her voice was seductive as if she was offering him something more intimate. She flicked through the pages.

'Eloise has bought it now,' Lawrence said, trying to get up from the seat but somewhat trapped by the table and Aurelia.

'Pity, but there's plenty more in my brochure. Let's see what other things I can tempt you with,' she purred, snuggling even closer to him.

12

The past week's guests left in the minibus for the airport with Theo. To his dismay, Bert had to stay behind in case, 'the new lot are dog haters,' Theo muttered to Eloise before he left.

Lawrence and Eloise went outside to wave the guests on their way. There were effusive yet rather staged goodbyes, except from Celia and Neil who scurried into the bus, heads down as if terrified that Eloise might produce a town crier's bell and finally expose their bedroom antics.

With any luck Harvey too would have left today, Saturday being changeover day for most of the chalets.

It seemed to Eloise as she went back inside Jacaranda with Lawrence that the parting guests had taken the relaxed atmosphere of the chalet with them. He seemed preoccupied. He opened the door for her to go back inside and then disappeared downstairs to his office without a word to her, making her feel discarded. She scolded herself, he had so much to think of, namely to chase up the Christmas tree that should have arrived last night, and after all it was not his role to boost her ego.

She went upstairs to her room. She hadn't had time to sort out her clothes, just jammed them into the cupboard, so she took everything out now and began to sort them, jerseys one side, shirts and jeans the other, and the one skirt and smartish dress she'd shoved in her case as an afterthought, she hung up.

In the wardrobe, there were some books on the top shelf and a faded dark red box pushed to the back that sparked some long-ago memory. She pulled the box out, put it on the bed and opened it and there, wrapped carefully in tissue paper, were Christmas decorations for the tree.

She unwrapped one, a tiny house with a red shiny roof and the black boots of a mini Father Christmas sticking up from the chimney. She smiled as she remembered it and the Christmas she had spent here as a child. Opening this box with the spun-glass decorations evoked the joy of that time; she'd take them downstairs and get Theo to help her decorate the tree when it arrived.

There was no one around when she went downstairs, so she left the red box in the kitchen and got ready to go out.

Lawrence had agreed on her menus and Eloise drove down to the village to buy the fresh food for the dinner this evening. It was a dull day, very cold, the sky heavy with snow, like a grey blanket bearing down on them. She parked the jeep and went into the butcher's to place her order and almost bumped into Aurelia, who was just coming out.

'Oh, it's you,' Aurelia said dismissively. 'Hear you've got those terrifying new guests arriving today. Lawrence is frantically worried that it won't work out and they'll complain to the agency and they will only send him the dreggy clients, if any, in the future.' She glared at Eloise as if Jacaranda's ruin would be all her fault.

'I expect they'll be fine,' Eloise said coldly, though her stomach churned with anxiety. She moved to go into the shop but Aurelia barred her way.

'I do hope so; Lawrence cannot afford to lose money over it. I mean,' she laughed disparagingly, 'I don't know if you are aware but Jacaranda needs a complete makeover, it's wiring must be a fire risk by now, it's so ancient, and the plumbing...' She raised her eyebrows. 'It must be done soon too and that will cost a fortune, which I don't think he has.'

The tone of her voice infuriated Eloise. She'd overheard Lawrence telling Theo about the old wiring and she'd noticed that the bathroom she'd used on the first floor was looking tired, but she wasn't going to agree with Aurelia. 'Jacaranda looks fine to me. It was properly built and has far more style and class than any of the newer chalets I've seen. Apart from the kitchen but...'

'I planned the kitchen and it's exactly what you need if you're doing this job professionally,' Aurelia said icily. 'Cosy kitchens provide cosy cooking, which any discerning guests definitely *do not* want.' She tossed her head in the air and walked away.

Eloise let her go, she'd sensed a touch of desperation in her voice, perhaps she'd hoped her 'Tempting Delights' would win over Lawrence. What did Aurelia feel for him? He was attractive, more than Eloise remembered, but then he'd been very young and arrogant when she'd last seen him. Did Aurelia care for him or just want to get her hands on Jacaranda?

Eloise wanted to fight for Jacaranda herself, stop Aurelia muscling in and changing it – and snatching Lawrence, a small voice said inside her, though she hurriedly dismissed it. Somehow he touched her heart, but that was just foolishness; it was Jacaranda and all the happy memories it held for her that made her want to fight. But when she returned home, it would leave the path clear for Aurelia, who she feared was already well ahead with her plans to move in.

If only there was something she could do to persuade Lawrence that Jacaranda didn't need Aurelia in order to be successful. Eloise was going home in a few weeks, would she have time to persuade him to keep Jacaranda in the family?

*

She finished her shopping and drove slowly back to Jacaranda, her shoulder still throbbing, although it was almost better now.

Eloise's heart sank when she arrived at the chalet and saw Aurelia's red sports car parked in her place. She struggled to control her frustration. Jacaranda's fate wasn't anything to do with her, she reminded herself as she heaved out the shopping. If Lawrence wanted to keep Jacaranda, he had to run it as a business and go with the flow of today's requirements. Her sentimental memories were not part of the plan.

There was a Christmas wreath on the door and when she went in she saw the tree wedged in the hall, still in its netting; it had arrived. She clumped along the passage to the kitchen, dumping down the box of groceries. There was no sign of Aurelia or Lawrence. Vera was having a cup of coffee and she insisted on helping carry in the rest of the shopping. As they passed the stairs down to the lower floor, they could hear Aurelia's voice drifting up to them from Lawrence's office.

'But if you really want to make a success of Jacaranda, Lawrence, you've got to up your game. Believe me, I know these sorts of people; they come to my shop all the time. They don't want sausage and mash and shepherd's pie.'

'And nor will they have it,' they heard Lawrence say, but they were back in the kitchen, out of earshot, before they could hear Aurelia's next set of instructions of how to turn Jacaranda into a place to tempt the rich clients.

Vera muttered, 'That woman's always telling Lawrence what *she* wants. But the people who come here always seem happy with their holiday.'

'The guests arriving today though are very rich and spoilt. They're already disappointed they didn't get a more luxurious chalet to stay in over the holiday,' Eloise told her.

Vera shrugged, 'Everyone who comes here is very rich. They are only people, and we will take them as they are. You do good food and the place is clean and comfortable and the mountains are beautiful, that should be enough.'

'You're right, it should be.' Eloise had the same thoughts as Vera, finding it incomprehensible that people coming to this lovely chalet should complain. But for Vera, who'd told her a few facts about her life – how she'd been in circumstances where she hadn't known where the next meal was coming from or where she would sleep that night – such dissatisfaction was unforgiveable.

A few minutes later they heard Aurelia leaving. 'So take my advice, I know what I'm talking about,' was her parting shot, sending an icy blast of air down the passage as she opened the front door to go outside.

Lawrence came into the kitchen; he appeared uneasy. 'Oh... Eloise, could I have a word with you... if you're not busy,' he added as if he hoped she was and he could put it off.

There was a sinking feeling in her stomach, had Aurelia persuaded him her 'Delights' were better suited to these multi-millionaires? Well, she would not go without a fight.

She followed him down to his office. He stood back to let her go in and shut the door behind him, which she took as an ominous sign that he didn't want Vera to hear him dismissing her. She sat down and faced him.

He stayed standing, one hand fiddling with his mobile that lay on the desk. 'Aurelia was here and...' he began, his eyes fixed on the papers on his desk as though they held some vital information.

'I know. I saw her in the butcher's; she made it quite clear that I am not up to cooking for the clients arriving today. I suppose you want me to go home and she will provide you with her "Tempting Delights" instead.' There, she'd made it easy for him, she half rose to leave.

'No,' he looked stricken, 'that's not going to happen. I'm sorry.' He raked his hands through his hair, his face anguished. 'I shouldn't burden you with this, but Jacaranda needs a lot spent on it, those dull but necessary things – plumbing, rewiring. I should have done it before, but somehow I kept putting it off. These clients coming today are very important in ensuring Jacaranda's future, but they wanted a far more luxurious chalet than this one, so it's not going to be easy to satisfy them, and if not...' He left the sentence hanging in the air, clearly anxious about the alternative.

'We'll just have to be extra nice to them then,' Eloise tried to raise his spirits. 'I promise there'll be no sausages and mash.'

He smiled, guessing she'd heard Aurelia's comments, and just for a second Eloise felt they were united, their eyes catching in a moment of intimacy.

13

'Sorry to snipe at you, Desmond, but I've things to do before these clients arrive.' Lawrence felt bad about interrupting his father's questions as he waited for the first lot who'd arrive from the heliport.

Aurelia's warnings still buzzed in his head like an annoying wasp. It had been partly due to her that he had got on the agency's books, as they were very particular on whom they included in their list of luxury chalets. Some people, as the firm's representative told him when he came to inspect Jacaranda, did like the charm of the older chalets, though they still expected the highest quality of care. He needed to attract the upper echelons if he wanted to succeed in this ever more competitive business and carry out the repairs Jacaranda sorely needed.

'I'll bet Eloise's cooking is better than that poncy stuff some of the exclusive restaurants kid their clients is what they should be eating,' Desmond said with feeling. 'I'd hate to see the sort of people poor Jacaranda has to put up with today – with more cash than taste. I don't suppose I'd like them.'

'Unfortunately they are the ones with money and to keep Jacaranda going we have to cater for them and they expect the best.' He knew he sounded impatient but really he didn't need his father's views at this moment on something he didn't understand.

'If dear Maddy was there, she would know what to do,' Desmond said mournfully. 'She knew how to make the place happy and comfortable. She just had a feel for it.'

'I know, but times have changed, Desmond,' he said quietly, knowing how much his father still missed Maddy, he missed her himself.

'For the worse,' Desmond said sadly, and after telling him to send Eloise his love, he rang off.

He heard the front door open, announcing the arrival of the first batch of guests. Being occupied with his father's call, he hadn't moved the Christmas tree in time and he hoped they'd get into the hall. Doing his best to ignore the squeeze of anxiety, he shut a disappointed Bert in his office before going upstairs to greet them. Franz, the taxi driver he often used on these occasions, stood by the open door and two men and a woman came into the chalet.

'Welcome,' Lawrence pinned a smile onto his face. The woman was the first in, sidestepping the tree, moving into the hall and leaving room for the others to follow her. She was very young and beautiful, dressed in a short fur coat with a matching pair of honey-coloured earmuffs, which she took off now, shaking out her blonde hair while she looked round the hall with interest.

For a moment he saw the hall through her eyes and though he loved the pictures and the old wooden skis on the wall by the cuckoo clock – which told the time but no longer cuckooed – he now thought it rather untidy, almost shabby, though she didn't remark on it, just smiled, exclaimed at the warmth and took off her coat. Vera had tidied out the cupboard by the door, so some of the coats could go tidily in there.

'Come in out of the cold,' he said to the others, knowing their names in his head but not knowing who was who.

He took the young woman's coat, wondering if he should put it in the cupboard or take it to her room. He'd never worried about this before but these people could make or break him. The two men had come in and were also looking round, squeezing in past the tree. If only it had arrived yesterday, as he'd been promised, then Aurelia would have decorated it. She was not free to do it today, but she had promised to come tomorrow, but he was annoyed it was delivered so late when he wanted everything to be perfect for these guests, and he hoped they wouldn't grumble to the agency about it.

He snatched a look at the men: one middle-aged with a weary look of someone who was always being called upon, the other was younger, tall and rather gangly, reminding him – for some odd reason – of a heron, with his long legs and pointy face, though he had beautiful blue eyes.

The two men looked around dispassionately, not seeing the charm of the place. No doubt they'd feel happier with something more lavish that shrieked money – minimalist probably, with a strange lump of something classed as 'art' carefully arranged in a prominent place – the sort of thing that the new chalets were doing.

Lawrence led the young woman into the main room where a fire blazed in the grate, giving the room a focus, a warmth that made her exclaim with pleasure and go towards it, hands outstretched.

'How lovely,' she said and smiled at him and he felt better, wondering how she fitted into this group. He only had a list of their names and this young woman had been added at the last minute.

He turned back to welcome in the men while Franz brought in the luggage – expensive cases that looked as if they had never been used before and most likely bought especially for this trip.

'Travis Ormond,' announced the short middle-aged man who had not much hair when he took off his fur hat. He stuck out his hand towards him and Lawrence took it.

'Lawrence Maynard,' he said, 'welcome to Jacaranda.'

'Thank you.' Travis followed the girl into the main room, scrutinizing it as if he were a potential buyer, prowling round the room examining the pictures on the walls.

The 'heron' man – unmuffled from his winter clothes, high-necked ski jacket, hat and scarf – had a pale morose face and a thatch of dark hair. He sloped into the room almost as if he was incognito. Lawrence supposed he was one of those rich people who lived in terror of being robbed, or challenged about the amount of money they had, while so many in the world went without. If being rich was so painful, Lawrence was glad he was not, though he needed more money to keep Jacaranda going.

'Welcome,' he smiled at the man, his hand ready to clasp his, but the man only nodded, thrusting his hands in his pocket as if afraid to be contaminated.

'Jerry Simpson,' Travis gestured towards him, 'and this is Gaby' – he nodded towards the young woman – 'his fiancée.'

'Hi,' she said, throwing herself down on one of the chairs, 'what a journey, thought I'd be sick in that helicopter. I'll go back with the others in the minibus.'

'Would you like some tea, or something stronger, or to go straight to your rooms?' Lawrence asked them. These first hours were always difficult while the guests got their bearings and settled down... or not, as the case may be.

These three had requested single rooms, while the two couples about to arrive with Theo from the airport had asked for doubles. In fact, all the bedrooms on the upper floor were double, though some had two single beds, which did for people who wanted a room on their own.

'Tea, please,' Gaby said.

'Tea with a shot of brandy to warm me up,' Travis said, still prowling round the room, reminding Lawrence of an anxious, moth-eaten wolf he'd once seen at the zoo.

'Thank you, I'll have the same,' Jerry said, sitting down on the arm of Gaby's chair, staring into the fire.

Lawrence left the room and went down the passage to the kitchen to ask Vera to take tea in to them.

When needed, Vera became a parlourmaid. She enjoyed the role and Lawrence paid her extra for it. She waited at table and hung about ready to iron any clothes as required, and even would have unpacked for them if the clients requested it.

She was in the kitchen washing up at the sink – he could never get her to put everything in the dishwasher – while Eloise arranged some untidy mince pies on a plate, the mincemeat having escaped from the base, leaving brown, sticky trails on the pastry during the cooking. There were some home-made biscuits and a sponge cake with vanilla icing standing ready for tea.

Eloise looked up when he came in. 'Have they all arrived?' she said, her eyes searching his face to gauge his reaction.

'No,' he said, 'just three of them, two men and a young woman.' He didn't add that he wondered why that beautiful woman was engaged to such a morose man. He had written their names down and memorized them. Some secretary had made the booking for Mr and Mrs Collins, their son and daughter-in-law; another relative whom he guessed was Jerry, and Travis the colleague. The young woman added at the last minute was the mysterious Gaby Jenson.

'The others will be here with Theo soon and I expect they'd like tea' He regarded Eloise's mince pies with dismay. They probably tasted delicious but their rather battered appearance was off-putting and they would probably need to be eaten with a spoon. He turned to Vera, 'That's tea for seven, please, Vera.'

'Something to eat?' Eloise asked, her face anxious.

He eyed the mince pies doubtfully, 'Let's send in those biscuits and the cake.'

'I know these look a bit messy,' Eloise said sadly, 'I think I put too much fruit in and it sort of exploded while they were cooking.'

'They taste good though,' Vera said, 'and they are home-made, much better than bought pies.'

'I'm sure they are, but we'll have them later,' Lawrence said, Aurelia's warning of the amateurism of home-cooked food compared to the sophisticated, well-presented dishes this sort of guest expected, nudging painfully at him. He picked up the tray of plates, the cake and biscuits and made for the door, telling Vera to bring enough cups and plates for the rest of the party and a pot of tea.

Vera had just brought in the tea and was pouring it out when the rest of the party arrived with Theo; she stayed in the room, fussing round with cake and biscuits, surreptitiously inspecting everyone. He hadn't confided his fears to her, but he knew how loyal Vera was and how she would fight for Jacaranda's future with all she had, not only to keep her own job but also because she was so grateful to him for rescuing her from a life of virtual slavery and paying her a decent wage which restored her dignity.

Debra Collins was also clad in furs, an elegant woman he guessed to be in her sixties. She glanced contemptuously towards Gaby who barely acknowledged her. Her husband, Ken, was friendlier and threw Gaby a warm, rather lecherous look, causing his wife to glare at him before she sat down on the sofa and began to talk earnestly to Jerry. Their son, Radley, was a rather effeminate-looking man, though he had his mother's good looks, his hair still glossy black while his mother's, though obviously tinted, was now a paler brown. His wife, Pippa, with pretty doll-like features and a cloud of chestnut hair, hovered uncertainly on the threshold, causing her mother-in-law to say brusquely. 'Do sit down, dear, and stop hovering. It's getting on my nerves.'

Lawrence watched Vera assessing them as she handed round cups of tea and the cake and biscuits. Theo having done his duty in delivering the guests had disappeared. He hoped he was taking their luggage upstairs but suspected he had gone to the kitchen to see if there was anything to eat as he'd missed lunch. He'd go there himself in a minute and see that Theo took the luggage upstairs, and when the guests went to their rooms, he must help him move the tree in to the corner of the living room.

He surveyed the party. It was obvious that Debra was the dominant person here. He wondered if she worked, was responsible for their wealth or was just another wife, perhaps once a trophy one, keeping her worker husband in order and spending his money.

He thought it would be prudent to introduce Eloise now, she could tell them what she planned for dinner and ask if there were any special requests. He put the idea to them and Debra said that would be a good idea. Ken, her husband, asked to see the wine list.

Vera went back to the kitchen to refill the teapot and after a few minutes Lawrence followed her. He could hear the soft drone of their voices, but the minute he entered, Vera stopped talking.

Theo, not caring what the mince pies looked like, was busily eating them. He looked up when Lawrence came in. 'They're delicious, and I haven't had any lunch,' he said as if to explain his hunger.

'You need to take their luggage to their rooms and then we must get the tree in the living room, it can't stay in the hall.'

'I will in a sec when I've finished this pie,' Theo said. He lowered his voice, 'Vera says one of the women is a prostitute... a sex worker.'

'Vera, what do you mean?' Lawrence turned to her in horror, not only was he in danger of getting a black mark at the agency if these clients complained about the chalet not being up to scratch, but Vera was now insulting them.

Vera, guessing his thoughts, protested, 'I won't say it to them, but I know. That young woman she is high-class, I have seen it before, these men, they bring this kind of girl with them.'

He'd heard the stories, there was even a place here called Cocaine Castle where all sorts was said to go on, but so far he'd never had anything like that here, not that he knew of anyway.

'You must not talk about such things, Vera. She is Mr Simpson's fiancée.' But even as he said it, he felt cold. What if Vera was right, would he have to turn a blind eye? No, that would be too much, and yet what was he to do? If he questioned these guests about it, they would no doubt complain to the agency, even leave and demand their money back, and yet nor did he want Theo to be exposed to such behaviour, or set such a precedent for Jacaranda's future. These mega-rich people could buy anything – or anyone – they chose, but Theo, he didn't want him to be among such people, people who bought and sold others for their greedy pleasure.

Theo appeared to be unperturbed, shoving another mince pie into his mouth before going to collect the luggage and taking it upstairs.

'You are not to mention such a thing again, Vera,' he repeated sharply. 'Now, Eloise, please come and let me introduce you to the guests and bring with you the menus in case there are any allergies or whatever, though I did ask them to let me know if there was anything when they booked. I'll introduce you and then I'll go and fetch the wine list.'

'OK,' Eloise said reluctantly, going to the sink to rinse her hands.

He wanted to say something to boost her morale but he felt as nervous as she did, worried that these people would demand culinary skills from her she did not possess. They walked down the passage in silence, Eloise following slowly behind him to the living room. They could hear the chatter of the guests, describing their journey out here, each one trying to outdo the other.

He waited at the door for Eloise to join him, turned and put his hand gently on her shoulder to guide her into the room before him, to give her courage. There was a sudden silence as they all saw her and he introduced her, 'This is Eloise Brandon our... chef, who will be...'

Before he could finish, Gaby shrieked, 'Oh, Mrs B, what a laugh, are you here doing the cooking? Are Kit and Lizzie here too?'

14

Eloise stared at Gaby, Vera's words drilling into her. Gaby, a prostitute, surely not, she must be mistaken. It must be a language mix-up; there were many words that described a young and beautiful girlfriend of a rich, and not very attractive man, who was sitting close to her, his hand on her leg.

Gaby was a year or so older than her twins and used to live in the same street as they did until her father died and she, her mother and her three younger brothers had moved away, struggling to make ends meet in London. Gaby, Kit and Lizzie often went on the bus to school together, and later, Eloise heard that Gaby had got into Oxford, or was it Cambridge, she couldn't remember, but she was a bright girl and surely destined for greater things than being a rich man's plaything. Vera must have got it wrong.

'Lovely to see you, Gaby,' she said, as Vera whisked past her with a fresh pot of tea and an inscrutable expression.

How pretty Gaby was, fresh-faced with shining eyes, her lips now clamped together to hold back laughter. She almost felt like laughing at the realization that one of the terrifying guests that could make or break Jacaranda's future was this young woman, one-time friend of her twins. Perhaps they wouldn't be so demanding to cook for after all.

'So you know each other?' The older woman threw Eloise a look of contempt as if by knowing her she was somehow complicit in Gaby's relationship with her nephew. She was swathed in a lilac cashmere shawl and seated on the edge of the sofa as though something nasty might be hidden in the depths of it and could spring out and bite her.

Eloise held her gaze. She'd known Gaby since she was eight. 'Yes we do. What a wonderful surprise that you're here, Gaby. I hope we have time to catch up.' Eloise was amazed to see her, then catching Lawrence's stern eye, she went on, 'I've come with the menu for tonight's dinner to make sure it suits everyone.'

'I'll get the wine list,' Lawrence escaped.

Apart from Debra saying she never touched fat or white sugar – though she had just eaten a large slice of cake with vanilla butter cream icing with relish – there were, to her surprise, no complaints about the dinner menu and Eloise thankfully went back to the kitchen.

Soon she heard the guests clump up to their rooms. Lawrence remained out of sight, and Vera, who'd also been out of the room, now appeared with the tea things and began to wash them up. Neither woman spoke for a while, then Eloise, not wanting to offend Vera if she'd inadvertently used the wrong word to describe Gaby, said quietly, hoping no one would overhear them, 'What did you mean, Vera... about... prostitutes?'

Vera came closer to her, watching her spread fruit cream between the baby macaroons she'd made in various soft colours to go with the fruit compote for supper – she left some plain as a token for Debra, who she suspected wouldn't be able to resist them.

'I don't tell lies,' Vera said as though she'd been accused

of a major crime. 'You should see what I have seen in places I've worked. Some of these girls are very intelligent, far more intelligent than the men they go with. To train for a good job, you need university and it is expensive, and not always possible to pay for. If they are pretty like that girl, and find a rich man to pay, it is better than cleaning, working all hours like me... until Lawrence rescued me,' she said, making Eloise feel ashamed that she had never been so desperate that she'd been forced to sink to such depths. Gaby's father had died young, leaving them with little money – was Gaby giving out sex to pay her tuition fees? Could she really be engaged to that dreary-looking man? Her own children came to mind. It would be a struggle to get them both through uni but the thought they'd ever have to succumb to such things filled her with fear.

Vera said, 'Those men in there look quite harmless and you know many are very lonely and all they want is someone to talk to, keep them company.' She laughed hoarsely, 'I do not judge these girls, and that Gaby doesn't look kept down, there are worse things than having sex with someone who is kind. You do what you do to get what you need.'

'I suppose so.' Eloise felt humbled by Vera's explanation. In many ways she'd been lucky. She may have lost the love of her life when Harvey had left her but she'd had a safe, comfortable life. She hoped she'd be able to have a heart-to-heart with Gaby, make sure she was happy and was not being used, though if Vera was right, Gaby could be the one who was using that morose young man to pay her university fees, though she hoped things were not that desperate for her.

When the guests had gone up to their rooms to unpack, Theo and Lawrence – with Bert, who'd escaped from his den downstairs, jumping around barking with excitement –

hauled the tree into the living room, took it out of the netting and set it up on its stand in the corner of the room. It was a beautiful tree, the fresh scent of the pine filling the room, its branches stretching out, begging, Eloise thought fancifully, to be decorated, and she fetched the box she'd found in the wardrobe and showed the decorations to Lawrence and Theo.

'I remember these when I stayed here once for Christmas, when I was about ten. They are so pretty. Have we time to put them on now?' She unwrapped a delicate angel and then a shining ball with a coloured pattern sunk into the centre of it, and a stunning egg covered in glowing beads like something by Fabergé. 'I remember these, Maddy made them, she blew the eggs and painted and decorated them.' Eloise recalled Maddy telling her how she made them. She hung it carefully.

Theo exclaimed in delight, 'They're fab, perhaps there are some more.' He dug his hands into the box as if he was doing a lucky dip. 'Look at this glittery tiger and this elephant, can't think what they have to do with Christmas, but hey... what's it matter?' He hung them both on the tree, his face flushed with delight like a small boy, enchanted, before delving into the box again to find more decorations and picking out another egg, which he hung reverently on a branch. Lawrence watched them in silence.

'Don't you like them?' She turned to him, smiling, 'Or are you worried about the dinner? It's all fine, I'll go back to it in a few minutes.'

'No... it's not that... it's just...' He turned to Theo who was excitedly unwrapping more decorations from the box, exclaiming at each new treasure he found.

'Mum bought this one, I remember that.' Theo took out a large opaque ball with a glittering snow scene inside. 'Great to see it again, a little bit of her for Christmas.' He hung it carefully on the tree.

His mother? Eloise wondered where she was, *who* she was, but Theo seemed more happy than sad to be reminded of her and she felt glad he'd found a small memento of her for Christmas.

Lawrence said, 'You were very young then, I'm surprised you remember it at all. But you know Aurelia does the decorations, Theo. She came to do it earlier but the tree hadn't arrived – she's coming to do it tomorrow.'

Eloise dropped the golden bell she was unwrapping back into the box. Of course, it would be Aurelia. She seemed to have far more than a foothold in Jacaranda. A whole leg, a shapely hip, her whole self. Aurelia was well on her way to getting her hands on Jacaranda and so too Lawrence. What could Eloise do? She was only here until after Christmas and then would go home and Aurelia could saunter in unchecked.

'She needn't do it this year. I want to use these beautiful ones Maddy made and the one Mum bought. They are much nicer than that pink and gold theme Aurelia did last year,' Theo said firmly, digging deeper into the box with pleasure. 'I want these, so does Eloise,' he smiled at her, 'so that's two against one, Dad, bad luck.'

Lawrence sighed. 'OK,' he said, 'I'll tell her. I expect she'll be glad to have some extra time for all the other things she has to do.' He did not sound convinced and left the room, going downstairs to his office to ring her, leaving Eloise feeling surprisingly jubilant.

*

The first supper went well, or at least it didn't go badly, as no one complained, not to Eloise at any rate, though Debra asked Lawrence rather pointedly if the dog was allowed in the kitchen, Lawrence assured her he was not.

'I'm relieved to hear it. Animals, even domesticated ones, are so dirty, especially dogs, sniffing around everywhere,' Debra announced with a shiver of disgust.

Eloise, who had just brought in the pudding, was glad that Theo had not heard this remark, for he would have surely jumped to Bert's defence and upset Debra. She sneaked a look at Lawrence who was explaining that Bert lived in the basement, but never, ever, in any circumstances was he allowed in the kitchen. Eloise wondered if he were crossing his fingers as he said this.

The arrival of these guests had put Lawrence in an odd mood; Eloise had caught him looking at her once or twice in a sort of pensive way as though he was trying to assess her. She understood his concerns and realized there was far more at stake than just a chalet full of grumpy guests put off by her cooking – Jacaranda's future was on the line. And she was sure Aurelia was standing by to be a part of it. She wondered how Aurelia had taken the news that she would not be decorating the tree this year. No doubt Lawrence had gone to see her after dinner to console her, as she heard him telling Vera he was going out to meet someone.

The kitchen was tidy thanks to Vera, but apart from her bedroom Eloise had nowhere else to sit if there were guests. Lawrence hadn't said anything, but she sensed that a mere cook like herself was not supposed to loll about in the living room fraternizing with these particular guests, and though it was past ten and she'd heard some of them go upstairs to their rooms, she felt she better not go into the living room to read. She decided to sit in the window seat in the kitchen with her book – a complicated historical saga. The room felt cold and clinical and she stared out of the window at the blackness of the night lit with pinpricks of stars, and the occasional sliver of light from the chalets scattered below them. She wondered if Harvey were still here. He might be staying in one of the chalets nearby, but with luck, he had gone home.

She tried to get back to her book instead of thinking of him, but it was a story that needed time and concentration and she found it difficult this evening, feeling unsettled now by thoughts of Harvey.

She heard someone coming down the passage to the kitchen and tensed, wondering if it were one of the house party – Debra seemed to be the one most likely to come and ask for something, or worse, to complain, but to her relief it was Gaby.

'So glad it's just you in here,' she exclaimed, coming and sitting down on the window seat beside her. 'It's so good to see you, Mrs B...'

'Eloise, please.'

'Eloise. I thought it was going to be a nightmare here with all of them, but with you here it might be fun.'

'I doubt it; I'm working, doing the cooking.' Eloise was cheered by Gaby's enthusiasm nonetheless. 'Anyway aren't you here with your fiancé?' She felt maternal towards her, so young and almost naïve.

Gaby blushed but regarded her defiantly. 'You'll be horrified, I know, but I'm only wearing his ring so his family aren't shocked. He says he's in love with me – he's mega rich and is paying my uni fees.'

'Oh Gaby. Does your mother know?' She immediately wished she hadn't asked. She remembered Gaby's mother,

Annie, and her panic when her husband, Garth, had died suddenly and she discovered he hadn't paid the mortgage for ages and there was little money left.

'Not really. She doesn't know the truth about our relationship, thinks he's just a boyfriend. She quite likes him and he's very generous to her, helping out with things. It's one of the reasons I stay with him. He hasn't got much of a family of his own.'

'But what about the others here, aren't they his family?' Eloise asked.

'Well the dreaded Debra...' Gaby raised her eyebrows, 'she's married to Ken, mother of Radley, mother-in-law to Pippa, Jerry is her nephew. But they've only really been in contact since Debra's sister, Jerry's mother, died a couple of years ago, and she's got him into the family business. It's not like a normal family, they work together, but they don't seem to have much fun together.'

'I guessed that, but who is the other man?'

'Travis, he's always been around, apparently. He's their Mr Fixit, arranges travel and things, a sort of business partner to Ken.'

'How are your mother and brothers?' Eloise was more interested in them than the party here. 'I'd love to see them again.'

'Oh, Mum's got a new man; I know I should be happy for her, but I don't like him very much. She and the boys are staying with him and his bratty children in Cornwall for Christmas, so I chose to come here with Jerry and get in some skiing.'

'And how long have you been with Jerry?' Eloise asked.

'Six months... and what about Kit and Lizzie?' Gaby rushed on as if fearful Eloise would delve deeper into her situation. 'Pity they're not here for Christmas.'

'I wish, but they're on their gap year in Tibet and finishing up in New Zealand with my parents. Harvey and I are divorced now and I'm here,' she went on quickly, pre-empting any questions about her marriage and getting the topic over and done with, 'because my godfather, Lawrence's father, thinks that because I once did a Cordon Bleu Foundation Course, I'm a trained chef. The last chef he had ran off with one of the rich clients staying here.'

Gaby laughed, 'So I'm not the only one living off ill-gotten gains.'

Eloise ignored her remark, though if there were a choice, she'd far rather cook than have to share a bed with that morose man Gaby was involved with. She wondered how she'd met him.

As if she could read her thoughts, Gaby said, 'I suppose. I'd better tell you all about Jerry and me, but don't tell Mum, she thinks we met at a party. In actual fact I met him on a dating site, Sugar Dads. It's full of rich men willing to pay uni fees in exchange for a bit of time with them. It's not just sex, you know, they just want someone to be with, sad really, but lucky for girls like me.'

15

Apart from Gaby, the rest of the house party kept closely together. There were copious phone calls and time spent on the Internet, causing Eloise to wonder why they had bothered to leave their own homes at all. True it was very cold and there was a whiteout on one side of the mountain range, so only a few intrepid skiers were out there, but Savoleyres was clear, but only Theo and Bert tumbled out of bed and set off to ski. Even if it had been clear and sunny, Eloise doubted if many of their guests would have bothered to venture far. Perhaps they didn't trust their businesses and investment brokers to go on making money for them without staying in constant contact. Instead of their wealth giving them freedom, it seemed to her to imprison them.

Eloise felt trapped too by them being inside all day. They wanted lunch, which meant extra work, but more importantly she wanted to escape Aurelia's visits.

Despite no longer being needed to decorate the tree, undeterred Aurelia had appeared the following morning at breakfast time, clutching one of her pink boxes containing some mini croissants and chocolate breads which she'd offered to the guests 'for their opinion'.

'I have my own little catering business,' she said coyly, smiling at Travis, who went all pink and squirmy under her scrutiny. 'I know you have a *wonderful* cook here.' If her glance aimed at Eloise had claws, she'd have needed major facial surgery. 'But this air makes you so hungry, and breakfast is not often enough to sustain you all morning, so if you feel like a teeny snack you'll find me just off the Place Centrale, beside the photo shop.' She handed round her box as the rest of the party wandered into the room for breakfast.

The tree stood in all its glory in the corner by the window, its branches twinkling with ornaments. Maddy's jewelled eggs had attracted many compliments but Aurelia shuddered as she passed it as though some vulgar person with atrocious dress sense had gatecrashed the party.

Lawrence had long since had his breakfast and was downstairs in his office on the telephone. Vera had let Aurelia into the chalet and Eloise had just come into the room with a dish of eggs and bacon. Apart from her cutting glance, Aurelia ignored her and began on her selling spiel, trying to seduce the guests with her pastries with their sweet vanilla and chocolate aroma.

Debra said she didn't touch white sugar or fat but just this once she'd take a tiny bite out of one, they smelt so good.

Vera began to offer coffee and tea, dodging round Aurelia as if she were an annoying piece of furniture. Eloise knew from her set expression that Vera wanted her gone and was not at all taken in by her box of delights.

Eloise escaped to the kitchen and heard Lawrence come up the stairs and go into the living room. She heard the buzz of his voice as he greeted the guests, but she couldn't hear what he was saying, though to her relief Aurelia left soon after.

She hoped that would be the end of Aurelia's visits, but she had reappeared that evening with yet more boxes – this time canapés, which she handed round, making a beeline for Ken now, who she assumed was the person paying for this holiday. Minutes before, Eloise had brought in the ones she had prepared, raw vegetables with a freshly made blue cheese dip, almonds roasted in oil with herbs and tiny asparagus tarts.

'Forgive me for bringing my small offerings for you to try,' Aurelia simpered, 'but I knew at once you are very discerning people and I would welcome your opinion on whether these are good enough to serve to those who expect the best. I have orders, you see...' she paused, lowering her eyes in pretence of modesty, 'well, you may have read in the papers that some of the royals come here to ski and...'

Ken perked up, 'Do you cater for them?'

Before Aurelia could answer, Lawrence, who was going round with the drinks, said, 'I expect they bring their own staff. Thank you, Aurelia, so kind of you to drop in when I know how busy you are.' He put his arm out to steer her towards the door, smiling, but Eloise saw a determined expression on his face as if he disapproved of this charade. Whatever his relationship with her, it obviously did not include letting her gatecrash with her wares, and for that she was grateful to him. Vera, who'd been hovering outside, came into the room with her coat, holding it open for Aurelia, who laughed rather sharply.

'Well I must fly,' she said to the guests, as if she were an important actor leaving the stage. 'I hope to see you all again soon.' And she swept from the room, snatching her coat from Vera as she went.

Lawrence opened the front door for her.

'I'm only trying to help you keep Jacaranda, Lawrence,' she said. 'I'm used to these sorts of people and they expect extremely sophisticated catering and style, you know.'

'Thanks, safe trip home,' Lawrence said, going out to see her to her car.

Eloise, feeling crushed by Aurelia's sales spiel, scurried back to the kitchen to put the last touches to the dinner. She felt worse when Lawrence, having seen Aurelia out, came in to sort the wine, his shoulders sagged and he did not look at her. At first she'd been cheered by his swift dismissal of Aurelia, been about to thank him, but now she felt that she had let him down so she stayed silent, concentrating on the sauce for the meat. Her insecurity, never far away, kicked in. Was he wishing he had splashed out on Aurelia and her expensive delights, instead of *her* less exciting ones?

*

All this she poured out to Saskia, when they met up the following day. They sat in a corner of the Milk Bar in the main drag, drinking hot chocolate with swirls of whipped cream on top. Harvey had probably gone home by now, but still, wherever Eloise went she found herself surreptitiously looking out for him so she could duck out of his way and avoid further heartache.

The Milk Bar was crowded as the snow conditions this morning were not for the faint-hearted. Though, thanks to Pascal, her shoulder was much better, Eloise was relieved when Saskia suggested they meet up for a drink today rather than ski.

'I warned you, Aurelia has got her eye on Jacaranda and, not surprisingly, Lawrence. He's very attractive,' Saskia giggled. 'Well, you must find him so, living under the same roof.' She paused as if waiting for Eloise to confess she was in love, or anyway in lust with him.

'I don't see him that way,' Eloise said, not meeting Saskia's eye. There were times when she'd caught him looking at her, or their eyes had met and she'd felt a sort of frisson of desire, but what good would that do her as she was going home in a couple of weeks or so, and, she suspected, she would not be coming back again. Besides, she thought it best to take a sabbatical from love, she'd been hurt enough by Harvey. 'Lawrence is my boss,' she went on firmly, 'and I've got enough on my plate trying not to mess up. He's been very quiet since these guests have arrived. He gave me a pep talk about how important they are for Jacaranda's future, the place needs mammoth work on it apparently, and these guests are the key to bringing in enough money to pay for it.'

'Yes, he was telling Quinn about it. Because Jacaranda's so old it costs more to rewire without spoiling it. Aurelia has different ideas, she wants to build more chalets there and extend Jacaranda, so it won't matter if the old walls have to come down,' Saskia said.

'How do you know this?' Eloise's stomach cramped with despair.

'Oh, we all had lunch together at the Relais des Neiges, the other day. I don't know why she was there, she just sort of appeared,' Saskia added quickly, seeing Eloise's expression.

Eloise bit the bullet. 'Are she and Lawrence an item? I can't make it out.'

'I'm not sure. There used to be a man Aurelia was with, Malcolm, though we haven't seen him lately, so maybe whatever their relationship was is over. I told you she wants Jacaranda. She, and possibly Malcolm, put quite a lot of money into starting her "Tempting Delights",' she emphasized the words, 'and it's doing well, but think how much more she'd make if she had a lovely chalet too? She could build sheds or whatever to cook in and store it all in the garden, and perhaps have dinners, or keep to the chalet parties in Jacaranda and force-feed the clients with her "Tempting Delights",' she giggled, 'and having a devilishly sexy man to curl up with would be the icing on her "Delights".'

Eloise was hit with a sick despair. She felt a sense of loyalty to Jacaranda, for Desmond's sake with his precious memories of Maddy and, of course, for Lawrence and Theo.

Saskia saw her face and said firmly, 'We can't let that happen, but Aurelia, apparently, does have access to money, perhaps she's made a huge profit, I don't know, and Jacaranda urgently needs to update its plumbing and all. But *you* have the advantage of being there, in the chalet… with Lawrence,' Saskia emphasized his name as if Eloise was slow off the mark.

'Oh Saskia, don't be silly. Our relationship is nothing like that at all, and even if it was I can't help out with money, I hardly have any myself after the divorce and buying the new house, and don't forget I'm going home very soon.'

'Well then, let's hope these clients at Jacaranda now are so impressed they tell the agency to send Lawrence all their richest clients,' Saskia said. 'It seems as if a lot hangs on whether they enjoy their time there. If they don't he may have no choice but to turn to Aurelia to save Jacaranda.'

'Don't say that,' Eloise said with a sickening heart, even though she knew that it was true.

16

There were two days until Christmas and at last they woke to blue skies and golden sunshine. To Eloise's relief, as she and Vera were fed up with some of the guests – namely Debra, Ken and Travis – lurking about seemingly glued to one electronic device or another as if they were oxygen masks, everyone except Debra wanted to ski. Lawrence organized a couple of ski guides to accompany them, though Gaby, who'd skied a lot as a child before her father's death, announced that she and Jerry had made plans to ski with Theo.

Theo had taken them out a couple of times already and Eloise guessed that Gaby wanted to get away from the group, and Theo was only too willing to take them and be out on the mountains himself. She wished she could go too, but she supposed she'd have to stay here and produce lunch for Debra. But to her surprise and delight, Debra said she'd join Ken and Travis for lunch on the mountains and as Lawrence was tied up, Eloise was detailed to take her to find them there and then she was free to ski herself.

Lawrence hurried impatiently into the kitchen while pulling on his coat. 'Are you up to date with your cooking?'

'Just about,' she said cheerfully, hoping to tease him out of his mood. Theo was collecting the turkey and the ingredients for the stuffing from the butcher later. The puddings were done and she'd had another go at making mince pies, leaving the pastry lids off and covering the tops instead with slivers of almonds and they looked and, she thought, tasted delicious.

'It's got to be more than "just about",' he snapped wearily, making her feel guilty that she wasn't the top chef his father had persuaded him she was.

'I'm sorry Desmond exaggerated my skills,' she said. 'I am doing my best, but I'm aware that my best is not good enough for these sorts of people. Have they complained much?'

He regarded her in surprise. 'No one's complained to me, have they to you?'

'Well, no, but I just thought they'd expect… top restaurant food, all tarted up.'

His face relaxed, his mouth quivered with the sliver of a smile. 'I think they would if this was one of those luxury chalets, instead of just plain old Jacaranda…'

'Jacaranda is far more than that,' she retorted. 'Those places have no atmosphere and are completely false, like a film set, not the real thing at all. I couldn't bear it if this chalet became like that.' The words 'if Aurelia got hold of it' hung in the air between them, though she'd stopped herself saying them in time.

His expression tightened again, his mouth now set in a grim line, 'Things have changed since we were children, Eloise. People expect far more today, and if I want to keep Jacaranda and maintain it properly, we need to attract people at the top of the market, there's a lot of competition now.'

'I know that, but what about ordinary families, people with children.'

'It doesn't really work. We need to make a certain profit

each year for Jacaranda to survive and that means setting the right price for each stay, which is usually out of the question for most families, especially when you need a car to get to the ski stations and the village. As you know, there's quite a walk to the bus stop and we charge extra if we taxi them about. Then there's parking fees, and all that costs more money which many families can't afford.' He turned back towards the door, 'We've got to offer more to get the right people.'

'Like zillionaires who seduce your chefs,' she joked, hoping to lighten his mood.

'Well no.' He studied her a moment, and she was about to say he needn't worry, she had no intention of going off with any of this lot, even if they managed to glance up long enough from their laptops to notice her, when Vera came into the kitchen and they could hear the bustle of the others searching for coats and boots in the hallway and Ken calling him.

Lawrence sighed and marched out of the kitchen as if he were on dangerous manoeuvres, ready to drive the skiers down. The outside door was left open as the party tramped in and out getting their belongings together. The blue minibus started up, its wheels crunching over the icy snow as Lawrence turned it round to go down the road and the front door of the chalet closed at last, cutting the creep of the icy cold air coming down the passage, and they were gone, leaving only Debra behind.

Almost at once she came into the kitchen, walking in as if she owned it. 'I'm to meet the skiers for lunch at 1.30,' she announced, 'and you are taking me there, Eloise, are you not?'

'Yes,' Eloise said, 'we'll leave about 12.15, if that's suits you. Do you have a pass for the ski lift?'

'No,' Debra said, 'and I'd like to do some shopping first,

so perhaps we'll leave earlier?' She smiled, though her eyes were hard, wary, as if she wouldn't stand for a different plan to the one she'd made for herself.

Eloise nodded, suppressing an oath. That meant she'd probably have to curtail her skiing this afternoon to finish off the dinner, a task she hoped she could finish this morning, but like Theo and Lawrence, she must accept that the clients' wishes came first.

Half an hour later they were in the jeep. The minute she was settled in her seat, Debra said, 'How extraordinary that you know Gaby. Have you known her long?'

'Yes, I suppose I have. Her family used to live in the same street as us and she was friends with my children.'

'Was? So she's no longer their friend?' Debra turned to Eloise as if she were interrogating her.

'No, but only because her family moved away when her father died.' Eloise slowed down as the road felt quite icy, being sheltered by the trees, and the sun hadn't had enough time to soften it.

'I'm sure she's very nice,' Debra said in a voice that implied that she wasn't, 'but she's not the sort of girl I expect my nephew to marry.'

Eloise bit back her opinion that she didn't think Debra's nephew was the sort of man Gaby should spend her life with. He reminded her of a lovesick dog following her round, which would surely drive her mad in time, if it hadn't already. If he weren't bankrolling her studies, she probably wouldn't have looked at him twice.

'Jerry's easily led,' Debra went on. 'When his mother, my sister, died, he came into a lot of money, not that he hasn't also worked hard for it, he's always worked since he left school,' she added quickly as if Eloise would despise someone who had inherited money. 'So he's easy prey for fortune-hunters.'

'And you think Gaby is one?' Eloise felt awkward, as Gaby had confessed to her that she was using Jerry's money to get her through uni. Studying law, she'd probably end up with a good job and a good salary and wouldn't need his money after that.

'Yes I do,' Debra said firmly. 'I've told Jerry in no uncertain terms that she's not for him, but he's besotted with her, fool that he is, and he won't hear a word against her. I didn't want her to join our party for Christmas, but he insisted, paid for her ticket, so there was nothing I could do to stop it.'

Eloise was torn. She liked Gaby and knew she was only trying to get a better life, earn her own way in the end, but she was using Jerry to get there, and though people used each other in all sorts of ways, Eloise did feel it was wrong, and would be furious with Lizzie or indeed Kit, if they did the same. Yet she knew Gaby's family had suffered financially since Garth had died and had been left in serious debt. Perhaps seeing her mother struggle to get by had fuelled Gaby's determination not to get caught in that trap herself. Without Jerry's help she might not have been able to go to university at all. Debra probably didn't know what it was like to worry where the next tenner was coming from and to be ground down by unending debt and anxiety about how to pay it back.

As if she could read her mind, Debra said, 'You probably think I married a rich man and go about spending his money, but you're wrong. *I'm* the one with the money. My sister and I went into property, built up a good business, and then we sold it. I married Ken for love, he was in the letting business himself, bought flats in what were then unfashionable parts of London, did them up and sold them on for a good profit. I now have various Internet businesses, as do Jerry and Radley.'

'And Travis and Pippa?' Eloise asked, rather admiring Debra now for not being a kept woman.

'Travis works with Ken, his right-hand man, and Pippa,' Debra paused, sighed, 'Pippa is really a passenger, riding on the backs of the rest of us.'

'I see.' Eloise felt rather sorry for Pippa for not having the drive of her mother-in-law. They reached the square and she parked the car and asked Debra which shops she wanted to go to.

'I'd like a warmer ski jacket,' Debra said. 'It's much colder than I thought and it will be worse up the mountain.'

She was wearing a well-cut wool jacket in dark green that looked warm enough. But it was what Debra wanted and Eloise was here to help her, though she wished she knew which shops to take her to. She'd only been shown the food ones and hardly knew where well-dressed women like Debra went to buy their clothes around here.

'Hello… it's Eloise, isn't it?' A man came up and greeted her; it was Quinn, Saskia's lover.

'Oh Quinn, how nice to see you. This is Debra Collins who is staying in Jacaranda. Quinn Pearson,' Eloise introduced them.

'Not *the* Quinn Pearson, the restaurant writer,' Debra exclaimed, her face glowing more than Eloise had ever seen it.

Quinn, no doubt used to such adulation, smiled, 'The very one, my dear lady. Now, are you here for Christmas, enjoying the skiing?'

'I don't ski, I never got round to it, though I love the mountains,' Debra said in a sort of cooing voice. 'But the rest of my party are up there and Eloise is taking me to join them for lunch. Are you going up today?' She twinkled at him; quite surprising Eloise who hadn't imagined this powerful lady with her millions would be impressed with a mere cookery writer.

'No, I'm lunching elsewhere, Chez Dany, walking up there with some friends.' He smiled, turned to Eloise. 'Saskia is thrilled you are here, someone her own age,' he chuckled, 'though she's very good with an old man like me.'

And you are very good to her, Eloise thought, before bidding Quinn farewell and getting back to the business of shopping.

There were quite a few clothes shops around and to Eloise's relief Debra found a jacket that pleased her in the second shop they went to. It was mouth-wateringly expensive, in a soft blue with a blonde fur collar and a matching hat. Clothed in those and a new pair of gloves, Eloise took Debra up in the gondola to the mid stop on the mountain where she was to meet the others for lunch.

With the exception of Theo, Jerry and Gaby, the others had just arrived and Eloise left Debra with them, join-ing the queue to take a gondola further up to the top of the mountain.

It was quite crowded, people jostling to get in, and she just managed to squeeze in the lift in front of her before it turned away and the door snapped shut. It set off, swinging a moment before climbing with a sudden surge high above the mountains.

'Eloise?' She heard her name; his voice hesitant as if he could not believe that she was there. 'Eloise, whatever are *you* doing out here?'

17

Eloise glanced up, her hand tightening on her skis, her stomach riddled with knots. She'd convinced herself that Harvey had left the resort, gone back home for Christmas.

There was hardly any place to move in the gondola with people and skis stacked close together, she was pinned against one of the side windows. A couple beside her were holding on to each other, the woman, her head snug in a cream wool beanie, craned forward every so often to nibble her companion's neck, or he leant to kiss her. Between them and their two bobbing heads, she saw Harvey staring at her, his expression a mixture of dismay and disbelief.

He was shocked to see her. At least she had glimpsed him in the village so knew *he* was here, though suddenly seeing him like this was most unsettling.

His face was lightly tanned, though quite pouchy around his eyes, and there were deep lines round his mouth. The glowing skin of the young couple beside her cruelly showed how much older he had become since she had last seen him in the divorce court. He was wearing the red and blue stripy hat Lizzie had given him the last time they'd been skiing – the family all together. She didn't want him here, want the memories of those family skiing holidays to swamp her, when the children were small and Jacaranda was cosy and familiar and Harvey loved her – or anyway she thought he did.

'You must be staying with your godfather,' he said, his voice loud above the chatter around them. He seemed pleased that he had found a reason for her being here, dodging his face between the kissing couple. 'Are you here for Christmas?'

She nodded, tried surreptitiously to see who he was with, but it was difficult in the scrum to see who was with whom. She felt slightly panicky now, as if she were imprisoned with him in this small and crowded place, without an escape route. What if she'd been standing next to him, pushed against him by the other skiers, feeling the shape of him, the familiar scent of his skin?

The couple between them snuggled closer, they were very young and obviously madly in love. It took her back to her and Harvey in their early days when they couldn't stop touching each other, reaching out as if to confirm the other was there. Then, as their life together went on and the children were born, he had become more and more restless until he had eventually drifted away.

She gazed out at the mountains and the hard light, with the brilliant blue sky and the white, white snow. In the spring, marmots came out of their burrows on these slopes and she remembered watching for them from the gondola, hoping to see one, though she never had. They wouldn't be there yet; they'd be snug beneath the ground in hibernation. She tried to think of them instead of Harvey, standing large as life just a few steps away from her.

She wriggled round so her back was to him while she struggled to calm herself. If only she could escape. She didn't want to talk to him, see who he was with. He was quiet now, no doubt wishing he'd tried to avoid her.

They arrived; the gondola shuddering into the dock, the door sliding open, and everyone clattered out. Eloise followed them and, to her dismay, Harvey was waiting for her by the stairs to go down to the snow.

'I'm so surprised to see you here,' he said, slightly awkward now, the way he was if he'd been up to no good with some other woman and he knew she suspected him.

They were stuck in the crowd of skiers all trying to get down the narrow stairs to the snow. 'Me too. How long are you here? Where are you staying?' She needed to know so she could lie low, keep out of his way. Her heart was beating fast, she wanted to get away from him, to cut away the memories of the good times that pained her so. She would not go out again until he had left.

'Down by the old church, in a chalet with friends,' he said.

She waited for him to tell her their names, wondered if they were friends they had shared when married, or people she had never known and he had kept from her, or new friends that now she would never get to know. Or did he mean he was in a chalet with a lover, the woman in pink? He did not venture any more information and she was not going to question him.

'So how long are you here?' he asked, his voice neutral, no doubt checking on her too, wanting to keep out of *her* way.

'I'm here as a cook at Jacaranda.' She moved away from him in the melee of people heading towards the stairs, longing to be skiing, escaping from him, dashing down the slope, though he could easily catch her up, but surely he would let her go, be relieved that she had gone.

'Cook?' he frowned. 'What do you mean?'

'The chalet's let out now for rich clients, their cook – or rather chef – ran off with a millionaire, so Desmond suggested I come out and cook for Christmas.'

'But that's... quite a job.' He looked incredulous, his mouth twitching with a smile.

'It is and I've got it,' she said firmly. Once she would have told him how precarious the job was, how she worried that Lawrence might think her not up to scratch and about Aurelia lurking in the wings willing her to fail, but now she said nothing, not wanting to add to her insecurity.

She moved as quickly as she could towards the stairs, frantic to get away from him, but she couldn't pass the other people, their heavy boots clanging on the metal steps as they went on down carrying their skis. Harvey was swept up by other skiers impatient to be down the stairs and back on the slopes and he was right behind her and for a moment they were trapped on the narrow stairs. He asked about Jacaranda, saying if he'd known they let it out he'd have told his friends, tried to rent it instead of the cramped place they were in now. She stayed silent; praying he and these friends wouldn't come up and visit.

Finally, she reached the bottom of the steps and joined the group of skiers putting on their skis. She wondered where Harvey was skiing. She wanted to go up to Tortin and ski down that way, have a good and challenging run, but she feared he'd planned to do the same.

To her relief, he said, 'I'm stopping here for a quick lunch. Have you heard from the twins?'

'I talked to them last week, I'll ring them for Christmas.' She didn't look at him, keeping her eyes on the run down to the lake now invisible under a deep covering of snow. It was so strange to be here standing beside him, the man she'd loved but now had lost.

'Are they all right?'

'Yes, don't you talk to them?'

'I will, I've emailed them.'

She turned to face him then, saw a sliver of guilt in his eyes. Now they were divorced and the children grown and gone, did he pretend he was a free spirit with no ties at all? He'd adored the twins when they were young but found it difficult to cope with them growing up, becoming independent, glowing with youth and good looks while his were fading. But whatever games he played, he was their father and despite everything, they loved him and they had many happy memories of the good times they'd shared. She'd done her best not to run him down in front of them but now they were here together her anger rose.

'You may be able to get shot of your wife but you must never desert your children. They are part of you and they love you,' she said, the words 'and you don't deserve them' hung between them.

'Of course I won't desert them,' he protested.

'I'm going,' she moved away from him to a clear patch in the snow, dropping down her skis ready to put them on and be off. 'Please don't come to Jacaranda, it's a business now and I am working there.'

'OK, enjoy your cooking.' He spoke, she felt, with relief, and he turned towards the restaurant.

A man she didn't know called to him, 'Harvey, we're here.'

From the muddle of people and skis propped in the snow outside the entrance to the restaurant, Eloise saw, with a sinking heart, Aurelia emerge and head towards them. How had she got involved with him, just by chance or had she already been after him with her 'Tempting Delights'?

'There you are, Harvey,' she said. 'Come on or we won't

get a table.' She had obviously seen them talking and she eyed Eloise curiously before saying, 'Do you know Harvey?' Her hand was on his sleeve as if she owned him, a look of condescension on her face as if she couldn't believe that they'd been talking together.

Eloise snapped her feet into her skis, her gloves were on, poles in hand ready to depart.

'Yes, I know him very well, he's my ex-husband, the father of my children,' she said, feeling a tiny burst of pleasure, which was quickly replaced with anger at Aurelia's obvious amazement.

'You two were married?' Aurelia said, unable to curb her surprise, staring open-mouthed at them both.

Harvey said, 'Yes, that's right.'

Eloise didn't hear any more but pushed off fast down the slope, the wind catching her tears and turning them to ice.

18

For a moment Lawrence felt that he was the king of the world, standing on the top of Tortin, the largest glacier in the district, his body surging with energy. He'd begun to wonder if he'd ever get the guests out of the chalet, them all being obsessed by keeping in touch with their various businesses and seemingly oblivious to the call of the mountains, though it was true the weather had not been good earlier in the week.

He'd hate to be like them – he'd seen it before in other rich clients. They never quite trusted other people, never dared to leave their work behind in case it crumbled without their attention.

But then he supposed he was a little obsessive with Jacaranda. He'd lost money this season with the chef dramas, having to fly more out when Denise had done her runner with that multi-millionaire. He'd managed to find another chef, Paddy, whom he'd had before; only he wasn't free until the second week of January. So far, Eloise was working out better than he thought she would, though he still felt nervous that there would be some culinary disaster. His father meant well, wanting to help, but he hadn't been here for so long and he had no idea of the standards needed at the top end of the rental market today.

He started on a long traverse across the top of the glacier.

He'd go on down now, get back to the village before the rest of them, so he could pick them up when they finished for the day. He hoped Theo would not take Gaby and Jerry too far away and would be back in time to help out if necessary.

Turning, he began to whip his way through the moguls; they were pretty relentless here and became more arduous nearer the bottom. There were quite a few other people on the slope, some not realizing how hard this run was, and having started off, they were now committed and were gingerly picking their way down, others just barging through, almost out of control, to get to the bottom.

He heard someone call his name and there was Eloise, pulling up her goggles so he could recognize her.

'I'm on my way back,' she said as if he might be annoyed that she was out here instead of slaving over the stove back at the chalet.

'Me too, in case the guests need picking up, and I've an appointment this afternoon,' he said. He noticed that her nose and eyes were red from the wind, giving the appearance that she'd been crying, but it was surely just the cold making them water, though she was wearing goggles. It made him say, 'I hope you're not finding it all too much, Eloise. I'm so relieved they all went out today. I thought we'd be imprisoned with them in Jacaranda for the whole time.'

She smiled, 'I thought the same. I wonder if they care if they're in the mountains or on a beach or wherever, being so glued to their laptops.'

'I know, hardly worth having all that money if you can't enjoy it.'

'I agree, though I suppose the weather wasn't very good the first few days, and Debra doesn't ski but she likes shopping.' She told him about her buying a new jacket. 'She's the one with the money. I had imagined it was Ken who was the rich one, but it's all hers and she earned it herself.'

'She did pay the full amount for the chalet herself, though it could have been a shared account. Good on her. So does she keep Ken?' He smiled. Eloise had lovely eyes; he hadn't really noticed before, blue-grey with long lashes.

'I don't think so. She said he does up flats and sells them on.'

'Property, if only we'd bought up some of those houses in London before various districts were "discovered", we'd have made our fortunes. Or even bought more chalets out here before the place became so fashionable,' he said. 'Well, I must get on. Shall we go together or do you want to take your time? Depending on how far you are with the dinner, you don't need to be back until five or six, though of course it will be dark before then, but you might like to stay out and have a drink or something. Vera will see to the tea if the guests come back for that.'

She hesitated and he thought she was wondering whether he wanted to ski home with her or if he preferred to go on alone at his own speed. Skiing was a tricky sport and two people not being compatible on the slopes ruined many a day and even, in some cases, romances. He wondered why that thought had come into his head.

'You start off and if I can't keep up with you, go on,' she said, pulling down her goggles. 'Just go at the pace you want, there's nothing worse than having to wait for someone who's struggling.'

'If you're sure,' he grinned at her, relieved that she understood. This could be the last time he had a good ski this week, what with the weather and having the guests and Christmas and all.

To his surprise she kept up with him and he was struck with the feeling she was driving something from her, getting rid of some inner demons. Perhaps they were her anxieties about being a good enough chef, or perhaps she, like him, was so glad to be here, finally out on the mountains in the clean, cold air. He remembered how when he'd first seen her at the top he'd wondered if she'd been crying.

He didn't know much about her; she was his father's goddaughter, though he couldn't remember meeting her before, at least not when she was grown-up, although they'd often had a collection of people staying at Jacaranda over the years. He knew she'd recently got divorced and her children had left home, perhaps she was missing them, remembering the times she'd spent here before, when they were young.

He hadn't treated her very well, he thought with shame. He was just so anxious about Jacaranda, it needed urgent repairs and he had three choices, as far as he could see: to shut it after the skiing season and get the refurbishments done then, or go in with someone else who could offer some finance, or, worst case scenario, sell it. He would *not* ask Desmond for money, he had given him enough already and he needed a comfortable income to enjoy his old age, but he must do everything to keep Jacaranda, for if he lost it, it would break his father's heart. But whatever his worries for Jacaranda's future, he should not take them out on Eloise, he owed her a lot for stepping into the breach and she'd done it with good grace.

As they neared the end of the run back into the village, he noticed that Eloise became nervous and kept shooting glances at the other skiers. When they reached the muddle of skiers taking off their skis at the bottom of the run, she offered him a lift in the jeep, but even as she asked him she was walking away as if she were in a hurry.

He followed her. 'No thanks, Eloise, I've got things to do down here and I'll hang about with the minibus for the others, or Theo can take them in the other jeep. He should be down soon. But are you all right... you seem troubled.' He put his hand on her arm.

'I'm fine,' she said, trying to smile. 'Just a bit tired, I haven't skied much these last years and that's quite a run.'

'It is... and your shoulder's holding up, I hope.' She was hiding something, he was sure of it, some secret sorrow, but he wouldn't probe, he sensed she wanted to keep it close to herself.

'Yes... Pascal did a wonderful job. Thank you for sending me to him.'

'I'm glad it's better.' He wanted to say more but he felt she'd put a barrier up between them to protect her secrets. 'I must just check my mobile, see if any of the guests want to be given a lift back,' he said. 'Would you like a drink before you go? You've got time, haven't you? It's not yet four.'

There was something about her stance that touched him. He'd probably been too hard on her, especially now with these particular guests, who expected so much for their money, and whom he, egged on by Aurelia, felt were so important for Jacaranda's future.

'Thanks, Lawrence, but I think I'll get back.' She kept glancing nervously about her, studying the other skiers who were coming down the last few yards, spilling out down to the car park. She gave him a quick smile before making hurriedly for the jeep.

He wondered what... or possibly who, was troubling her, but he soon forgot it as he went to the office of the firm that dealt with some of the chalet lettings to catch up with the bookings that had come in and any queries. Theo texted him to say they were all on the way down and was he still there to take some of them back in the minibus. He texted back that he was and went to have a drink in his favourite bar while he waited for them.

It was a good meeting place and he enjoyed dropping in there when he could. He saw a few people he knew and joined them for a drink. Aurelia and a couple of men passed by. When she saw Lawrence she stopped, told the men she'd catch up with them and came to join him.

'You'll never guess,' she started, with the air of someone bursting to pass on some gossip.

'But you're going to tell me,' he said wearily, wondering what bombshell she was going to drop on him now. It was usually about some law or plan the Swiss were rumoured to be implementing over tax on chalets or land belonging to foreigners, or a new right of way or something that would surely put Jacaranda in jeopardy unless he looked sharp and took precautions to avoid it. Her remarks concerning Jacaranda were beginning to annoy him. It was almost as if she got some pleasure from taunting him with some real or imagined drama that could affect his chalet business.

She ignored his tone of voice, 'I saw your little cook on the slopes and, guess what, her ex-husband was there. He used to stay at Jacaranda with her and he was very interested when I told him how you let it out and how if – like I'm always telling you,' she smiled proudly, 'you'd enlarge it, fill up the garden with little flats, you'd make a fortune.'

He'd heard Aurelia's plans all before and he didn't like them, but Eloise's *ex-husband*. What was he doing here? He didn't know her ex's name or what he did for a living. Was he a property developer, and might he hope to worm his way into Jacaranda? He knew he'd stayed there in the past, so he could drop in any time. Did Eloise know he was here and was that why she kept looking about, wary of seeing him? And what was Aurelia to do with it all?

'She never said he was out here,' he said weakly, remembering her red-rimmed eyes, her furtive looks at the other skiers and her wish to get quickly back to the chalet this afternoon.

'I don't think she knew; he certainly didn't. He was quite shocked to see her, but he's interested to see Jacaranda again, though she told him not to come, but you know...' she shrugged as if Eloise's request did not matter and anyway this man was a free agent, able to go where he pleased.

He felt a slow burn of anger grow in him but he banked it down. 'How do *you* know him, Aurelia?'

'Oh, I don't, not really. He's staying near the old church in one of the chalets Frankie – you know Frankie Butler – owns. We all met up for lunch and I saw Eloise talking to him, I must say I was quite surprised he was her ex-husband.' She had a mocking smile on her face that annoyed him further. He'd got too involved with her and he was tired of Aurelia always belittling people she felt were somehow inferior to her. 'They've been married for ages and they've got twins who are on their gap year, so she's now home alone.' She said the last two words with derision.

He knew about Eloise's situation but now he felt ashamed, he'd been so focused on getting a chef to keep his house party happy he hadn't asked Eloise anything more about herself, though also he did not want to pry, perhaps open wounds that were halfway healed. But Christmas was coming the day after tomorrow and she must be missing her children and perhaps she'd want to see this ex-husband to be able to talk to him about them, remember happier days. But maybe she didn't, maybe it was all too painful for her. Either way, though, he should have made an effort to think of her feelings and try and help her through what would be, in more ways than one, a difficult day for her.

To his relief his mobile rang, announcing that the chalet guests were down.

'I must go.' He got up, glad to be taking his leave of Aurelia, but she stopped him.

'I thought I'd give a little party, Steven said I could have one in his bar and I'll invite you all. I'm sure you'd be very interested to meet Harvey, he's worked in the travel business – upmarket holidays – for some time and he's got some wonderful ideas to put Jacaranda on the map.'

Lawrence didn't answer her as he hurried off to find his guests. He did not want to meet Harvey and hear any ideas he might have concerning Jacaranda. He also had a feeling that going to such a party, especially to meet him, was somehow betraying Eloise.

19

'What's happened, Eloise, you look upset?' Saskia called, as Eloise was about to get into the jeep. She was carrying her skis, having just come down from the slopes herself; she quickened her pace to catch up with Eloise.

Eloise looked round, 'Oh... Saskia, nothing, just tired after skiing down Tortin.' She wanted to get in the jeep and scurry away from the increasing crowd of skiers, fearful that Harvey, and worse still, Aurelia, would appear.

'Well come back with me to our chalet, have a drink. Quinn has gone to Geneva for the opening of a new restaurant, and I'm home alone.' Coming closer and picking up on Eloise's reluctance, she added, 'It's not far, just across the road and down, takes seven minutes at a brisk walk. Please, or do you have to go back to cook a banquet?' she teased.

'No... but...' Eloise longed to escape back to Jacaranda, and yet it was tempting to go with Saskia and confide in her. She felt so alone with her distress at having seen Harvey, spoken to him – he shouldn't be here, especially as she had just been getting used to the idea of spending her first Christmas alone as a single woman. Just knowing he was here made her feel lonelier and more bereft without her family as it was. Almost worse was him knowing Aurelia. She supposed she knew everyone out here, but her scorn at not believing that Harvey had married her dug deepest, bringing back her feelings of inadequacy which she'd struggled with over Harvey's infidelities and then their divorce.

Saskia came close to her and took her arm. 'Come on then or, if you'd rather, we can drive there.' Without waiting for her answer, Saskia dumped her skis into the back of the jeep and clambered in.

Eloise started it up and backed out, forcing herself to concentrate on not hitting anything instead of keeping an eye out for Harvey and Aurelia in case they were threading their way through the car park.

'Quinn and I had lunch up at the top then he came down early to go to Geneva and I stayed on to ski. We've got his son and his girlfriend coming tomorrow for Christmas. I think I've got most of the stuff in. What about *your* guests... are they as demanding as Lawrence feared they'd be?' Saskia asked, eagerly watching her reaction.

Eloise felt even more crushed. Was Lawrence going round stressing about her ability to cook for his guests?

She said, 'They're all right, spend most of the time glued to their laptops.' She paused as she joined the road and then, at Saskia's instruction, turned down the next road towards Saskia's chalet. Not knowing where her chalet was she went slowly in case she overshot it.

'There, that one, park next to the Mercedes.' She stayed silent while Eloise carefully parked and turned off the engine. 'There's something you're not telling me.' Saskia turned to face her.

Eloise sighed, 'It's just I saw Harvey.'

'What, here? Did you know he was out here?'

'No. I saw him a few days ago, where we were just now,

and then I heard his voice when I was waiting to see Pascal, he'd dropped some woman there, but he didn't come in.'

'Oh, love,' I'm sorry,' Saskia said. 'What a bummer.'

'I thought he'd be gone by now, go back for Christmas, but at lunchtime I saw him in the gondola. It was crowded but he saw me and called out and there I was, stuck high in the sky with him, but what was worse, when we arrived at the top Aurelia was there and she knows him too.'

'Oh, God, well she would, wouldn't she?'

'She looked… well she seemed amazed that someone like him would have married me.' Her mouth wobbled and she dashed the tears away.

Saskia leant over and hugged her. 'Don't take any notice of what that bitch says. She can't bear anyone else having a boyfriend or a husband – even when Malcolm was around she flirted with other men. She's even tried to snatch poor Quinn, only he's so vague he didn't notice.' She laughed, then added seriously, 'But you don't think they are together, do you?'

'I don't know. The first time I saw him he was with a woman in a shocking pink ski suit, and it was her he dropped off as Pascal's, but I didn't see her face. He's not alone that's for sure, he left me for some bosomy sexpot – it could have been the pink woman, I don't know.' She did wonder if there was anything intimate between Harvey and Aurelia, but then she had always wondered who among their female friends and acquaintances he was involved with, and now they were divorced it should no longer be her concern.

'I'm so sorry, Eloise. Let's go in and drown your sorrows.' Saskia opened the jeep door. 'So I suppose he's here for Christmas?'

'He didn't say and I didn't ask. He's with friends some-where by the old church.' She got out of the jeep and followed Saskia down a snowy path to a small chalet overlooking the valley. Saskia unlocked the door and they went inside.

'I suppose you'll be stuck in Jacaranda cooking for your guests, but Quinn likes to give a party on Boxing Day, drinks around six, everyone's invited, but not Harvey of course, nor Aurelia, though she often just appears. I expect Lawrence and Theo will come and whichever of your guests want to.' Saskia led the way to the main room with its stunning view right down the valley. 'I hope you'll be able to make it.'

'Sounds great but I don't know what's happening that day, or any day really.' Eloise sank down into a large comfortable chair, watching the smoky dusk creeping up the valley and the lights from the chalets below glowing through it.

'Lawrence knows about it, so we'll see.' Saskia poured her a glass of wine and sat down on the sofa near her and lifted her own glass in a toast, 'To you, and may you find love again with a better man than Harvey.'

Eloise took a sip, she felt better now, having shared the load of her misery with Saskia. 'So where are your children?' she asked, wanting to steer the conversation away from herself.

'They are with Toby and his parents,' Saskia said. 'They come out here for New Year. It works quite well: Quinn's family one year, mine the next.'

'How many children does Quinn have?'

'Two sons, one lives in the States. He's a grandfather of two adorable girls,' she giggled, 'and I'm a step-granny, can you believe it?'

'I suppose once one's children reach puberty any one of us could be a grandparent,' Eloise said, hoping her two would wait awhile before having babies. She wanted them to have a bit of a life first before they embarked on marriage and parenthood, though today everything was different and they might not marry and have children at all.

'Well I hope mine won't just yet, get into their careers first,' Saskia said, echoing Eloise's thoughts. 'Toby had another baby with his new wife.' A shaft of pain crossed her face. 'I shouldn't mind, she wanted a child of her own after all, and I was the one who left him first, but I *do* mind, I'm dead jealous, though I know I've no right to be, and it's not that I want another baby. Silly isn't it?'

'I would be jealous too.' Eloise was bitten by the same anxiety, though she didn't think Harvey wanted any more children as he'd always said twins, one of each, was perfect. But then one of his woman friends, this bright pink-clothed ski bunny might want one before her fertility clock ran out.

'So have you got all your Christmas stuff in?' Saskia asked. 'Do the guests eat normal food or are they those strange leaves and grains people, always on some health kick?'

Eloise laughed. 'It might be easier if they were. Only Debra, the matriarch, says she can't eat sugar or fat, but she eats enough cake and pudding.'

'She's only human, like the rest of us, can't resist a few goodies. So, I suppose this Christmas is your first without Harvey or the twins, perhaps it's a good thing you'll be so busy here, somewhere different,' Saskia said with sympathy.

'I'm trying not to think of it,' Eloise admitted. 'I loved Harvey, but I never really trusted him,' she confided now. 'At first it was all passion, that feeling of overpowering love... or probably lust,' she smiled.

'Oh yes, lust but love too,' Saskia said, 'and we were young and thought we were different to those dreary middle-aged couples who hardly even spoke to each other any more, and that for us it would last forever.'

'To be honest I never thought that... I never felt sure of him, though in the beginning he was so loving, and then we had the twins and he loved them and I told myself not to be so foolish and I was ashamed that I didn't really trust him.'

'I understand how you might feel like that about him,' Saskia said. 'Unlike many English men, certainly like Toby, Harvey felt comfortable with women, almost understood them, and so I suppose he wanted as many of them as he could, and they were drawn to him, but I think he truly loved you,' she finished, leaning over and squeezing Eloise's arm.

'Anyway, it's finished now and I'm here and I'm going to enjoy it, as long as Lawrence doesn't freak out over something I've done or haven't done.' Eloise smiled, feeling better now. 'I'm so glad you're here, Saskia,' she said warmly. 'I don't know how I would have coped without you.'

'You would have been fine, you're a coper,' Saskia held up her glass 'and let's drink to your new, independent life.'

20

As soon as she got back to Jacaranda, Eloise went to the kitchen to check on her preparations for the dinner. The joint of lamb had been marinating all day, sealed in a plastic bag with honey, fresh lime and herbs. She took it out of the bag and put it in the oven to roast, adding a little more of the marinade. The dark red fruit compote, which she'd cooked earlier, was now at room temperature and the brandy snaps made. She had just the starter to do and some canapés to have with the drinks and they wouldn't take long.

Theo came in carrying the tea tray from the living room. He put it down before cutting himself a huge slice of cake, saying he was going out but had to leave Bert here downstairs. 'Away from that dog-hater woman,' he added with contempt.

'I'll keep an eye on him,' Eloise said as he left, promising to be back soon.

A few minutes later Lawrence came in to the kitchen, he stood by the door facing her, watching her carefully as if he was about to say something important. Her stomach cramped and she turned away from him, pretending to concentrate on preparing the pudding, while she struggled to remain calm. He was going to tell her these people had complained about her cooking. It didn't surprise her, she guessed they were the sort who were always finding something to complain about.

'I'd like a word...' he began and she turned to face him, determined not to be cowed by him.

'Sure... what's up?'

'I... I didn't realize your ex-husband is out here.'

'Oh I...' She was caught off guard; this was the last thing she'd expected him to say.

'Aurelia told me.'

'I suppose she would,' she sighed, wondering if she'd only told him to make him think she'd be so traumatized at seeing him here, she'd be unable to cook. She said firmly, 'I didn't know he was coming here and it's been something of a shock. I saw him in the crowd the day I hurt my shoulder and I thought he'd have gone home by now. But then today I saw him in the gondola and later with Aurelia.' She busied herself with chopping the vegetables for the crudités, thinking of Aurelia as she did so. Had they seduced each other? she wondered grimly. They were both attractive people, but something told her that Harvey, who had brought that pink clad woman with him, would not be terribly tempted by such a forceful woman as Aurelia.

'I knew you were divorced, Desmond told me, and you have children. You must miss them and I suspect this Christmas will be hard for you, even worse with your ex hanging about. I'm so sorry Eloise, if there's anything I can do.'

She stopped her chopping and regarded him. There was a warmth about his manner as if he cared for her feelings. 'It will be difficult, but because I'm here, in a completely different place, it won't be so bad. My children, Kit and Lizzie, are on their gap year. It was arranged before we got divorced, in fact I think it freaked Harvey – his children being grown-up and able to go off across the world on their own – so he upped and left before they did.' She hoped she sounded cool about it though it still hurt. 'I'll try and telephone them on Christmas Day, I don't know what the signals will be like,' she said, going back to her chopping to hide the sudden tears that rose in her.

'Of course, use the landline, just get the time right.' He smiled, 'Where are they?'

She swallowed, said, 'Not sure, they were in Tibet but they could have moved on to China.' It was kind of Lawrence to consider her and she said so.

'I've been so focused on finding a new chef and stressing about these guests, I didn't think about your life and concerns, and I'm sorry, Eloise,' he said. 'Is your... husband, ex-husband...' he floundered, biting his lip, and even though she didn't feel comfortable that the conversation was going back to Harvey, she waited for him to say his piece while she arranged the chopped vegetables on the dish. 'Is he in the travel business, holiday lets, things like that?'

She stared at him in dismay. Was he going to say he'd invited Harvey here, wanted him to help rent out Jacaranda, or worse, he was in cahoots with Aurelia and wanted to help bring about her changes to appeal to more clients? Her warm feelings towards Lawrence's concern for her cooled.

'Yes he is... but... not really this sort of thing.' She gestured round the room. 'He finds beach resorts, really, sea and sun. He gets hotels and rented accommodation together for holidays and wedding venues, things like that, for the travel firm he works for. It's... quite upmarket, advertises in the top newspapers and magazines.'

'So he doesn't do skiing holidays?' He regarded her intently.

'I don't think so, though he might include those now.'

He'd have told her if he was out here scouting for business, wouldn't he?

Saskia had warned her that Aurelia wanted to get her hands on Jacaranda and now she'd met Harvey and found out he was in the travel business, finding holiday venues, would she try and use him to persuade Lawrence to let the agency he worked for manage Jacaranda, and was Lawrence now tentatively trying to suss her out to see if it would work?

'Whatever the reason's he's here,' she added firmly, 'I'm sure it's not to look for holiday places. I don't know what Aurelia told you, but he knows Verbier and he's probably here to ski.' With a pang, she thought of the pink-clothed woman who'd almost knocked her flat, Skiing wasn't his only sport either.

A look almost of relief crossed Lawrence's face. 'That's fine then. Sorry, I didn't mean to pry. Verbier is a very popular place, so you're right, it's probably just one of those things. But, all the same,' he touched her arm, 'it can't be easy for you.'

They could hear the others coming downstairs and going into the living room and Lawrence, with a quick smile, left to join them.

She finished preparing the canapés to go with the drinks and because Vera was coming in a bit later this evening she took them down to the living room herself. Ken, as usual, keeping one eye on his wife, leered in her direction; she ignored him, leaving the room and shutting the door behind her, glad to be able to escape to the solace of the kitchen.

A mournful howling stopped her in her tracks. It was coming from Bert shut downstairs. Poor little dog, she felt sorry for him, perhaps he needed to go out, she'd pop down and reassure him. Theo had found him abandoned in the village and adopted him. Perhaps he felt insecure, wondering if he'd been abandoned again.

She had a few minutes before she had to take out the lamb and Lawrence was occupied with the guests in the living room. She went downstairs and carefully opened the door to the main room where Bert was lying in a cosy corner. She spoke softly to him as she went in, so as not to scare him.

Bert stopped his howling at once but before she could catch him he made a bolt to the open door, ducked past her and ran upstairs with her in hot pursuit, hissing, 'Bert, stop, come here.'

He ran into the kitchen, sniffing around for morsels on the floor. Following him in there, she shut the kitchen door and set about catching him but the timer on the cooker went off, and not wanting the lamb to overcook, she opened the oven quickly to inspect the joint.

She'd no idea how it happened but she tripped and the leg of lamb, glistening under its marinade coat, fell to the floor. In a second Bert seized it by the shank – the joint was almost bigger than he was but he dragged his prize with him under the table by the window.

'Oh no, Bert, give it back.' Horrified, Eloise went down on the floor and crawled half under the table to retrieve it.

At that moment the door opened and Lawrence came into the kitchen where he was faced with Eloise's backside halfway under the table. 'What the devil are you doing...' he started, while Bert, annoyed at being disturbed in his feast, growled.

'Why is Bert in here, Eloise?' His voice was cold. 'He was shut in downstairs and you know he's not allowed anywhere near the kitchen.' He moved closer and bent down, 'And what is that in his mouth?'

'The dinner,' Eloise said, she knew she couldn't hide it. This was the end for her; Lawrence had caught them both red-handed.

With a supreme effort, she managed to get hold of Bert and snatched the joint from him, though it was hot. She backed out from under the table, bottom first, and stood up. Juggling the joint in her hands, she crossed the kitchen and dropped it back in its dish and inspected it.

'We can't eat that.' Lawrence was horrified.

'We're minutes away from serving dinner and the butcher will be closed, and even if he wasn't, it would take ages to buy something and cook it, it's this or ham sandwiches,' she said firmly.

She inspected the joint closely. There was a small bit chewed off by the bone and much of the sauce was on the floor and on her hands and down her apron, but fortunately she had some of the sauce left over, so if she wiped the joint clean, added more sauce and put it back in the hot oven, no one but her and Lawrence would know what had happened, and any germs Bert or the floor – which was cleaned daily – might have left would be killed by the heat in the oven.

Lawrence stared at her in fury. 'How did he get out?' he said. 'I heard Theo shut him in, he knows the rules.'

She faced him, she might as well tell the truth. Things could not get much worse. 'I let him out, I didn't mean to, but I heard him howling and he sounded so sad I went to see him, but he escaped.'

'And now he's ruined the dinner. Everyone's very hungry.' He glared at her, snatching his mobile from his pocket. 'I don't know if Aurelia could bring something, at such short notice.' He sighed. 'Yet another expense,' he added tartly.

She imagined Aurelia's glee if she had to come rushing

round to the rescue with boxes of her dratted delights. Talk of making a meal of it.

'This joint will be fine,' she said. 'I'll wipe it down, add more sauce, then put it back in the oven to kill any germs. Bert only chewed the bit at the end, and the floor's clean, Vera saw to that.'

'We can't do that,' Lawrence exclaimed in horror.

'Only you and I know about it.' She regarded him defiantly. 'All sorts of dreadful things go on in some kitchens in the top restaurants.'

'But not here, what if they are poisoned and they become ill... I can't believe this of you, Eloise.' His face was stricken; he raked his hair in desperation, his other hand still holding his mobile.

'Listen, Lawrence, it's not as if Bert's licked the whole joint. It was too hot and he's only chewed the end and I've cut that off. I'd eat it myself.' She felt impatient with him now, any moment one of the guests might appear asking where their dinner was and, of course, if they found out, there would be hell to pay, though she didn't believe the meat would harm them.

Bert was happily licking up the sauce from the floor while keeping a weather eye on Lawrence. They heard footsteps coming down the passage and threw each other frantic looks. Lawrence snatched up Bert and pushed him out in the cold among the dustbins.

The door opened and Vera came in. Seeing the consternation on their faces, she said, 'Something wrong?'

'Eloise let Bert out and he snatched the dinner and we can't eat it now and we're about to sit down to the table,' Lawrence said in despair.

Vera looked from one to the other and then saw the joint. 'What did he eat?'

Was he not able to keep this to himself? Eloise was annoyed, though she knew how close he and Vera were and she knew Vera would not say anything to anyone.

'I was going to put it back in the oven for a while. There's time, they still have to eat their first course.'

'They'll never know unless you tell them.' Vera came over and inspected the meat. Eloise pointed out the bit she'd cut off, relieved to have Vera on her side.

Vera faced Lawrence. 'Some people have no dinner; this is a feast. It won't kill them. Don't stress so much and don't say anything.' She smiled at Eloise, raising her spirits, 'You can't throw out a lovely piece of lamb just because that little dog took a tiny bite of it.'

Before he could answer, someone else came down the passage; it was Ken. He saw the joint by the stove.

'So that's what smells so good, can't wait to eat it.' He smiled at Eloise, and turning to Lawrence, said, 'I've come to see what's happened to the white wine you were fetching, I'll take it back if you're busy here.'

'No, just coming.' Lawrence went over to the fridge and took out a bottle and, with one last furious look at Eloise; he went back with Ken, who hadn't seemed to notice the smears of marinade on the kitchen floor.

'It will be all right,' Vera said. 'What you don't know can't kill you, don't they say that? Let's hope it's true.'

21

There was much praise about the lamb later from Ken and some of the others, especially Gaby. Lawrence said nothing as he helped to bring the empty dishes back to the kitchen and carry in the pudding. Eloise didn't look at Lawrence in case she giggled, so much fuss over such a small thing. She'd taken off the one bit Bert had chewed and the heat from the oven would have cauterized any germs left behind.

Vera, with a wink at her, said to him, 'You see all is well.'

'Unless they die in the night,' he answered darkly.

'Then they will die of something else, if their time is up,' Vera said. 'You worry too much, Lawrence. These are lucky people, do not worry about them.'

Theo turned up, clumping down the passage in his boots and still in his coat, saying he was going to take Bert out. Eloise dithered about telling him now about the evening's fiasco, or waiting until they were away from any eavesdroppers, or even until these guests had left Jacaranda. But Vera decided it.

'Poor Eloise has had a shock, Bert tried to eat the dinner,' she started.

'What, what dinner? I gave him his before I went out,' Theo protested, frowning at her, so she had to tell him the story.

'I just went to see him, I didn't think he'd rush out like that, bolt up the stairs, and I dropped the joint and Bert took off with it...'

'So they had no dinner? Dad must be livid.' Theo was shocked.

'No, they ate it, it didn't show and we didn't say anything, but your father is furious, well I suppose rightly, but...'

'Oh, wow, disaster,' Theo said, grinning now.

'You mustn't say anything,' Eloise said, still anxious about Lawrence's reaction about it later. He was obviously not amused and she worried that he might tell Aurelia who'd somehow freak him into using her, no doubt germless, delights.

'No worries, Bert's clean, cleaner than most of them, I'd have thought,' Theo said, leaving to go down to him. 'Don't worry, I'll cope with Dad, and will keep quiet.' He giggled as he left and they heard him running down the stairs, calling to Bert that he was back.

Later Theo brought Bert to Eloise 'to apologize', though Bert was not the slightest bit contrite, in fact he seemed delighted with her and enthusiastically licked her fingers as if she had presented him with the joint herself. So at least one of them went to bed happy, Eloise thought as she put out the light.

No one died or was ill in the night but Lawrence was decidedly frosty towards her the next morning, appearing in the kitchen while she was having her breakfast.

'What if I hadn't come in and seen it all?' he said, as if inferring that there must have been other disasters she had covered up.

She felt she'd apologized enough and she kept out of his way for the rest of the morning, carrying on as if nothing had happened.

When she told Saskia about it later she shrieked with laughter.

'Pity he caught you in flagrante, as it were. Ask Quinn about some of the restaurants he's been to, quite famous ones too; you'd never eat out again if you knew what goes on in some of them. Now relax and get ready to enjoy Christmas.' She hugged her.

'I will.' She smiled, trying not to think of the Christmases she'd spent before, always with her family: her parents and then her own children. Even now she was past the hype, there always seemed to be a touch of magic to it lingering from childhood.

Despite the wintry surroundings, it was not so blatantly Christmassy out here as it was back home. Lights were laced through trees or glowing from windows, but Eloise hadn't – yet anyway – seen any huge lit-up Santas complete with sleighs and reindeer rampaging over the roofs of any chalets.

The ski runs would be open as usual on Christmas Day and so it was decided by everyone at Jacaranda to have the main meal in the evening.

Eloise made some dark chocolate mint fudge for Lawrence and Theo, cooking it that afternoon when she returned from seeing Saskia and everyone was out. She made a pomander orange for Saskia and Vera and a few more to put in a bowl in the hall, sitting in her room in the evenings carefully cutting designs on oranges with a fine peeler and filling the pattern with cloves. She ran a coloured ribbon through the centre of them with a loop for hanging and wrapped them in paper with ground spices until Christmas Day.

The following evening was Christmas Eve and Theo came into the kitchen to tell her the plans. It had been arranged that they'd all go down to the village to sing carols in the square and have supper at one of the restaurants there, later there was midnight Mass for anyone who wanted to go. Lawrence or Theo and possibly her would ferry people up and down.

'I think I'll stay here,' she said, not wanting to face a grumpy Lawrence across a dinner table – he'd said no more about the joint, though she'd done her best to keep out of his way. But worse would be seeing Harvey and Aurelia.

'You can't, you'll be the only one not there. Vera comes as well, everyone is there, you can't miss it.' Theo's young face creased with disappointment. 'It's not really religious,' he added as if that was the reason she wasn't coming.

'It's not that. I…'

'And you won't have to cook; we're eating out, all of us. It's part of it, we always do, it's a Christmas tradition.' He went on, 'You have to come… Dad wants you to.'

She wondered if that was true, but how could she explain to Theo her fear and pain at seeing Harvey and Aurelia, or whatever woman he was with. But there would be crowds of people, so she might not see him. Was she really going to hide here alone while everyone else was having a good time, just in case she saw him again? She must not let him dominate her life. Saskia had told her the same thing.

'I… I will come.'

She was rewarded by Theo's grin. 'It's great, all of us together,' he said. 'And tomorrow the weather looks good and I'm skiing with Gaby and Jerry and possibly some friends, so maybe you'd like to come too? We thought we'd dress up in Christmas gear – I've got a reindeer hat with antlers,' he laughed and she smiled at his joy. She was not going to spoil his pleasure by not joining in with everyone else.

She didn't remember everyone congregating in the square singing carols when she was here that Christmas as a child. There was something magical about the crowd of people of many nationalities all singing together in the darkness with, here and there, a flicker of candlelight. Whether Christmas was seen as religious or just a holiday, everyone seemed to be affected by it.

She stood away from Lawrence; he had not ignored her and yet had not said anything to her either, though she caught him watching her sometimes with a pensive look on his face, making her wonder what he was thinking. She stayed with Vera, Theo and Bert, who snuffed around hoping to find something delicious to eat. The air was crisp and cold, but they were warmly dressed and were soon enveloped with the ambience and the singing of familiar carols. When the songs were over, Lawrence rounded everyone up and they went on to a restaurant near the church in the old village for supper. Theo dropped off Bert with a friend on the way, saying he'd freeze to death if he left him in the car.

Eloise, not knowing they were going there, kept her head down and used Theo as cover when they entered the restaurant, afraid that Harvey would be there as he was staying in this part of the village. Every time the door opened she furtively watched the people come in, afraid he would suddenly appear, but to her relief he did not.

The restaurant was famous for its fondues and everyone except for Debra, who said hot cheese caused her indigestion, ordered it. Eloise sat in between Pippa and Jerry, with Gaby on his other side. Pippa and Jerry were quite silent, so Eloise struggled to keep the conversation going. Theo fared better, sitting opposite Jerry, discussing their ski plans for tomorrow. Debra sat next to Lawrence and Ken. Eloise noticed how she kept throwing impatient looks in Pippa's direction, as if expecting her to add something intelligent to their conversation which was about finance and the world markets, a subject she noticed Lawrence joined in with, though his views were more about spreading the largesse around than keeping it for just a few people.

'But it's people like us who generate it,' Ken said jovially.

'And people like me who spend it,' Pippa said under her breath, but Eloise heard her, and feeling sorry for her, said quietly, 'But by spending it you give others work in shops, restaurants and things.'

'You could look at it that way,' Pippa said, 'but this family doesn't.' She concentrated on dipping her cube of bread into the bubbling fondue pot.

Eloise didn't know any of this family. She'd spent a short time with Debra and had rather admired her for doing so well in her life, but she understood she had little patience with people who she thought 'free-loaded'.

'I was a teacher before I met Radley,' Pippa went on quietly as if she needed to explain herself, 'only it didn't fit in with our life.'

'I see, so is Radley in the family firm too?' Eloise said. Radley hadn't made much of an impression on her, he seemed to be rather intimidated by his mother, who barely hid her disapproval of his choice of wife.

'Yes, he is, but he has a few of his own ideas. He's just bought a publishing company for trade journals,' Pippa said, before lapsing back into silence.

Trade journals, did they include glossy holiday mags on places to stay? Eloise glanced at him sitting in silence as if he was in his own world. Was he a journalist, perhaps he was writing a review of Jacaranda?

'Does he write some of the articles?' she asked Pippa.

'He'd like to, but he doesn't really have time just now, but he might write about being here, skiing at Christmas.'

'Good idea,' Eloise said weakly, wondering if Lawrence knew. She studied Radley again, he seemed perfectly innocuous, but if his forceful mother got at him, she guessed he would write whatever she told him to.

After supper those that wanted to went to church, Lawrence drove the others back in the minibus to Jacaranda. Travis, Radley and Ken were getting quite edgy as though feeling as if they didn't get back to their laptops and check in on things, there might be some catastrophe.

Eloise, who'd brought the jeep, went with Debra, Theo, Gaby, Vera and Jerry into the church and Pippa ran after them at the last minute.

It started to snow as they headed to the church. Huge flakes falling silently down like soft feathers, adding to the Christmas atmosphere. The church was very crowded but they found a seat and Eloise thought of Kit and Lizzie, wondering what they were doing and wishing they were with her. She'd had a text from them earlier telling her they were now in Thailand having met up with friends. She texted back saying she'd try and telephone them tomorrow.

She sat quietly, trying to reach out to them in her thoughts on this first Christmas they'd spent apart. She wondered if Harvey was suffering pangs of regret about leaving their children… breaking up their family. She hoped he wasn't here, in the church, but she didn't look round to check. Instead she tried to concentrate on being here in this wonderful place. But her thoughts soon turned to what would happen when Christmas was over and she had to return to the house that did not yet feel like home. Her job was there when she wanted it, there were always pictures that needed to be restored and good friends to see but sitting here, the thought of leaving Verbier made her sad. She wished she could stay longer among the beautiful landscape, the majesty of the mountains where she felt so much at home.

Lawrence turned up during the service and when it was over met up with the guests to take them back. But Theo, Gaby and Jerry said they wanted to go on for a drink. Eloise couldn't help noticing that Jerry perked up, was almost amusing, joking with Theo. She was going to head back in the other jeep behind Lawrence. Vera, who had a room close by, said goodnight and slipped away.

It was still snowing, thickly covering the ground, and Eloise was relieved to follow Lawrence's taillights as he drove the others back to Jacaranda.

'Happy Christmas, everyone,' Lawrence said when they were all inside the chalet.

The guests returned his Christmas greeting, and Debra and the men went into the living room, whilst Pippa escaped upstairs.

'Happy Christmas, Lawrence,' Eloise said, smiling yet feeling strangely sad.

'Happy Christmas, Eloise.' He smiled back and she wondered if he'd forgiven her for the lamb fiasco. 'Would you like a drink with us?' he added.

'No thanks; I'll go to bed now. Goodnight and thanks for dinner, it was lovely to go out.' She smiled at him, resisting a foolish desire to kiss him – and there wasn't even any mistletoe about to excuse it. She turned towards the stairs, and he called after her.

'You can ski tomorrow if you want to; there will be powder snow and dinner's not until the evening. Everyone seems to want to go out, even Debra wants to join them for lunch.'

'Thank you, Lawrence, I'll see what the day's like,' she said. Theo had asked her to join him, Gaby and Jerry, so that might be fun, better than moping around here at the chalet missing her children.

She slept badly, tortured with images of her children so far away. She always gave them stockings, though of course she hadn't this year. Kit said it was his favourite thing of the day and she wondered what their day would be like. At least they had each other and that was a comfort. She closed her mind to thoughts of Harvey.

'Don't think,' she kept saying to herself, 'just don't think.'

She had just dropped off when she heard Theo coming back, stumbling into his room. She didn't bother to look at the time.

22

Christmas Day dawned bright, with a fresh blanket of snow clothing the trees and roofs and covering the ground. Lawrence and Theo dug out the cars. Bert jumped around barking and trying to catch any stray snowflakes in his mouth.

Travis, Radley and Pippa, who were not very strong skiers, were leaving later with Lawrence to meet up with their guide to ski the lower runs. Ken said he'd go up with Debra, and Lawrence said he'd drop them at Medran when they were ready and go on and do a couple of runs himself, so if Eloise wanted to spend the morning skiing she could.

'I hope you're coming with us, Eloise,' Theo overheard him, pulling on his reindeer headdress, complete with bells and a red nose.

'Oh yes do, then we can gossip,' Gaby said eagerly. 'We've hardly had time to talk at all.' She had a wreath of silver tinsel round her fluffy hood. Jerry was looking rather self-conscious in a red Santa hat. Not to be left out, Eloise put a couple of gold stars on her beanie and they all set off, with Eloise driving them down in the jeep.

'We're meeting up with some others after lunch, Bert's staying here with Vera, a whole day's too cold for him,' Theo told her. 'It's just us, the intrepid ones, this morning.'

Eloise smiled at his enthusiasm. She'd got her ski legs back and she'd ski with them this morning, and then see what happened at lunchtime. If Theo went off with friends, she might continue to ski with Gaby.

The snow was new and soft and many of the skiers were dressed like Santas or reindeer. Two colourful characters had a sledge and were handing out chocolate bars, there was much laughter and nonsense and Gaby, her eyes shining, said to Eloise that it was the best, the maddest Christmas she'd ever had.

Theo suggested that they ski at Vallon D'Arby where the powder snow would be magical and they might not get the same conditions again while they were here.

'I'll just check it's safe after the heavy snowfall,' Theo said, going over to a ski guide waiting with a group of clients, who agreed it should be fine, but as always to take care.

Jerry, who'd become much more animated away from the rest of his family, laughed when he heard this. 'Course, it's safe, they'd have closed the run if there was any danger, you know how cautious the Swiss are. Lead the way.' He stamped his skies on the piste like an impatient horse.

Eloise caught sight of a warning sign, a series of flags denoting the level of danger. She couldn't remember how to read them but Theo would know, she called out for the others to stop and check them but they just waved and sped on, she pushed on, not wanting to lose them as she hadn't skied on this particular slope for some time.

They skied round the back of the lake in the new snow, leaving the busy slope behind. The slopes here were almost empty as it was a secret place not easily found by people that didn't know it. It was beautiful and still, bringing a peaceful silence, enhancing the power of nature.

Eloise increased her speed easily, catching up with Gaby who was a competent but more cautious skier than the rest of them. Theo stopped before Eloise reached him, standing on the top of the slope, taking in the scene. Two snowboarders came up behind them, paused an instant before starting down, both skiing in unison as if performing a graceful dance. Theo watched them, glancing round again at the fall of the snow.

'What are you waiting for?' Jerry, who'd been just behind him, pushed past him to follow them down.

Theo stayed where he was, his face half hidden by his ski goggles, holding back, which was so unlike him, he was usually the daredevil, king of the slopes.

'What is it?' Eloise asked.

'You two wait here,' he turned to her and Gaby, his voice firm. 'When I'm almost down, follow me one at a time. That guide said it would be okay, but there's been a big snowfall overnight and the snow's quite heavy here. I think it would be safer to go down this bit one at a time, just in case we set off anything. I'd have liked to have waited a moment longer after those boarders went but Jerry has already gone.'

'Surely there won't be an avalanche today, it's so sunny,' Gaby said, determinedly not looking at Jerry who had stopped just beneath them, urging them on and trying to get her attention by waving his ski poles in the air.

'We'll do what you say, Theo,' Eloise said, not at all nervous but not wanting to ridicule him by teasing him for his fear in front of the others.

Theo moved away from them, turned and started down to join Jerry. 'Wait a moment, Jerry,' he called to him but Jerry just laughed.

'Come on, slowcoach, race you,' he dared him, setting off at speed.

Eloise and Gaby watched them go a moment, getting ready to follow them. But there was a strange whoomping noise, and they saw just beneath them the snow begin to slide.

'Watch out,' Eloise screamed, her voice lost in the noise of the tumbling snow. It rose like a cloud in front of them, taking a few small trees with it, a wall of white that hid the others from sight.

'Oh God, will it catch them,' Gaby clutched at Eloise's arm.

Eloise started screaming and shouting, 'Avalanche, avalanche.'

All around them was silence, the fall of snow settled and for a moment the silence was terrifying, as if the two women were the only two people left in the world.

Eloise was rooted to the spot, staring at the white mound of snow beneath them.

Gaby turned to her whimpering, her face stark with fear.

Eloise forced herself to take charge and overcome the cold fear that had gripped her. She must not think the worst, but all she could see was white snow and the trees. Theo and Jerry had disappeared.

'Are they dead?' Gaby whispered.

Eloise struggled with a surge of terror; she took off one of her gloves, dropping it in the snow and searched in her pocket for her mobile to ring for help. They heard a shout, and to their great relief a group of skiers with a guide appeared at the top of the slope.

Gaby waved frantically at them. 'There's been an avalanche,' she screamed, trying to struggle up to them.

The guide skied down to join them, leaving his clients

behind. 'Is anyone caught in it?' he asked, taking in the scene when he reached them.

'Two of our friends went down just before it... and oh, some snowboarders, but they were quite a bit ahead,' Eloise said, relieved that they were no longer alone.

Gaby clung to the guide who was pulling a mobile out of his pocket. 'We can't see them; they must be under the snow. We have to find them.' She was crying now.

'Let him call for help, Gaby,' Eloise said. 'They might have outskied it and be waiting for us further down.' It was so hard to take in. One minute they had been in heaven, the snow like silk under their skis. Now they were in hell, terrified the two men were dead or gravely injured.

The guide telephoned for help and far below them they heard a shout.

Eloise moved closer to look. She could see a figure waving a pole, but it was too far away and covered with snow to make out if it was Jerry or Theo, or indeed someone else.

Gaby saw him. 'Jerry, Jerry?' she screamed.

Telling them to stay where they were, the guide skied down to the figure. Gaby, disobeying him, followed, and Eloise, determined to know the worse, snatched up her glove, shoved it in her pocket and skied down too.

To her enormous relief she saw it was Theo, covered in snow, the red nose of his reindeer hat still visible. He was saying something to the guide while undoing his backpack and pulling out a shovel. The guide had already taken off his backpack and was pulling a probe out while asking Theo if he was hurt.

'If Jerry activates his transmitter and it's on him, we'll find him,' Theo said when Eloise and Gaby reached him. His face was clenched with terror as he searched the piles of snow around him. 'Unless he outskied it. There's a possibility he managed that, I suppose, but he should have waited.'

'Where's Jerry?' Gaby was sobbing now.

Eloise put her arm round her. 'Theo is here and Jerry was skiing close to him, and look they've started digging,' she said to comfort her, forcing herself not to think that he was lost. The beautiful snowy scene before them was as still as if it were a picture.

Gaby, still crying, began frantically poking through the soft snow with her ski pole.

Eloise said a silent prayer of thanks that Theo was alive, but she felt so useless, so afraid that Jerry was trapped under the snow, dead or badly injured. She pulled out her mobile; she wanted Lawrence, needed his strength. Dialling his number, she hoped he'd pick up and not be out of range.

'Eloise?'

'Lawrence, we're at Vallon D'Arby, there's been an avalanche, Jerry has disappeared, the rest of us are fine.'

'Oh, God, when?'

'Just now, but there's a guide with us, he's called the rescue service. There's a great pile of snow beneath us, Jerry could have skied through it, but we don't know.'

'I'm not far away, I'll come over. Stay safe and keep out of the way in case there's another.' He rang off and the two women stood there, clinging to each other.

Theo, looking slightly ridiculous in his reindeer hat, appeared to hear something and pointed to a patch of snow a few feet from them. He and the guide began to dig frantically. Eloise wondered if she could help, she'd been to a talk a long time ago about surviving an avalanche and remembered that being tumbled by the falling snow was often the killer, the next being running out of air, poisoned by carbon monoxide.

Gaby was sobbing as if her heart would break. 'What can we do? If only more people would come, dogs that would find him,' she cried.

'I think they've found where he is, or at least his transmitter, they've just got to get him out.' Eloise struggled to bank down her terror of what they would find. Was it Jerry or just his rucksack torn away from him? Or it could be one of the snowboarders that had gone down just before them. What if Jerry hadn't been able to activate his transmitter and they were not able to find him in time? She couldn't bear to think about it, such an ending to a day which started with so much promise.

23

The two skiers who'd been with the guide now made their way cautiously down to them. They were French, middle-aged men and offered to help dig with their guide and Theo, but the guide told them it was safer for them to wait, so they stood there silently as if mourning over a grave.

'Many killed on ski slopes,' one of them remarked, causing Gaby to cry out. The man just shrugged as if it was a fact of life.

'Very dangerous,' the other agreed. 'How many lost?' he asked Eloise, who tried to comfort Gaby by telling her not to listen to them.

'We don't know how many people were caught, but we are worried for our friend. But we hope for the best, he could have outskied it,' she added, more for Gaby's sake.

The man's answer was lost by the clattering throb of a helicopter hovering overhead, and Eloise saw to her great relief the ski patrol were coming over the slope towards them and the helicopter then circled and moved off.

'Why won't it stay with us?' Gaby cried, stretching out her arms as if trying to claw it back.

'It's OK; they are probably just assessing the situation, checking where we are and leading the ski patrol to us. Look,' she pointed to the ski patrol, 'here's the rescue team.

They'll soon have Jerry out.' Eloise put her arm round Gaby, though she too was worried.

The ski patrol quickly took charge, Eloise told them about the snowboarders, but they said they'd escaped it, the helicopter had seen them much further on. They took out their equipment and, with sensors, tried to check for movement and began digging where they picked something up. The ski guide stepped back and after a quick discussion, returned to his clients, suggesting they ski down. Now help was here there was no more he could do. He asked Eloise if she and Gaby would like to come down with them.

Eloise refused; Lawrence was coming and she must stay here to support him and Theo, who was digging frantically now, aware time was running out.

'Thank you, I'll stay... but,' she turned to Gaby, 'perhaps it would be better if she went... in case...' No, she *must not* think that a body would be found and certainly must not say as much in front of Gaby. 'Would you like to go with them, Gaby,' she said. 'I'll stay here and I'll text you with any news.'

'No... I must stay,' Gaby said. 'I must know what's happened to Jerry.'

'If you're sure,' the guide said, sensing the impatience of his two clients, perhaps nervous another avalanche was imminent.

'Yes, thank you, and thank you so much for helping.' Eloise tried to smile but her face was stiff with fear and cold. She turned to Gaby, 'Are you really sure you don't want to go down with them?' She thought it would be better if she did, in case Jerry was not found in time.

'I want to stay,' Gaby said, though her face was clenched with fear.

'As you wish.' The guide pressed her hand to offer her courage, his two clients bowed to them and they set off. After they had gone, Eloise wondered if she should have asked them to telephone Debra, if Gaby had her number, but Lawrence might have done that already.

She heard her mobile ring and she scrabbled for it in her pocket, nervous of dropping it in the snow. It was Lawrence.

'Has help arrived? I'm trying to get to you. I'm at the top now, tell me where you are.'

'Wait, I'll ask. A helicopter came but now it's gone, but the ski patrol are here digging for someone – we hope it is Jerry. Theo is helping,' she added, wanting to reassure him that Theo was safe. 'Do you want to talk to him?' she added, watching Theo, his skis and jacket off, digging with great energy.

'If you're sure he's not hurt, I'll just get there. Tell me exactly where you are.'

She went closer to the patrol and asked him their location. Without pausing with his digging, the man told her and Lawrence said, 'I heard him; I'm on my way. Ring if there are any developments.'

Eloise imagined him making his lonely way here, his mind tortured by wondering if Theo really would be all right, or whether he may have some sort of delayed injury. She thought of Kit and Lizzie, young and vital but who could be wiped out by some freak accident in an instant. As soon as she got back she would ring them, she was going to anyway for Christmas, but she could not wait to hear their voices to reassure herself they were OK.

How fragile life was, and what of Jerry, would they find him alive? Time was surely running out before he suffocated, or he could already be dead, killed by the force of the snow, but she must not think like that, imagine the worst until she was faced with it.

She had never imagined such a Christmas: she and Gaby standing here watching the patrol desperately digging in the hope of finding a man who moments before had been full of energy, racing down the slope, revelling in the snow.

Gaby was crying beside her, her ski goggles on the top of her head, her tears falling unchecked. 'I didn't love him,' she said. 'I used him to get my degree.'

'But you did care for him, Gaby.' She leant over and hugged her. Both of them were still in their skis. 'You were kind to him and he was happy with you,' Eloise tried to reassure her, guessing how hard it was for her to manage her own guilt at using him when now he could be dead or badly hurt.

'Yes, but I wouldn't have married him, Eloise. I agreed to say we were engaged so his family wouldn't be shocked, but he's behaving as if we really are. I'm twenty-one, I want to get a good career and perhaps marry and have children when I've got everything on track. He didn't understand that.' She wiped her eyes with the back of her hand. 'He's never known what it's like to be poor, really poor, like we were when Dad died. We had a roof over our heads but Mum had to juggle with bills and work so hard.' She sniffed. 'I did try to get a grant but it wasn't enough, which made Mum worry. I don't want to be poor like that and I want to help her so she won't need to be with shitty men like Roger.' The words poured out of her.

'I understand, Gaby.' She held her close. Eloise was finding it difficult to keep positive and time ticked on and there was no sign of Jerry.

Suddenly, there was a shout and Lawrence and two other

men skied into view. Eloise turned to greet them. They skied down to join them, Lawrence's face twisted in concern.

'Any news?' He glanced at the ski patrol working a few feet away.

'Not yet.' She longed to hold him, take away his fear, a fear that ate into her bones that Jerry was dead and Lawrence would have to break the news to Debra and the rest of them. But his eyes were on Theo, watching him dig, his face taut with concern as if he could not believe that his adored son had escaped and was alive.

'And you two, are you all right?' He put his arm round her for a moment. 'You weren't caught in it?' He turned to Gaby, 'Either of you?'

'No, we were behind them, behind it.' Eloise forced herself not to fall into the comfort of his arms.

'I'll join them,' he said, moving away from them and skiing down to join the rescue group, his two friends following behind. Theo leant against him a moment, Lawrence hugging him before he and his two companions took shovels from their own backpacks and began to dig.

At last there was a shout and more frantic digging. Eloise and Gaby, who'd kept out of their way as they'd been told to, hurried closer.

'Bloody hell, get me out, it's cold down here,' Jerry said, his voice like music though there was a crack of panic in his tone.

'Oh Jerry,' Gaby sobbed.

The men pulled him out.

'And you've still got that stupid hat on,' he said to Theo with an attempt at a laugh, holding on to him for balance.

'Are you hurt?' Theo regarded him anxiously as if he expected bits to fall off him.

'Don't think so,' Jerry gingerly flexed his limbs. 'Bloody cold though. I remembered to make a hole so I could breathe, but very glad to see you all.' He glanced round at them, tears in his eyes. Gaby, almost falling in her hurry to get to him, cried even harder, clinging to him as if he might slip back under the snow.

Lawrence, relief in his face, questioned Jerry on his state of health and then after conferring with the rescue team, it was decided he could not ski down – one ski was lost anyway – and it would be prudent to go to hospital to be checked over.

'I don't need to go to hospital, I'll be fine after a hot shower and a drink,' Jerry said, 'though I could do with another ski.' He tried to sound upbeat but Eloise could see his exhaustion and knew he couldn't manage the journey back.

Lawrence insisted that he went to hospital to make sure he wasn't suffering from delayed shock or an injury to his head or his heart. 'Your aunt would say the same,' he added firmly. 'I'll come with you and Theo.' He turned to Theo, 'Are you really all right?' He put his hand on his shoulder, his face anxious. 'Perhaps you should have a check-up while we're there.'

'No, I'm OK,' Theo said. 'I was knocked over and rolled about a bit but nothing like Jerry.'

'You never said you were knocked over, I thought you escaped it?' Eloise said. He'd been covered in snow but she thought he had just fallen. She was fearful now that he too might be hurt but in his concern for Jerry had disregarded it.

'We'll get you checked too, better safe than sorry,' Lawrence said firmly, holding on to his arm as if he might escape.

'I'm fine, just wet.' Theo leant against his father, craving comfort. 'I don't know what happened. The guide said it was safe,' he said now as if finally taking in the seriousness of what had happened. Lawrence held him closer, murmuring reassurances.

Eloise remembered the flags she'd spotted. Were they spelling a danger of avalanche and Theo hadn't seen them, or worse still had he disregarded their warning? This was not the time to say anything but it worried her that he could be blamed for taking them all into danger.

The ski patrol called for a helicopter to take them to the hospital. Theo walked to it with Lawrence's arms still round him and Jerry, with Gaby hovering round him, silent now, staring at him as if she could not believe he was alive.

As the two men were helped in, Lawrence tried to telephone Ken; he had not been able to get through to him or Travis. If Ken and Travis were skiing they might not hear their phone; he didn't have Radley's number, nor did he want to ring Debra. He didn't like to leave a message on voicemail, but Ken didn't pick up and he had to say something. 'Hi Ken, it's Lawrence. Jerry and Theo have been involved in an accident, but they seem fine. We're just going to go to the hospital to make sure. I'll try and contact you when we get there. Ring me when you get this.'

He turned to Eloise who stood with Gaby close to the helicopter, the fear still in his face. Lawrence put his arm round Eloise again and hugged her to him for a second, to offer comfort, and she fought a sudden desire to rest her head on his chest. She must be suffering from delayed shock she warned herself sternly.

'Do you think you can both ski down? My friends, David and Marcus,' he introduced his two companions, 'will go down with you. They know the route well, so you'll be safe with them.'

176

Gaby looked longingly at the helicopter, but Eloise, not seeing any alternative as there was only room for the injured and Lawrence, assured Gaby she'd be fine, they'd take their time and would make it down.

'I'm sorry to ask you, Eloise,' Lawrence leant closer to her, his breath soft on her cheek, 'but if you see Debra or Ken or one of the party can you tell them what happened. I'll keep trying to reach Ken on his mobile, or hopefully he'll pick up the voicemail and get back to me. Jerry is still in shock and said to wait to tell them, but I think it best to let them know as soon as we can.' He sighed, moved away from her. 'We don't want them to think we're trying to hide anything from them. I'll keep you informed, I guess we'll go down to the hospital in Sion.'

'Are they going to be all right?' she asked him, wishing he would hold her again, they'd been through such a shocking experience and she craved comfort too and it was so long since she'd been held in someone's arms. 'I thought Theo had escaped it.' She felt guilty now she knew he'd been tumbled about in the snow. 'It was all white and we couldn't see anything at first. If I'd known he'd been caught in it too I would have stopped him doing all that digging, the guide was there after all.' She felt she'd let Lawrence down again.

'You weren't to know and Theo would have done it anyway unless he was incapacitated,' he smiled at her. 'They are safe now, but we can't really tell how it has affected them until they've been properly examined,' Lawrence said. 'Sorry you have all this to deal with but thanks for ringing me.' He touched her hand, glanced at Gaby, 'You'll both be all right skiing down, won't you, and it's not a difficult run.'

'They'll be fine, we'll see they get down,' Marcus said as Lawrence left them to board the helicopter.

'There won't be another avalanche, will there?' Gaby said fearfully, her love of the mountains now filled with terror. Eloise was afraid too, but it was the only way they could get down, there was no room in the helicopter, which would fly straight down to the hospital.

Lawrence's two friends reassured them.

'The worst is over and we ski down to the road where there is a lift, or we can take a taxi back if you've had enough, but let's get started,' Marcus said.

The helicopter roared away, Eloise wondering if it could start another avalanche with its whirling blades. The ski patrol set off to another call. Gaby, pale with fear, stayed close to David and they started off back home.

Eloise tried to enjoy the run down. It was all so beautiful, the intense blue of the sky, the sparkling snow – a Christmas-card scene, peaceful and serene. It was impossible to believe the nightmare they had all been through, the sudden fall of snow coming so unexpectedly.

'Had there been warnings of avalanches today?' Eloise asked Marcus when they at last reached the road and started to walk along it to the lift. Gaby seemed lost in herself, and Eloise, though keeping a watch on her and occasionally giving her words of comfort, thought it best to let her come to terms with the event, undisturbed. They could discuss it later.

'Not that I know of,' Marcus said, 'they usually cordon off areas if they think there could be danger and you didn't cross any barriers, did you?'

'No, we didn't.' She tried not to think of the flags she'd seen at the beginning of the run.

'The danger is always there, especially at this time of year when there's been a heavy snowfall. But as you probably know, it's your own decision where you ski off-piste as long as the run is not closed – we saw the warning flags, but they gave the warning as three – five is the worse, so...'

'I don't think I saw those,' Eloise lied, wondering if Theo had seen them but thinking three was safe enough, didn't mention it to them. At least three was passable and surely they would have shut the run if a real danger were predicted?

'Although it was very scary and potentially life-threatening, the rescue service said it was not a very large avalanche,' Marcus went on.

'It was large enough to bury Jerry and if he hadn't been dug out...' Gaby broke in.

'That's why most of us carry a shovel,' David said. 'Some people think we are overcautious but they were needed today.'

'What a Christmas Day,' Eloise said with feeling.

Marcus grinned, 'None of us will forget it but at least it ended well.'

'They'll be all right, won't they?' Eloise asked nervously. What if there were unforeseen side effects or internal damage and both men were more badly injured than it had appeared?

'They're both young and fit. They'll be a bit shaken and bruised and it might haunt them for a while, but I'd say they'll get over it. It was a good thing you called Lawrence and a relief he was close enough to be here.' Marcus shrugged, 'It's not worth stressing about now. It happened and we all got away with it.'

Eloise felt suddenly faint, not wanting to think it could so easily have been Gaby and her lost under the snow. How would Kit and Lizzie cope if she left them so soon?

'You all right?' Marcus put his hand on her arm.

'Yes, thanks... just... I won't think of what might have happened. We're lucky, it ended well.'

'I hope so,' David, who'd been listening to them, said. 'I mean, let's hope those rich clients at Jacaranda won't try and sue, or whatever.'

Eloise was horrified. 'They couldn't make trouble, could they? Surely they know there are risks on the mountains and the run would have been closed if there was a great danger?' Again she thought of Theo, if Debra and the rest of them made trouble for him ignoring, or not seeing, the warning flags, his whole future as a ski guide and instructor could be in jeopardy.

'It wouldn't surprise me if they tried it on, it wouldn't be the first time rich clients did it,' Marcus said. 'They could state negligence, or something. It would cause some damaging publicity, which could be the last straw for Lawrence and Jacaranda.'

24

They reached the safely of the village at last, Eloise having to urge Gaby on. She was obviously traumatized by the events, but they had to get down to the village as at this time of the year the slopes iced up early in the day.

Marcus and David offered to drive them back to Jacaranda but Eloise said she had the jeep and she wouldn't bother them further. It was not far to go and she felt up to it.

She wanted to get back to the familiarity of the chalet to process the drama of the morning. She needed to be somewhere quiet to try and come to terms with what had happened.

'If you're really sure,' David said.

'Do you need help with the guests... telling them about it, I mean,' Marcus said, 'and dealing with any problems it might throw up?'

The fear lurking inside her intensified. The avalanche *was* a fact of nature, but Debra – for if anyone was going to take this further it would be her – might twist it and suggest that Theo had led them into danger. Eloise decided not to mention the flags until she'd spoken to Theo about them. Just because he had seemed not to notice them didn't mean he hadn't and had thought that, as the run wasn't closed, it was a risk worth taking.

She'd read of people being bankrupted over cases taken against them, even if they'd won or the case had been thrown out. These things could drag on and on, ruining reputations before they were concluded. Then there were ambulance chasers, people persuading others who might have had even a small accident to push for compensation, killing small businesses – small businesses just like Jacaranda.

She was about to accept Marcus's offer, afraid she'd make a mess of it and put Jacaranda in peril by inadvertently saying the wrong thing, when she heard someone call her name and, to her horror, she saw Debra crossing the street towards them, smiling.

'Good time skiing?' she said. 'Are you going back to the chalet now, can you give me a lift?'

She obviously didn't know about the horror that had engulfed them. Gaby gave a little cry, causing Debra to look at her sharply, seemingly annoyed to see her. 'Is there a problem, Gaby?' she said sternly.

Eloise took a deep breath, 'Debra... Lawrence tried to ring Ken...'

'He left his mobile in the chalet, he says there's often not a signal, though I had mine,' she added, as if hers was the important one. 'We've just had lunch and he and Travis have gone for a walk. I thought I'd go back, was going to take a taxi, but finding you here...' She watched Eloise keenly, 'Is something the matter?'

'Yes... but let me explain,' Marcus stepped forward.

Eloise said at the same moment, 'Jerry is fine, but he and Theo were involved in an avalanche.' Just the word shocked Debra, she stumbled and Marcus shot out his hand and steadied her.

'It was a small avalanche and both men are safe, but

they've been flown down to Sion to hospital, just to make sure,' David chipped in. 'Lawrence has gone with them.'

'Lawrence tried to ring you, Travis and Ken. He managed to leave a message with Ken but of course if he's left his mobile in the chalet he wouldn't have got it,' Eloise said breathlessly.

'And you were both there?' Debra scowled at Gaby as if *she* had somehow set off the avalanche. Gaby was very pale, struggling to keep herself together.

'Yes, we were skiing behind them, they were sort of racing each other, it was lovely powder snow,' Eloise finished, realizing from her expression that Debra had no idea of the magic of powder snow or even what it was.

'Where's Ken when I need him,' Debra said in annoyance. 'I can try and contact Travis if he's in range.' She took her own mobile out of her bag then dropped it back in again. 'More sensible to go straight to the hospital, not hang about for them to come back. Can you take me there at once? I must be sure the doctors are competent, give Jerry X-rays and a thorough check-over. He could have had a head injury, was he conscious?' She had snapped into a commandeering role. No wonder she was so good at business, Eloise thought, few people would dare argue with her. Then to her relief Eloise's mobile went and it was Lawrence.

'They've both been thoroughly checked and, thank God, there's no harm done. I'll bring them back in a taxi. Are you at the chalet yet?'

'I'm still at Medran and Debra's here. Ken left his mobile in Jacaranda...' Before she could say any more, Debra put out her hand and almost snatched the mobile from her.

'Lawrence, what do the doctors say?' Debra demanded 'I hope they've given Jerry a thorough examination. He probably imagines he's all right but he could be suffering from internal injuries or a bleed on the brain.'

Her list of prognoses spooked Gaby, who started to cry again.

'Let me talk to Jerry,' Debra was saying and the moment he was on the line she began to question him, barely letting him answer before she fired out the next one. Where were they skiing, what were the conditions like, did they know there was a danger of an avalanche? When he had answered as best he could she demanded to talk to the doctor. She had to hang on while he was fetched before she interrogated him as if she doubted his qualifications, demanding to know every test and examination he had carried out.

Marcus took Eloise's arm and pulled her aside. 'The Swiss doctors are very thorough, they are used to seeing hundreds of skiing accidents and will have taken all precautions,' he said.

'I know but, well,' Eloise glanced at Debra, dropped her voice, 'I'm worried for Theo, in case she blames him for taking us there.'

Debra clicked off the mobile, having reluctantly agreed to Jerry's discharge, and handed it back to Eloise. 'I'll have to get this looked into,' she said. 'Why were you anywhere near an avalanche, Eloise?'

Her mouth felt dry, her worst fears were coming true. If she said after a heavy snowfall and at certain times of the year there was always a slight chance of an avalanche, Debra would pounce and remind her that there was a heavy snowfall last night and turn the blame on to Theo. She said carefully, 'We did not know we were near one, it's just one of those hazards of the mountains.'

To her relief David broke in. 'If the sécurité des pistes

thought there was a real danger they would have closed the runs. They check the main runs every day and...'

'But they weren't on the main run,' Debra said. 'Were you?' she accused Eloise.

'Theo took the precaution of asking a guide if it was safe before they set off and he said it was, though one must always take care while on the mountain,' Marcus said. 'If a run's not closed, people can make their own decision whether to go on it or not. That particular run is well known to the regulars and, after a snowfall, Theo would know that it usually has the best powder snow.'

'It doesn't sound safe, you can't ski where you like in Canada,' Debra said.

'Perhaps not, but you can here in Europe,' David said.

'I'll get my lawyer to look into it.' She caught sight of Gaby's tear-streaked face. 'Why are you crying? Is there something you're keeping from me?'

'No,' Gaby said, 'I'm just scared, it was such a shock, one minute they were there, the next... and I... I didn't love him enough.' She blurted out in shock as if it was time for a confession.

'Well, that much was obvious,' Debra said coldly. 'So you can leave him alone now. I suppose planes fly tomorrow, you can go back to London, get out of his life.'

Gaby gasped but Debra turned her back on her as though that was the end of it and as far as she was concerned she'd cut Gaby out of her life. 'I'd like to go back to the chalet, now,' she said to Eloise, 'and wait for Jerry to return to see for myself if he needs another check-up. I can take him to Geneva tomorrow if I have to, they have the top doctors there.'

Marcus opened his mouth to speak but thought better of

it. Eloise too knew there was no point trying to talk Debra round, and anyway she was so shocked that Gaby was to be sent home, she turned to her instead and put her arm round her in support.

Marcus and David asked again if they could do anything to help, but Debra dismissed them with a flick of her hand and the three women piled into the jeep.

Eloise drove them slowly back to the chalet, forcing herself to concentrate on the road and not be distracted by Debra trying to get through to Travis, grumpily asking why he wasn't picking up as she needed him to look into this incident. She felt drained, wrung out not only by the experience on the mountain, but also by Debra's determination to take further action to attribute blame. She was not going to let this go easily and Eloise worried that Jacaranda would be in the firing line.

Pippa and Radley were already in the chalet having just skied back, when Eloise, Gaby and Debra returned. Debra immediately cornered Radley, spewing out the details of what had happened as if she had been there herself.

'Jerry could have been killed or at least disabled or brain damaged for life,' she said it as if the avalanche had somehow been arranged, poised on the rocks to fall on him just as he passed. She didn't mention Theo – the fact that he had been taken to the hospital too to get checked over – as if he were of no consequence.

Gaby had retreated into herself; she stayed silent, took off her boots and went upstairs to her room. Eloise followed, longing for a hot shower and some sleep and to escape from Debra's torrent of accusations, not wanting to be dragged into any interrogation. She was also worried about Gaby.

She passed her room, and seeing the door was ajar she

went in. Gaby was lying on her bed. 'So I'm to go home,' she said, 'the old cow, she hates me being with Jerry.'

Eloise sat down on a chair facing her. 'You did tell her you didn't love him, Gaby,' she reminded her gently. 'Maybe because you thought he'd been killed it made you feel...' She was about to say guilty, but perhaps that was too harsh just now. 'I suppose it made you admit that you don't love him enough to marry him, but you're fond of him aren't you?' she asked. It was obvious that Jerry loved Gaby but she did not love him in the same way and the accident had made her face up to her actions and she felt guilty about using him. She must work out how to deal with it herself, though Eloise would support her as she would her own children if she asked for it.

'I don't know why I said it to her,' Gaby said with a sigh. 'I didn't mean it to sound as if I don't care for him; I do, but not as much as he wants me to. I feel ashamed of myself now that I'm using him but I don't want to be sent home, though perhaps it is best that I do go.'

'You must do what you think best, Gaby, though I'll miss you,' Eloise said. 'But Debra might calm down when she sees that Jerry is all right'

'I doubt it. She's like a dog with a bone – once she's got her teeth into something she never lets it go.'

'What will Jerry say if you *do* go home?' she asked, Gaby's remark filling her with fear.

'He won't want me to; though he might have changed his mind after this. If Debra makes enough fuss he'll fall in with it, probably hate me for using him, I don't know.' She shrugged, looking miserable. Eloise took her hand. Gaby would have to sort this out for herself. 'Perhaps I should break it off with him.' Gaby faced her. 'I'd have hated it if he'd died as I'm fond of him, he's a good person, but I don't love him as I should, and this was perhaps my punishment for taking his money and not loving him enough to want to stay with him for life, have his children.'

'It's your decision, Gaby, but you've had a terrible shock, so perhaps it's best to wait until you're calmer before you decide, and wait until Jerry gets back, talk it over with him.' She got up. 'Why don't you have a long, hot bath to relax. I can't believe it's Christmas Day, I've got the dinner to see to, though I wonder if anyone is in the mood to eat it.' She bent over and kissed her. 'Try not to stress too much. It will probably all sort itself out in the end,' she said with a confidence she'd didn't feel.

She had a sudden longing to talk to her children. Lawrence had said she could use the landline and she crept downstairs to go to Lawrence's office. The door to the living room was ajar and she could hear Debra speaking on her mobile. 'I'm well aware it's Christmas Day, Travis, but I need to speak to Hugh at once, see if there is a case to answer.'

Afraid Debra would see her and pull her in, Eloise scuttled back upstairs, she'd ring the twins later.

In the bathroom, Eloise stood under the hot shower for ages hoping it would wash away her fears; it warmed her body but not the turmoil in her heart. Would the avalanche be the end of Jacaranda if Debra made trouble? Even if she didn't have a case against Theo, she could involve lawyers and Lawrence would have to do the same and it would cost him a fortune, and she could make trouble with the agency which would affect Jacaranda's reputation. Eloise couldn't bear to think of it. She dressed quickly and went downstairs, and to her relief found that Lawrence had just got back with Jerry and Theo.

Debra immediately snatched up Jerry, who seemed perfectly well, and she took him into the living room, firmly shutting the door behind them.

Theo grinned at Eloise. 'Rather hairy time,' he said, as she went to hug him. He hugged her back, the warmth; the living bulk of him comforted her. She released him, blinked away her tears.

'I suppose you're hungry,' she said to hide her emotion.

'You bet, we missed lunch,' he said, following her to the kitchen.

Lawrence said something about seeing to the champagne and came with them. He seemed subdued, gentle with her. He said, 'I hope you're none the worse, Eloise. It must have been a very frightening experience.'

'It was, but I'm fine now, relieved no one was badly hurt.' She wanted to say something about Debra trying to get hold of a lawyer but he went on.

'Have you rung your family yet?' When she shook her head he said, 'Use the landline in my office, you'll be undisturbed there.'

She wished for one mad moment that he would hold her close. 'How are you, Lawrence? It's been quite an ordeal for you too,' Eloise said, seeing how tired he looked, exhausted with the strain and shock of the day.

'Fine, thanks,' he said, though she sensed he didn't mean it. He paused as if he had something important to say, but instead said, 'We'll forget it all for now, try and celebrate Christmas, but tomorrow I'll need to find out from everyone exactly what happened and if you saw any warnings to keep you off the piste. I don't know what Ken will make of it but I get the impression Debra will not want to let this go.'

25

It was a great relief that she'd cooked the Christmas meal many times before; she could almost do it in her sleep, Eloise thought. She had already stuffed the turkey with an apple and pistachio mixture and made little balls of meat and cranberry stuffing to cook separately and it was now in the oven. She parboiled the potatoes to make them extra crispy when they roasted in a pan of goose fat.

It was comforting to have something familiar to do after their terrifying experience this morning, though she wondered if anyone apart from Theo would sit down to eat it, Debra and her party being in a fever after the events.

'They were not even there, on the mountain,' Vera said when she heard about it as she hovered round the kitchen. The table was laid in the main living room but the door to the room was still shut while the family conferred over what action they might take over the event. 'It's always the very rich who try to make money out of everything,' Vera went on. 'The men are alive and well, they should thank God for that. Give money in thanks to the sick and poor instead of trying to get it off someone else.'

Vera obviously didn't like these guests but Eloise kept her own feelings about them to herself. Lawrence had given Vera the evening off and she was about to leave to have Christmas dinner with her friends. Theo and Eloise – though both were summoned to sit at the table, something Eloise would have liked to avoid – were going to be the waiters with Lawrence filling in where needed.

It had been an unusual Christmas Day to say the least, and she'd be quite content to go to bed with her book. She was dreading spending Christmas evening with Debra and her family.

They heard the living room door open and someone come down the passage. Vera jumped up from the chair she had just sat down on and picked up her bag, ready to leave, as if afraid it was Lawrence telling her she couldn't go after all. Travis came into the kitchen and the sight of both women staring at him made him nervous. He jiggled on his small feet, attempted to smile and look friendly and failed. Eloise felt sorry for him.

'Do you need anything?' she said, her heart racing. Was he going to say they were leaving, or had sent for a lawyer?

He didn't look at her but fixed his eyes on a spot above her head. 'It's Christmas Day and you've obviously gone to a lot of trouble to prepare dinner for us, so it's Debra... and Ken's wish that we put the events of today to one side and enjoy the rest of Christmas.'

'Good idea,' Eloise said, wishing it was just her, Lawrence, Theo and Gaby sitting down together. 'Is eight thirty all right for everyone?'

'Yes, that will be fine,' Travis muttered and scampered away.

'He does their dirty work,' Vera said darkly.

'We don't know that, Vera,' Eloise said, though she suspected it was true.

Lawrence came into the kitchen, 'All set, Eloise?' He was

smiling but she could see the tension in his face. He came closer to her, putting his hand on her arm, looking into her face. His voice was soft, 'I'm sorry if you don't feel up to all this cooking for tonight, I could...'

'Bring in Aurelia's "Tempting Delights",' she said. 'No thank you. I'm fine, glad to keep occupied and not sit about and dwell on this morning, I'm just so relieved it all ended well.'

A shudder passed over him as if he could not bear to think of how it might have ended. 'We'll have to see, but let's try and enjoy this evening.' He moved away to deal with the wine.

He had put the champagne and some white wine in the fridge and he now opened the red wine to let it breathe. Theo appeared, having taken Bert for a walk, and asked if he could help, his eyes lingering on the glasses of chocolates and sugared almonds ready to go on the table in the living room.

Vera said, 'If they are finished in the other room, Theo, you can help me carry these in before I go. Don't eat any,' she smiled indulgently at him.

'I'm starving,' he said, popping a chocolate into his mouth and rearranging the others to hide the space it left. 'Only one and no one will notice.'

He reminded her so much of her own children, young and vibrant and always hungry. Eloise turned back to her cooking to hide her pain of missing them, the hollow feeling in her heart. She'd managed to speak to them, Lawrence leaving her alone to make her call from the landline in his office, shutting the door behind him to give her privacy.

To her disappointment the line had been bad, their voices lurching in and out of earshot as if they were being rocked forward and back by the sea, so they couldn't have much of a conversation. She did not tell them about the avalanche this morning or even that their father was here, but asked them instead about what they were doing, but their sentences came in broken bursts, though she gathered they were well and moving on to China. It was a relief after the trauma of today to hear their voices even though they were not clear. As she said goodbye she begged them to keep safe and look out for each other.

She had spoken to her parents in New Zealand too; Lawrence had insisted on that. 'You must ring your family. I've spoken to Desmond and he hopes I'm not working you too hard,' he said. 'I haven't told him about this morning,' he added in a quieter tone. 'No need to worry him just now.'

The line to New Zealand was clearer and she told her parents about the avalanche, starting the story by saying no one was hurt. Her mother took the news calmly.

'You are in the mountains after all, Eloise, and it's one of the hazards, but I'm so relieved everyone is safe. You know what I think about mobiles making people feel insecure if they are not constantly in touch with everyone, but in this case having one was a godsend.'

When her parents had rung off, leaving her feeling cocooned in their love though missing them dreadfully, Eloise told herself she only felt so lonely because it was Christmas Day and the people she loved best were far away.

After her calls she went upstairs to get the presents she made for everyone and when she returned to the kitchen she found Lawrence, Vera and Theo waiting for her.

Vera was very touched with her present of the orange pomander she'd made, saying she'd hang it in her wardrobe. Vera gave her a pretty bottle of body lotion. Theo gave Eloise a box of chocolates and insisted on trying one and the fudge she'd given him, saying it was the best fudge he'd ever tasted. Lawrence too was pleased with his fudge, saying he would hide it from Theo so he could enjoy it in peace. He gave Eloise a cashmere scarf which had been beautifully gift wrapped from an expensive shop. It was gorgeous and she was touched by his choice.

'I hope the colour's right, I thought it matched your eyes,' he said as she held the soft blue scarf to her face. 'It looks good.' He smiled, his eyes appraising her, making her blush, his look feeling warmer than the scarf. Ken, calling for him, quickly broke the moment, and throwing her a reluctant glance, Lawrence went to him, leaving her feeling bereft. *Remember you are going home very soon*, she warned herself, *leaving all this behind*.

*

The turkey was cooked to perfection and Eloise served the starters while it rested. They all sat round the table in the living room. Vera had laid out the silver candlesticks that Eloise remembered from when she was here before and made everywhere so elegant. In the centre was a glass bowl filled with golden balls and the glasses of chocolates and white sugared almonds.

Eloise sat next to Theo and Radley. She had brought one smart dress with her, it was cobalt blue, slightly fitted with a fullish skirt in a silky material which enhanced her figure. Lawrence did a double take when he saw her, and seeing her surprise he laughed.

'Sorry Eloise, you look so different out of trousers.'

'Not so different, I hope,' she said. Had she been looking a complete fright? Too unattractive to tempt any of his rich clients – though no amount of money would tempt her to go after anyone in this party.

At first the atmosphere of the dinner was awkward, everyone trying to be festive without much success, but after some champagne and then wine they loosened up.

Radley was shy but he tried to talk to her, asking where she lived in the UK. She told him and then asked about his writing. 'Pippa told me you've just bought a publishing company, for trade magazines, I think she said.'

As she spoke there was a lull in the conversation and Lawrence caught her words, and she saw the pinch of anxiety on his face. Was this yet another weapon to use against Jacaranda's reputation? He was watching her and she was spurred on to continue the conversation.

'Yes, that's right,' Radley said. 'I did the deal just before we left.'

'What do the trade magazines cover?' She could feel Lawrence's tension.

'Various subjects: art, travel, antiques, you know.'

'So will you be writing about Verbier?' Eloise said, smiling at him to hide her fear.

'I might,' he said, 'it's a lovely place.'

Debra heard his words and said bossily, 'You could do an article on the new chalets out here, the ones in that modern complex down in the village. Get a photographer up, that would go down well.'

Radley's face creased with anxiety and Eloise guessed Debra would persuade him to do what she wanted, perhaps even write a damning article about the danger of being led into avalanches, but before she could say any more to him, Ken started on about a car he had seen that afternoon.

Jerry seemed none the worse after his adventure and in fact he and Theo boasted about it. Debra ignored them and turning to Lawrence sitting beside her, began rather pointedly to question him about how early in the year one had to book one of the 'more luxurious' chalets in time for Christmas. Might it be prudent to do it now, while she was here?

'I've no idea,' he said smoothly, 'some of them are no doubt booked a year in advance, you must contact the ones you like, perhaps go and look round them and see how it goes.'

'I think we'll have next Christmas in the sun,' Ken said.

Jerry butted in, 'Well I like the snow, it's more Christmassy really, and it would seem odd to spend it in a swimsuit on a beach in the blazing sun.'

'Same here,' Theo said and Jerry began to say how he'd like to come to Jacaranda again, but he might as well have stated a liking for a shack in the middle of nowhere without food or drink for the enthusiasm Debra showed. Ken just smiled, glancing nervously at Debra. Travis, their Mr Fixit – though Eloise guessed he only fixed what he was told to fix – finished his wine in a gulp and looked anxiously round for more. Pippa hardly said a word; throwing nervous glances at Radley every so often, as if afraid he might suddenly disappear and leave her here alone to be picked at by her mother-in-law.

Gaby seemed completely withdrawn. Eloise tried to catch her eye, send her a smile of comfort, but she didn't – or wouldn't – notice, perhaps she too missed her family, her mother and her brothers. She pushed her food around her plate and not even when Theo brought in the Christmas puddings surrounded by dancing blue flames did she show much interest. Jerry was sitting away from her and perhaps he didn't notice her mood in the candlelight, or if he did he didn't know how to deal with it for he never said a word to her.

Eloise hoped to be able to speak to Gaby again that evening, try to make her feel better. But as soon as the dinner was finished she went upstairs, leaving the rest of the party sitting in the living room by the open fire drinking wine and coffee and eating the chocolates and sugared almonds.

Lawrence hovered about between the kitchen and the living room, helping carry through the dishes, and finally settled in the living room with Ken who was questioning him about other ski resorts. Theo and Eloise tided up the kitchen together and Bert crept in and hoovered up any morsels he found on the floor, though Eloise, still chastened by the lamb incident, asked Theo to take him away.

'Don't worry, the dinner's eaten and no one is going to come in here and see him. If Dad makes a fuss, I'll say it's my fault,' Theo said cheerfully.

'Let it be on your head then,' Eloise retorted. Then, changing the subject, she said, 'Have you heard that Debra is insisting that Gaby go home tomorrow, back to the UK?'

'No.' Theo frowned at her. 'Why should she, they're booked for the rest of the week?'

'She's annoyed with her because...' She paused, wondering the best way to explain Gaby's situation, and decided it was better to tell it as it was. 'Because she told Debra she didn't love Jerry. She was in shock after the avalanche, but Debra said she knew she didn't and is sending her home.'

Theo looked concerned, 'And what does Jerry think?'

'I don't know, maybe Gaby hasn't told him, though I suppose Debra has.' She put the leftovers from the two

Christmas puddings on a plate and stored them in the fridge.

Lawrence, coming in for more coffee, interrupted their conversation. Bert, seeing him, hid himself behind the curtain and if Lawrence noticed he didn't remark on it, he just made another pot of coffee.

Eloise was almost asleep on her feet and as the clearing up was finished, she said goodnight and scurried up to bed. As she turned off the light and snuggled down to sleep, she suffered a wave of loneliness, missing her children and her family as it used to be, but she'd got through her first Christmas without them and it had been the most eventful day.

She was down at half past eight the next morning to make breakfast. Vera was already there and had laid the table and was tidying before the guests came down. Everyone, even Lawrence, drifted down long past nine. The day was overcast, the sky heavy with more snow, and it wasn't until mid-morning that it was noticed that Gaby and Jerry had not appeared.

Debra sent Eloise up to wake Gaby. 'Travis has found her a flight at teatime and she must pack and leave for the airport. I assume Theo can take her, or you can call a taxi,' she said bossily.

Eloise didn't answer and went upstairs to give Gaby the news. 'Gaby, it's me, can I come in?' There was no answer; she knocked again before opening the door.

The room was empty, a pillow on the floor, the bedclothes in a tangle; the cupboard doors flung open showing they were bare. She knocked on the next door which was Jerry's room, there was no answer either and when she went in, apart from the unmade bed, there was no sign that he had ever been there.

26

There seemed to be a lot of commotion upstairs, raised voices, someone clumping up the stairs, the thud of a door closing. Lawrence sighed; it had been the strangest Christmas of his life. He still felt sick thinking of the avalanche yesterday, terrified at how near he had come to losing Theo.

It was not surprising that the mood on Christmas Day had been affected, though they had managed to enjoy a good dinner, having made a pact not to talk about the event until the following morning. Yet he felt that those of the party who were not on the mountain at the time – Ken, Debra and the rest of them – had not understood the possibility of an avalanche, imagining that the runs were constantly monitored, as if they were at a playground for small children, not a place governed by the elements. They wouldn't understand any more than they'd understand that a sudden squall at sea was a product of nature and could not always be dictated to by man.

Everything seemed to be conspiring against him this season – finding that he couldn't put off the extensive work of Jacaranda any longer; the chef drama, although Eloise had worked out better than he imagined as she brought something special to the chalet – though he wasn't sure what – and then the avalanche and the fallout from that; learning that Radley had bought a publishing firm and might write an article – possibly dictated by his mother – about Verbier, or even Jacaranda; and now some new ruckus seemed to be taking place upstairs.

He sighed, he supposed he'd better go up and see what was happening – how glad he'd be when this lot had gone – but before he could shut down his computer, Theo came running into his office, his face fraught with panic.

'Gaby and Jerry have gone.'

'Gone where? Skiing?' He put his hand on his shoulder as if to reassure himself that his lovely boy was safe. Theo seemed none the worse for his experience; in fact he'd heard him and Jerry joking about it last night before supper, though he suspected Jerry was more scared by the ordeal than he pretended.

'No... packed and everything, left the chalet,' Theo said as if Lawrence were slow on the uptake. 'Eloise says they've run away from Debra, you know she told Gaby she had to go back to London today...'

'I didn't know that.' He was annoyed he hadn't been told. It didn't matter to him financially if anyone left early as the chalet was already paid for, though he did expect to be told if there were any changes.

'Gaby was so stressed after the avalanche; she told Debra she didn't love Jerry and Debra ordered her to go home today. Travis has got her a ticket for a flight this evening.'

He struggled with the sudden burst of anger rising in him. 'So why has she already left, and where is Jerry?'

'I don't know,' Theo slumped down on a chair, staring morosely out of the window, one hand stroking Bert who'd left his bed in the other room and come to him, hoping they were going out. 'Jerry and I were going to ski the four valleys before he left, he even said he might stay on a few more days to do it if there was room here.'

Lawrence felt sorry for Theo. He'd thought Jerry a dull kind of person, probably under Debra's thumb, but Theo had brought him out of himself by taking him and Gaby skiing. Although Jerry was quite a bit older than Theo, they had got on well together and perhaps Theo had shown him what fun ordinary life could be, so it seemed churlish of them to just up and leave without saying goodbye to him.

'We must find out what's happened to them, perhaps Gaby has told Eloise where they are,' Lawrence said. 'No doubt someone has checked their rooms?'

'Yes, Eloise did and I went up too. The rooms are empty. Eloise knows no more than we do. Vera said she found the outside door was unlocked when she came in this morning, but it often is if you get up early or Bert is let out, so she thought nothing of it,' Theo said.

'I better go up and deal with it,' Lawrence sighed. There had often been dramas with the guests over the years, but this lot were some of the worst – if not *the* worst – they'd had, probably because Debra and Ken didn't really want to be here, at Jacaranda, at all.

'I suppose they ran away so they could be together,' Theo said. 'Debra doesn't like Gaby; she thinks she's after Jerry's money. Do you think she is, Dad?'

He smiled at him, knowing that Theo only called him Dad when he needed reassurance, he was just nineteen after all and though he liked to act older, there were times – especially like this – when he escaped back into the security of childhood.

'Who knows? But I'm sure they will work it out between them. I'm sorry if they have left, you got on well with them and they obviously enjoyed skiing with you.' The whole situation sounded a bit strange to Lawrence, especially if Gaby had said she didn't love Jerry. He couldn't have forced her to leave with him, could he? No, from what he'd seen of them, Gaby was too gutsy to allow that.

'Do you think the avalanche was my fault?' Theo suddenly blurted.

'No. I don't. You know after a large snowfall there is more risk, and Marcus, David and I were about to ski in the same place. It could just as easily have been us. It was just bad luck, you know the mountains well enough.' Theo must have seen the warning flags and made his own decision. If he hoped to be a ski guide he had to be able to assess the risks, and Lawrence knew his son wouldn't have knowingly put anyone in danger. He got up. 'I better go and deal with Jerry and Gaby's disappearance.' He lowered his voice and leant closer to Theo, 'Though I'd quite like to run away from Debra myself.' He reluctantly made for the door. Theo followed him, assuring Bert he'd be back soon, knowing that if Debra saw him she'd only kick off.

They were all, except for Pippa, who Lawrence had presumed had gone upstairs, assembled in the living room. Debra sitting on the sofa, Ken standing by the window looking as if he too longed to escape, and Travis hovering about anxiously as though Gaby and Jerry's disappearance was somehow his fault. Radley prowled by the bookcase looking grumpy, as if annoyed with the fuss being made. Eloise and Vera were not there but he could hear some clattering in the kitchen. He wondered if he should ask them both to come in so they could all discuss this together but decided against it – Eloise had told him she had no idea where they'd gone and Vera didn't know, so better to leave them out of it.

Lawrence said quietly, 'I understand Jerry and Gaby have left without your knowledge.'

'She is nothing more than a gold-digger,' Debra announced, making Ken say nervously, 'We don't know that, dear.'

'*You* might not, but I know one when I see one,' Debra retorted, as if she was constantly on the lookout for such people. 'She practically admitted it to me, said she didn't love Jerry enough.' She turned to Lawrence. 'I told her she must go back home today, Travis booked her a ticket for this evening, as he told her he would. Now I find she *and Jerry* are gone.'

'And you've no idea where?' Lawrence wasn't at all surprised they'd escaped; he was amazed they consented to stay here with Debra at all.

'Of course not or I would have gone and fetched him, talked some sense into him,' Debra threw him a withering look. 'I can't reach him on his mobile, I've left countless messages but he won't respond. I suspect she's taken his phone,' she added, as if Gaby was entirely responsible for this and had Jerry imprisoned somewhere.

How should he deal with this? Both of the fugitives, especially Jerry, were well over age and surely able to do what they wished. He suspected that Gaby had the stronger character of the two but this was hardly a case of a woman abusing a vulnerable person, though there was no doubt Jerry was in love with her. He addressed Ken, hoping to get a more helpful answer from him.

'Do you know where they could have gone, Ken?'

'I've no idea.' Ken glanced nervously at Debra, before quietly suggesting, 'Perhaps they just wanted some time alone together.'

'Huh! I'm sure *she* engineered the whole thing,' Debra proclaimed, her eyes boring into Ken's face. 'So what do you suggest we do, Lawrence? Perhaps you could telephone all the hotels, see if they are there.'

He was certainly not going to do that; Ken didn't seem concerned about them so nor would he be. 'I'll go and check with Eloise, I believe she knows Gaby,' he said hurriedly before leaving the room. Theo, who'd been standing by the window looking longingly out at the mountains, quickly followed him into the kitchen, relieved to get away.

Eloise was making a mushroom and leek filling for her interpretation of a beef Wellington. She looked up with an expression of sympathy. 'Did they – or rather Debra – give you a hard time?' she said quietly. 'I don't know where they have gone, but I would imagine Jerry wanted to go with Gaby, either back to the UK or somewhere else, he's desperately in love with her.'

'They are both mature, consenting adults,' Lawrence said, though he imagined that that wouldn't be enough to please Debra. 'How old is Gaby?'

Eloise thought a moment. 'At least twenty-one, possibly twenty-two, she's a couple of years or so older than my twins.'

He sighed, 'And she's obviously a clever, sensible girl, so I don't know what to do.'

'Let them go,' Vera, who was at the sink polishing the silver knives and forks, broke in. 'I would go if I had to stay long with that woman.'

Privately Lawrence agreed, but the sound of the door

opening, the chill of cold air and voices in the hall disturbed them.

Theo said hopefully, 'Perhaps they've come back?'

Lawrence started down the passage to see who it was. At the same moment Eloise's mobile announced a text, she peered at it as it lay on the table beside her.

Jerry and I have moved on. Tell you more later. Gaby xxx

She had given Gaby her number so she could pass it on to her mother. Eloise was about to show this text to Vera and Theo when she heard Aurelia's voice, loud and unmistakable.

'There you are, Lawrence. I've bought my new friend, Harvey Brandon, to see you, to give you some great ideas about making Jacaranda more lucrative.'

27

Harvey… Harvey was here? Shocked, Eloise rushed to wash her hands at the sink, frantic to escape.

'Oh that woman again,' Vera said impatiently, then seeing Eloise's consternation exclaimed, 'What has happened, are you ill? That woman makes me ill, coming here, trying to steal Jacaranda from Lawrence.'

Eloise forced herself to remain calm. She dried her hands and took off her apron. They might not come into the kitchen, or Lawrence might ask them to leave, perhaps to come back when he'd sorted out Gaby and Jerry's escape, for that's what it was, it was obvious from Gaby's message. At least she was safe… but she couldn't worry about that now, not with Harvey here. Why had Aurelia brought him to Jacaranda? How well did she know him – were they sleeping together? That was usually her first conclusion when she saw Harvey with an attractive woman, and Aurelia was glamorous and sexy, but what about the pink-clothed woman… no, she must not go there, Harvey's love life was nothing to do with her any more.

'It's my ex-husband… Aurelia's brought him here with her,' Eloise explained to Vera, her heart beating fit to burst. Perhaps she should escape through the door by the kitchen, though it would be so cold if she had to wait outside there long, and why should she risk freezing to death for Aurelia and Harvey?

'How she got him?' Vera frowned, glancing in the direction of the passage leading to the front door as if they would suddenly emerge.

Eloise and Vera could hear Lawrence asking Aurelia why she hadn't telephoned first, it was not a good time, and perhaps they could come back later. Then they heard Aurelia's laughter.

Eloise crept closer to the door so she could hear their conversation better.

'Harvey has to leave soon and he says he knows the chalet. It's such a surprise,' Aurelia sounded incredulous, 'that he was once married to your little cook.'

'I don't think we've ever met?' Lawrence said.

Theo, who had followed his father out of the kitchen but had only gone halfway down the passage to see what was going on, came back now.

'Is he your ex, Eloise?' he asked in surprise.

She nodded, furious now that Aurelia had barged in here with Harvey. Had she brought him here to taunt her? 'Excuse me, Theo.' She dodged past him and went down the passage.

Lawrence turned to her, an expression of incredulity on his face; did he think she had invited him here with some wild idea to turn the place into some millionaires' haven?

Harvey, seeing her, smiled awkwardly, 'Hello Eloise, sorry to drop in but Aurelia...'

'You should have rung first,' Eloise said sharply. Aurelia was grinning in a pitying sort of way, and now Debra came out of the living room and said imperiously, 'Are you here about Jerry? Do you know where he is?'

'Oh, no,' Aurelia said, not at all interested in Debra's distress. She had taken off one of her boots and was about to bend over to remove the other, she straightened, smiled at Debra and said, 'I've come to show a friend who's in the travel business this chalet, so he can suggest some ideas to make it appeal to a higher market.'

Debra, who obviously thought she *was* a member of the 'higher market', suddenly forgot about her own dramas and began, 'Well you need more bathrooms and...'

'Thank you,' Lawrence said firmly, 'now is not a good time, Aurelia, and I suggest you come back later... and please give us warning before you do.'

Harvey, as if he wanted to calm the atmosphere, said, 'We had some happy times here, didn't we, Eloise?' He threw her a look, and then addressed Lawrence, 'We stayed here a few times when our children were small.'

Eloise wanted to cry, remembering now those times when all seemed calm and loving, when she and Harvey were together and the twins were too young to leave home alone, be off in the wide world somewhere, open to untold dangers, but she pulled herself together, her dislike of Aurelia and her love of Jacaranda giving her strength.

'It's a wonderful chalet and people who really enjoy the mountains and nature and the true atmosphere of the place are happy here. Wouldn't you agree, Harvey? Don't you remember you used to ridicule those ponced-up places, as you called them, pandering to people with money but no imagination, no feeling for the natural beauty all around. Remember,' she threw him a stern look, 'your descriptions of some of the holiday places you visited in your job? The ones that didn't have the charm and beauty of Jacaranda.'

'I don't you know what you mean?' Aurelia looked offended.

To his credit Harvey looked ashamed, which was rare for him. Eloise suspected that dropping in here unannounced had been entirely Aurelia's idea. Having found out what Harvey did for a living had she thought she could get him on her side and persuade Lawrence to make changes to Jacaranda to suit *her*?

Lawrence said, 'I think it's best if you go now, Aurelia, we'll talk on the phone later.'

Debra addressed Harvey, 'Are you involved with the chalets in the new development? Can you put in a word for us to rent one next time *if* we should come to Verbier again?'

Harvey had the grace to say, 'No... I... that's not my line of work, I deal mostly with summer resorts.'

'But he's got very good ideas about skiing ones and Verbier attracts more and more summer visitors,' Aurelia tried again.

Theo looked worried, he said, 'We love Jacaranda as it is, are we changing it, Dad... Lawrence?'

'It needs more bathrooms and perhaps a hot tub,' Debra reiterated.

Lawrence's face darkened. 'I'm sorry,' he said to Harvey, 'you've been brought here under false pretences. I'd be grateful if you'd leave, make an appointment to come back if you have to... unless...' he glanced at Eloise, but she shook her head and turned away. It still hurt to see her ex-husband, imagining him making love to other women... to Aurelia? The last thing she wanted was for Harvey to come back to the chalet. Perhaps Lawrence thought they were like some of those celeb couples that divorced yet referred to each other as their 'best friends'.

'Go now, Harvey,' she said firmly, 'it's not a convenient time. In fact there is no convenient time for you to come to Jacaranda.'

'But Eloise...'

'No buts,' she said, 'we haven't been here for at least ten years and things are different now. Please leave and don't come back.'

Aurelia said sarcastically, 'Well if it's not convenient... but Lawrence, I'd say you're missing out on a great opportunity by not at least listening to Harvey's ideas to turn Jacaranda into a huge money-spinner.'

'That's not what I want,' Lawrence said, and then Bert, who'd managed to escape from his place downstairs, came flying down the passage barking excitedly.

'Oh, that dog.' Debra backed away as if he were a raging lion.

'Theo, control him will you,' Lawrence said, trying not to laugh.

Bert started to sniff at Aurelia and Harvey, but before he could decide if he liked them or not, Theo scooped him up.

'I'll take you out soon,' he said, going back towards the kitchen, making Debra remark that she hoped he was well out of the way of the food as animals were so unhygienic.

Eloise, in her nervous state, felt an urge to giggle when she thought of Bert and the joint of lamb but curbed it when she caught Lawrence's stern eye, though his mouth was twitching with a smile. She turned to go back to the kitchen.

Lawrence opened the front door and the freezing air drove Debra back into the living room, shutting the door firmly behind her. Left with them in the hall, Aurelia struggling to put on her boot, Eloise heard Lawrence say, 'You've come at a difficult moment. Two of our guests seem to have done a runner. I've got to sort that out before I do anything else.'

'What, like your last chef, run off with one of the guests, or run off without paying?' Aurelia asked. Eloise hovered in the passage to hear what Lawrence would say.

'No, nothing like that,' Lawrence said irritably, 'it's a family matter but I need to deal with it in peace.'

Theo, still holding Bert, said as she came down the passage, 'What's your ex-husband doing here, Eloise? Is he trying to get you back?'

'No,' she said, 'it's just a dreadful coincidence. I'd no idea he was even out here, I probably wouldn't have come if I'd known.'

'I'm jolly glad you didn't know then,' Theo said warmly. 'I'm sorry if you don't want him here, I don't either if Aurelia's trying to get him to change Jacaranda. We love it as it is.'

28

Eloise arrived at Quinn's chalet after tea. Saskia telephoned her to beg her to come early to their party so they could gossip before the other guests arrived.

'Most of the work's done. Quinn doesn't like too much to eat as he says it spoils the enjoyment of the wine,' she said, 'but I've done a few bits and there's bread and cheese if anyone's hungry.'

Eloise followed Saskia into the main room. There was a small tree in the corner decorated with shiny crimson baubles and gold stars and a swathe of evergreen and gold-painted fir cones and red berries draped over the mantelpiece. The furniture was pulled back to make a space in the centre of the room. The curtains were left open and the view down the valley was a picture of sparkling lights glowing through the darkness.

Quinn was 'resting' and his family, who'd come for Christmas, were visiting friends nearby but would be back for the party, so for the moment all was quiet. Saskia poured Eloise a glass of wine and the two of them sat gossiping.

'So,' Eloise finished, having told Saskia the whole saga of the avalanche, 'Gaby and Jerry seemed to have disappeared, but they are safe together. She sent me a couple of texts, not saying where she is, just that they are "nearby". They are going to stay out here for another week. I imagine that Jerry's furious with Debra for sending Gaby home and he persuaded her to stay on out here with him, and as her mother and brothers are with her mother's boyfriend I suspect she was easily persuaded.'

'Much more fun to ski than go back to winter in the UK, but frightening about the avalanche though,' Saskia shivered. 'You never know what will happen if there's been a huge snowfall but they are very good here, they usually close runs if they think they are dangerous, or even close the whole place and stop running the lifts. Good thing you were not caught up in it and could call for help.' She gulped at her wine. 'I always keep to the main piste if it's been snowing and I'm on my own.'

'Fortunately this wasn't as bad as it might have been. Theo warned us, said it would be better if we skied one at a time and to wait a little as two snowboarders had just gone, but Jerry laughed and crashed off. Theo was caught in the edge of it and tumbled about and luckily, because Jerry was wearing a transmitter, he was dug out in time.' Eloise went on, 'But just the word avalanche has sparked panic in Debra, and Lawrence is terrified they'll sue him or at least contact their lawyers so he'll have to bring in his, as if he is responsible for the avalanche.'

Saskia sighed. 'I doubt you can sue against the weather, but I suppose if someone knowingly goes out when it's dangerous, or goes on a run that's been closed or disregards warning signs, you could make a case,' Saskia said, her words chilling Eloise.

Those warning flags, if Debra found out about them, she would not hesitate in laying the blame firmly at Theo's door.

'It wasn't closed or anything, was it?' Saskia asked.

'No… there were other people there.' She would not mention the flags.

'The richer they are, the harder they push in such cases. Quinn, who's sometimes had to step in if someone sues a restaurant, thinks that some mega-rich people have a sort of complex that poorer people are trying to get at their money and take it as a personal slight if someone has crashed into their car, or given them food poisoning. Poor Lawrence, he's trying so hard to make Jacaranda pay for itself and he seems to be having nothing but bad luck this season, his chef running off and…'

'Having to employ me,' Eloise said.

'No! That was his good luck that you were free at such short notice,' Saskia said.

'Harvey's still here,' Eloise said to change the subject and to offload her concerns. 'Aurelia brought him to Jacaranda to give Lawrence advice on how to transform the chalet, no doubt to accommodate her "Tempting Delights",' she finished darkly.

'So he didn't go home for Christmas?' Saskia sounded surprised.

'No, I thought… hoped he might. He must be splashing out to stay here so long but it seems Aurelia's got her claws into him.'

'You mean they're together?' Saskia was shocked.

'I hope not, I don't think so. I told you I saw him with a woman in pink, but I haven't seen him with her since, but then he probably wouldn't have brought her to Jacaranda, knowing I was there. Despite his faults he never flaunted his other women in front of me and I wonder if he would have come at all if Aurelia hadn't brought him.' Much though he'd hurt her, Eloise wanted to be fair to him.

'I suppose once Harvey told her what his job was, finding venues for holidays, she latched on to him with her ideas for Jacaranda, no doubt hoping his expertise would help sway Lawrence to her ideas,' Saskia said.

'Fortunately he was far more concerned with placating Debra over Jerry and Gaby's midnight flit than to listen to plans to upgrade Jacaranda,' Eloise said.

'Aurelia's coming tonight, do you think Harvey will come with her?' There was a gleam of excitement in Saskia's eyes that Eloise tried to ignore. She'd become used to it; Harvey, despite now being quite paunchy, still had the gift – or perhaps the curse – of inducing excitement in women.

'Oh, I hope not.' Eloise hadn't thought of this, she'd seen more than enough of Harvey and she decided now that if he came here tonight, she'd leave, but she didn't say this to Saskia.

Before Saskia could question her further, Quinn appeared dressed in a bottle-green velvet jacket and a navy silk cravat.

'Ah, the chef,' he said smiling, lumbering over and kissing Eloise. 'How is it going at Jacaranda? Heard you have quite difficult guests this week.'

'Yes.' Eloise glanced at Saskia, wondering what she'd told him, but the doorbell interrupted them and Eloise and Saskia ran to answer it.

Quinn turned, ready to welcome people and Eloise, suddenly overcome with dread, looked round for a way of escape if Harvey and Aurelia should come in, but the only way out was through the front door.

To her relief it was a couple, Otis and Patsy, who, Eloise saw, were of the same vintage as Quinn and they remembered Desmond. They told her they missed him and of course dear Maddy, but they'd do their best to get him to come back to Verbier soon. They lived here full-time now, having lived in other parts of the world and decided that Verbier and the mountains was where they wanted to be.

Others soon arrived and then Lawrence, Theo and the party from Jacaranda, but there was no sign of Aurelia or, luckily, Harvey.

Eloise had told Lawrence about her text from Gaby and that they were safe together somewhere. She had left it to him to tell Debra, which she assumed he had done.

Theo, now standing beside her, keeping a wary eye on Debra as if afraid she'd insist on interrogating him about the avalanche or Jerry's whereabouts or both, said quietly, 'I've heard from Jerry. He wants to meet up tomorrow to ski, but he said I mustn't tell Debra and Ken in case they turn up and force Gaby to go home.'

'They can't force her,' Eloise replied, also keeping her eyes on Debra who was talking to Otis and Patsy. 'Has Lawrence told Debra about the messages I received from Gaby?'

'Yes and Debra was furious, called Gaby all sorts of names, which didn't please Ken, who I think rather fancies her himself, the old lecher. He said Jerry was old enough to choose whom he wanted to be with. Anyway, I hope I can slope off and you too and we can all meet up tomorrow.' Theo emptied his glass so Saskia could refill it as she made the rounds.

'That would be fun,' Eloise said, 'I think it's meant to be sunny tomorrow.' She did not add that there were only a few days left for her to ski before she went home and how she'd miss it.

She knew no one here but Saskia, Quinn and the Jacaranda people, but she found everyone very friendly. The guests at this party were fascinated to hear that she was the latest chef at Jacaranda, the locals having heard of Denise flying off with a pudgy millionaire. 'Love is indeed blind if it comes with a fortune,' one said with a laugh.

Eloise began to enjoy herself. Quinn's son and his girlfriend appeared and were as warm and friendly as he was. The wine was delicious and the cheese perfect, a large brie with a layer of truffles through the middle, laid out with loaves of fresh baguette, the wine changed to complement the cheese, and there were tiny tangerines and chocolates to finish.

She was filled with the warmth of being among convivial people, everyone shared the love of the mountains, and even those who no longer skied still went up to walk or did cross-country skiing. They told her of the summer when the mountains were green and scattered with wild flowers. She had never been here then, and when she was asked if she was staying indefinitely at Jacaranda, she wished that she were. She felt she belonged here, instead of going home to a new house – the week after next – was it really as soon as that? A house which would seem lonely without the twins giving it life.

It was painful to accept that her days out here were numbered, though she didn't say that to anyone who asked. She didn't want to provoke talk and perhaps questions to Lawrence.

Lawrence and Pascal were among the group she was talking to, discussing the summer sports here, when she became aware that people had become distracted and were turning towards the door. And there was Aurelia in her polar bear outfit, her eyes skimming the room to see who was here.

The joy ran out of Eloise like sand in a timer and she searched frantically for Harvey among the chattering crowd, but she couldn't see him.

Lawrence, watching her, said quietly, 'Are you afraid she's brought your ex?'

'Yes, but I can't stop him from being here.' She tried to smile as if it were no consequence that her ex-husband was gallivanting about the place where she felt happy, with at least one other woman, forgetting the life and love they had once shared together.

Lawrence moved a step closer to her. 'She's come alone. She always makes a late entrance and if she brings someone she leads them in like a trophy.' Lawrence smiled and touched her arm, 'Forget her, Eloise, and just enjoy yourself.'

But before she could answer, Aurelia spotted them and came towards them like a ship in full sail. 'Lawrence,' she breathed, kissing him on his cheek, her hand on his shoulder as if she was claiming possession of him. 'Just who I wanted to see, I've so much to tell you.' Ignoring Eloise and Pascal, she slipped her arm through Lawrence's and made to lead him away.

But Lawrence stood his ground. 'Good to see you, Aurelia, we were just talking about the summer season here, what do you think of it?'

She looked round at the rest of the group haughtily. 'You're missing a trick there, Lawrence. If you took some of my ideas on board for Jacaranda, it would be thriving summer and winter. You could make money, real money, and save Jacaranda from ruin.'

'I have plenty of ideas of my own, thank you, Aurelia,' he said, walking away.

29

Eloise and Theo met up with Gaby and Jerry at the Cabane du Mont Fort for lunch, an Alpine hut made of grey stone perched high on the mountain. It was too cold at this time of year to sit on the terrace so they stayed cosy inside, eating raclette and drinking wine.

Eloise was thrilled to be able to take time off to ski, it was cold but sunny and the conditions were good. She was also pleased to see Gaby, feeling as responsible for her as she would for her own children, and to check she was all right.

They'd chosen to meet here because Ken and Travis – if they did ski today – would not come this far, preferring to stay on the lower, more accessible slopes. They were not concerned about Pippa and Radley finding them if they should stop off here as they could trust them not to sneak on their whereabouts.

'I don't know exactly what they are planning to do about our adventure on Christmas Day, but I think they might try and make trouble,' Theo said, his young face taut with despair.

Eloise was afraid that Debra and Ken might make much of Jerry being led into possible danger, having never been to Verbier before and therefore reliant on Theo to keep him safe. If they did take some sort of action, Eloise would stand up for him. Theo had warned them to wait awhile after the snowboarders had gone down, but Jerry had not listened and shot off. Any adverse action would generate bad publicity for Jacaranda and, whatever the outcome, any legal dealings would cost Lawrence a fortune.

This morning Travis had asked to speak to Lawrence and the two of them had been closeted in his office for some time. Eloise, putting on her boots in the hall, had seen Ken prowling round the living room while Debra sat at the desk, mesmerized with her laptop. Lawrence, perhaps suspecting that Debra would make a thing of it, had told Theo and Eloise they could ski until after lunch and if Ken and Travis wanted to go out he could drop them down later at Medran. Eloise guessed he wanted them both out of the way while he heard what Debra and Ken planned to do. Neither she nor Theo had mentioned they were meeting up with Jerry and Gaby.

'They can't make a case if I don't agree to it,' Jerry said now. 'It is just one of the hazards of skiing. As far as I know, we didn't cross any barriers and other people were skiing there. We're alive, uninjured.' He lifted his arms as if to prove it.

Gaby, who was still subdued, stayed silent, but the glance she gave Eloise said it all. It wasn't going to be as easy as that. These people worked their guts out to make money and took advantage of every chance that came their way to make even more.

Vera had been the most strident in her condemnation of them. 'I know this sort,' she said, her mouth twisting as if it was tainted with something sour. 'They spend a lot of money to come here and they can't get the chalet they want, so if they sue they get the money back, have a holiday for free.'

'But if it hadn't happened they wouldn't have had anything to make trouble over,' Eloise argued and then said no more as Theo appeared, hungry as always, for a snack.

Eloise roused herself now as their meal came, raclette, warm and filling on such a cold day.

'But they don't know where you are,' Theo said to Jerry, 'and they might start something about the avalanche without talking to you first.'

'I'll contact them.' Jerry leant over and took one of Gaby's hands, smiling at her. 'Debra wanted to send Gaby back home, she doesn't approve of our relationship, thinks Gaby too young.' He smiled at her as if he obviously thought it a joke. 'So we escaped; we need a bit of time together, alone. But I will get in touch with them, tell them I'll have no part in trying to make something of it; they weren't there, they don't know what happened.'

Eloise felt a little comforted by this, but she could not help noticing how withdrawn Gaby was. Her hand lay like a trapped bird in Jerry's. Perhaps she had been severely traumatized by the avalanche, but would she not then have wanted to go home away from such dangers?

They finished their lunch; Gaby ate well, so perhaps she was just tired and hungry. Eloise and Theo had to get back to the chalet and she managed to snatch a brief moment with Gaby while the men were studying a map of the ski routes pinned on the wall.

'Are you all right, Gaby, you seem to be very quiet,' Eloise asked.

Gaby smiled weakly, 'I suppose I deserve it, but I feel I'm trapped with Jerry. After the avalanche and realizing that I couldn't carry on with him, I thought I'd back off, finish it, stop taking his money, but he won't listen. He says he loves me and it's only because I'm younger than him and involved with my studies that I don't feel ready to get too serious and settle down.' She bit her lip. 'He says he understands that. He wants to help me get my degree and he thinks I'll come to love him more as I mature. I'll always care for him but not as he wants. I know I should have gone home, only Mum and the boys are with Roger and I hate it there and don't want to be home on my own. Anyway,' she gave a little laugh, 'I do love skiing and I haven't been for ages.'

'Oh, Gaby.' Eloise squeezed her hand. She'd changed her mind about her opinion of Jerry. Her first impression was of him being a man overpowered by his aunt – Debra was what her father called a 'ball breaker', a woman who emasculated men – but he seemed different when he got away from her and could joke around with Theo. Perhaps he simply needed Gaby, wanted someone kind who depended on him. The avalanche had scared them all, thrust them into the cold, stark reality of life and death and perhaps made him more determined to hang on to Gaby, who he was obviously besotted with. But Gaby, being so much younger, understandably felt trapped and even guilty.

'He's twelve years older than me, and although I enjoy being with him, I don't want to be with him all the time, I want to hang out with my own friends.' She looked anguished. 'I don't know what to do.'

Theo and Jerry were now returning to the table.

'Perhaps suggest a few weeks' break from each other,' Eloise said quickly, 'time apart sometimes puts things in perspective.' There was no chance to say any more but she hugged Gaby tightly, urging her to keep in touch. She worried how it all might turn out, but underneath it all she felt that Gaby was strong enough to make the right decisions in the end.

Time was marching on, so Theo and Eloise skied quickly down, not stopping to chat. Not until they were both in the jeep on their way back to Jacaranda did Theo say, 'What will happen to Dad and Jacaranda if they do make a fuss? What if Debra makes Radley write something in one of his magazines that puts people off coming to us?'

'Let's wait and see if it happens,' Eloise said, a knot tying itself tight inside her as she considered the possibility. But whatever happened, it was out of her control; she was going home herself very soon, when the next chef Lawrence had booked arrived to take over. The thought tightened the knot. She didn't want to leave, she wanted to stay here. Despite the real concern of avalanches, a lurking ex-husband and a scheming woman, she had felt happy and safe.

Only Vera was at the chalet when they got back.

'They want to make trouble,' she greeted them darkly. 'I didn't hear much, but that woman said she was very dissatisfied' – Vera shrugged – 'though they still want to stay here... too lazy to move on, I suppose. If I had my way they'd be out in the snow with all their bags.'

'What sort of trouble?' Theo looked anguished.

'Bad I would think, knowing them, but Lawrence says can you make dinner as usual.'

'Of course,' Eloise said, she'd half prepared it already, and was glad that she had as the last thing she was focused on now was cooking.

'If I were you,' Vera said, 'I'd make a very strong curry so they cannot leave the bathroom, keep them quiet.'

Eloise felt that even the hottest curry would not keep Debra quiet.

30

Despite having had a good lunch, Theo set himself the task of eating up all the leftovers while Eloise prepared dinner. She cut oranges in half and carefully took out the flesh, planning to fill the empty shells with orange, shrimps and avocado and a sauce for the starter. The breasts of duck were marinating, and the puddings – brown sugar meringue vacherins filled with cream and the sweet chestnut puree that Aurelia had been so rude about – were already made.

Theo begged her to make some more shortbread. 'I'll miss it when you've gone home, please leave lots for us.'

Gone home. It hurt to think of it.

'I'll tell you how to make it yourself,' she said, 'I haven't time to make any now.'

'I'll never make them as well as you do,' he moaned, but he listened to her instructions, writing them down while she busied herself with the dinner.

Lawrence returned sometime later from wherever he'd been and found them both in the kitchen, Vera was laying the table for dinner in the living room.

'Look, made them on my own,' Theo announced proudly, hovering round some rather misshapen biscuits cooling on a wire rack.

'They look good, but you've made quite a mess.' Lawrence

snitched one, managing to bypass a mixing bowl, an open jar of sugar, a couple of wooden spoons and a scattering of flour that lay all around them.

'I'm about to clear it up,' Theo said, before lowering his voice and saying; 'Is Debra and that lot back? Are they going to make trouble for us?'

Lawrence sighed, put his hand on his shoulder. 'I don't know what will happen, Theo. We must wait and see.' He turned to Eloise, 'Jerry rang and Debra is livid, having found out that you were both skiing with Gaby and Jerry today, she thought they'd gone back to the UK.'

'Why shouldn't they stay where they like, they are not children,' Eloise retorted.

Theo said, 'We met up this morning, they are staying at Nendaz. What's it to do with Debra anyway?'

Lawrence said gravely, 'She doesn't like Gaby, thinks she's after Jerry's money and is annoyed she is still around, and worse, Jerry is with her. It upsets her that you and,' he turned his attention to Theo, 'especially you, Theo, met up with them as if nothing has happened.'

'But nothing has happened,' Theo said vehemently. 'I don't know what Gaby and Jerry are up to, we just ski together.'

Eloise thought of Gaby's confession about how she wanted to escape the relationship. She would say nothing about it in front of Theo. It was Gaby's business.

Eloise turned to Lawrence. 'I didn't tell you about meeting up with them today as it would have put you on the spot if Debra asked if you'd heard from them.'

'Jerry told me,' Theo cut in, 'and made me promise not to tell the others. Said it was none of their business… which it isn't.'

There was the sound of the outside door opening and the draught of cold air swooping in with it. Lawrence put his finger on his lips. 'They went for a walk,' he said quietly before leaving the kitchen to join them.

Theo crept nearer the kitchen door to eavesdrop. Eloise, on the far side of the kitchen, got on with slicing the potatoes into matchstick chips though she itched to know what was being said. She could hear the soft hum of voices; the clump of boots being dropped and, watching Theo's expression, guessed they were giving Lawrence a hard time.

Vera came into the room, her face creased with fury. 'That woman,' she said, her eyes flashing, 'no surprise she is rich, she tries to make money wherever she can. She wants lawyers, to ask their advice. I'll give her advice and I won't charge her either.'

Theo looked near tears. 'If she brings in lawyers, Dad will have to talk to his and it will cost zillions, which we don't have, and Jacaranda needs so many repairs.'

Eloise put her arm round him in sympathy, though she couldn't think how to comfort him. Even if Debra and co didn't sue, just the mention of possible negligence could ruin Jacaranda's reputation and Theo's dream of being a ski guide.

It upset her watching Theo struggling to be brave while obviously terrified that Jacaranda would be lost, and she suspected he blamed himself in part for the avalanche. She thought of Kit and Lizzie being held responsible for something out of their control and how hard she would fight for justice for them. Even though she was leaving so soon and the outcome would not affect her, she could not let Debra ruin this wonderful boy and his home without a fight. She dumped the potatoes into a bowl of water, wiped her hands and strode off down the passage. She'd had enough, she wasn't going to sit back and do nothing any more.

The group of walkers had taken off their coats and boots and moved into the living room and Lawrence was about to shut the door when Eloise put her hand out and stopped him and to his surprise, followed him into the room. Debra, halfway to the sofa, turned and seeing it was Eloise ignored her and carried on, sitting down and picking up her iPad that lay on the table beside her. Ken and Travis were standing by the window.

Travis said to Eloise now, 'We would like some tea and any biscuits you have, those home-made ones are delicious, and the cake if there is any left.' He gave her a tight smile, glancing round at the others to see if they agreed. Debra nodded, waiting expectantly for Eloise to go and fetch them, looking forward to a hot cup of tea after their brief walk in the cold.

Debra's attitude to her added to Eloise's anger, she may only be the cook but she would fight for what was right.

Lawrence watched Eloise with a slight frown, wary of her, suspecting that she was not here to offer tea and biscuits. 'Is that all right, Eloise?' he said quietly. 'Vera can bring it if you're busy.'

Eloise struggled with her feelings. She must remain calm and not become hysterical, though she felt hysterical, distraught at the prospect that Debra could destroy Jacaranda if she let fly her misinformed opinions about her nephew being led straight into the path of an avalanche through negligence.

Though Jacaranda is not yours, she reminded herself firmly. Jacaranda may be full of happy memories for her, but it was not hers, she was here as a cook and when her time was over, that was it.

'I will fetch some tea in a minute,' she said, her stomach cramping, 'but I want to say something about the avalanche. I was there, and none of you were. For all I know you might never have seen one before, I certainly hadn't. And perhaps you don't know much about the conditions in the mountains…'

'Of course we do,' Debra said archly, 'and we don't need you interfering, please fetch us some tea.' Her look was one she might give to some poor unfortunate illegal immigrant who had no business to be trespassing in such a chalet, such a life. Lawrence moved towards Eloise, his mouth open to speak, his arm outstretched as if to corral her, lead her away, but Eloise took a step away from him, Debra's words spurred her on, she turned to face Ken and Travis who were staring at her, Ken with shocked admiration.

'I know you've already asked Jerry about what happened, but I want to make sure you know all the facts, including what I witnessed. No lawyer of any sense is going to act on just one version of the event, especially from someone who wasn't there,' Eloise said firmly.

Lawrence started to speak, but Ken broke in, 'She has a point there, Debra.'

Debra dismissed him with a toss of her head. 'They were taken into danger. That my nephew was not killed or severely injured was just good luck. All night it snowed heavily, they should not have been there at all.'

Eloise snapped back, 'The people in charge here, the sécurité des pistes, obviously have good knowledge of snow conditions, their reputation relies on it, if there had been any great danger they would have stopped the lifts or closed the run and they did not. It was a fluke accident and, though very scary, not a great avalanche, in fact the locals would probably describe it as a snowfall.'

Lawrence said, 'That is the truth of it, Debra, and we haven't heard Gaby's side of the story yet, I'll get my lawyer on to it if you wish, but I think we'll find it a waste of time and money. If any of the people involved want to take action that is up to them.' He finished, 'Now Eloise, perhaps you could arrange some tea.' He smiled at her but she could see the warning in his eyes: you've done your bit now back off.

Ken said, 'We must get hold of Jerry and Gaby, hear all sides of the story.'

Debra, realizing that her word on the matter would not be enough, turned to Eloise and said coldly, 'As you seem to know where they are, you can tell my nephew to come here ASAP. He can leave that girl behind, she wasn't even caught in the avalanche, so we have no need of her side of the story. She is no good for him, a leach after his money. I've paid for her ticket home. Tell her she must leave as soon as possible.'

'My dear, that's a little harsh,' Ken bleated. 'I mean, Jerry...'

Debra ignored him, glaring at Eloise. 'I expect him here within the hour.'

Catching Lawrence's eye, Eloise bit back her retort that surely it was up to Gaby, and indeed Jerry, when Gaby went home. 'Theo is in touch with him, I'll pass on your message.' She turned to leave the room, but not before she saw Debra's furious expression at not getting her own way, but there was also a look of determination there.

'And one thing more,' Debra's voice stalled her escape. 'Take off that ridiculous apron, it's hardly professional to appear with such a vulgar slogan written across it.'

In her haste to fight for Jacaranda, Eloise had forgotten

to take it off. She caught the gleam of laughter in Lawrence's eyes. It did not comfort her; Debra held Jacaranda's fate in her hands. She was very much afraid she'd made it worse, a mere cook daring to question Debra's judgement.

31

He couldn't sleep. Lawrence pulled on a thick jersey and went onto the balcony outside his bedroom. It was freezing, the air like icy smoke gripping his face. The sky was black, deep as velvet, and dotted with stars, brilliant against the darkness. Beneath him splashes of light coming from some of the chalets hit the snow. All was still, like time suspended. High above the village as they were, any sounds from the clubs and bars rarely reached them.

He had sat here in all the seasons feeling comforted yet awed by the beauty and majesty of the world around him and the realization that whatever his problems they were puny compared to this universe. But what if he couldn't sit here any more, immerse himself in the power of the landscape? If he lost Jacaranda, he would never come back, he couldn't bear to see what others would do with the chalet, how they would change it, ruin its atmosphere. If he lost it, he would never set foot in Verbier again.

It was Eloise that had kept him from his sleep. He was tired, exhausted, and it was well past midnight, but he couldn't settle, his mind was full of her. The way she'd stood up to Debra at teatime, tried to explain that the avalanche was an act of nature out of their control, though Debra had not seen it like that. He couldn't help but admire Eloise.

He'd seen her as a chef, his father's goddaughter whom he'd thrust on him to fill the vital service of providing meals to his guests. But if he were honest, he felt she was more than that, he felt drawn to her; but she was going home in a matter of days, and she'd surely be relieved to get away from here and go back to her friends and her life.

He'd had reservations at taking her on as a chef – cook, as she preferred to label herself – her being Desmond's goddaughter, and the added difficulty of getting rid of her should she have been a disaster. But having been let down so badly by Denise and then those other girls, and it being so close to Christmas, there hadn't been any other options, except for Aurelia's expensive takeaways. To his relief, and surprise, he had to admit after she'd told him straight out that his father had exaggerated her cooking skills and she'd only cooked for her family and friends, Eloise had done well. There'd been no complaints. Her food – especially the puddings – was good, not top restaurant quality like the qualified chefs produced, but then as she said, the guests could go to a top restaurant for that. She just cooked good food with good ingredients and a bit of flair and the guests had been more than content with that. Even these difficult guests – though to be truthful only Debra was difficult – voiced complaints about various things, many he had no control over like the weather, and the service in one or two bars or restaurants, but no one had criticized Eloise's cooking. He'd heard Debra say there was too much sugar in the puddings and yet he'd noticed that she ate them quite happily.

Ken and Travis were easier to please and Radley seemed emasculated by his mother, though he'd noticed that he and Pippa kept out of her way as much as possible. He suspected that Debra had decreed that they would spend a family Christmas together and so they had all been forced to come along, though she had no love for Pippa, and even less for Gaby, perhaps because of the murky past Vera had referred to, though she didn't seem like that to him. He suspected that Debra despised women who didn't have a career, who sat back feeding off rich men, though he'd since discovered that Pippa was a qualified teacher and Gaby was studying law, but perhaps Debra was jealous of their youth or annoyed they had the full attention of her son and nephew. He wished he could have got rid of them at once, but despite their concerns they did not want to leave, probably because all the best places here were full to bursting. It would be a relief to see the back of them, or anyway Debra.

But Eloise. The way she stood there in the living room calmly telling it how it was. She knew the mountains and the dangers that lurked there and she had put Debra firmly in her place. Travis and Ken had also been impressed and had tried to convince Debra to let the matter drop, but she, perhaps unused to having her views ignored, or more likely annoyed by a mere cook telling her how it was, insisted she was taking her lawyer's advice on how best to deal with the situation. She had told Travis to track down Jerry at once as Eloise could not be relied upon to pass on her message that she must see him and hear his side of the story.

He had not imagined that Eloise held such fire, but then she'd come here to Jacaranda over the years, and Desmond was her godfather and no doubt she was fighting to save it for him. She was a kind, thoughtful woman, but he knew she was vulnerable too. He'd been affected by Eloise's obvious pain when Aurelia had brought Harvey round. It was the main reason why he had sent them packing. What shocked him most was that Aurelia knew they'd only recently divorced. How could she be so insensitive as to bring him unannounced to the chalet, knowing that Eloise was probably there preparing dinner?

He shivered; the cold crept into his bones, he'd freeze to death if he stayed out here much longer. He let his gaze linger a moment longer on the view he knew and loved so well. How much longer would it be his if Debra pushed ahead with her threat to take legal action over the avalanche? Despairing, he went back inside and got into bed still wearing his jersey and tried to sleep.

He woke late the next morning, showered and dressed quickly. He was halfway down the stairs when he heard the raised voices in the kitchen.

'I demand to know where Jerry and Gaby are staying, you have no right to keep the whereabouts of my nephew from me, I expected him here yesterday, I told you to tell him to come.' Debra was obviously on the warpath and he hurried on down, hearing the quieter tones of Ken's voice telling her to calm down. 'Go away, Ken, I can deal with this,' Debra said.

Lawrence nearly collided with Ken as he hurried to the kitchen.

Ken took his arm. 'She gets like this when she wants something, I've hardly slept a wink, she's been tossing and turning all night, determined to find out where Jerry is,' he mumbled, not looking at him. He seemed shrunk and at the end of his tether. Lawrence felt a mixture of sympathy and impatience for him for being so weak. Debra was a formidable woman, but surely he could stand up to her sometimes?

'I don't know where they are staying and I doubt Eloise

does either,' he said, wanting to save her from Debra's anger.

Ken wouldn't let him go. 'She's got it into her head that Eloise set the whole thing up, found them somewhere to stay in the village so she and Gaby could meet up. Gaby is a friend of Eloise's children and Debra...' He stopped, gave a frantic laugh, 'Well I'm sure it's not true, but Debra feels that Eloise is encouraging her not to go home and to hang on to Jerry.'

'I'm sure it's not quite like that but I'll find out.' Lawrence managed to shake him off at last and get to the kitchen, with Ken following closely behind.

'I did ski with them, but I've no idea where they are staying,' Eloise said. 'We met up at the Cabane du Mont Fort yesterday for lunch and a ski, then Theo and I came back here, leaving them there.' Eloise was crashing about with a frying pan, trying to fry some eggs for Ken and Travis's breakfast and Debra was standing close to the oven in grave danger of being hit by an egg or the pan.

'Please tell me what's going on,' Lawrence said firmly. 'Debra, you first.' He pretended he hadn't seen Eloise's furious look at him, defying him to make her take the blame for this client's madness.

Debra rounded on him, crossing her arms over her powerful bosom. 'I think Eloise should have had the courtesy to inform me where my nephew is staying. It was extremely bad manners for them to up and leave without telling me, I didn't invite him here to behave like that, though no doubt he was egged on by that girl, and she's probably stolen his mobile so I can't get hold of him.'

Lawrence fought to curb his temper. 'I understand you told Gaby to return home at once, perhaps they wanted to be together.' Lawrence braced himself for further onslaught.

'She's after his money. We all work very hard and deserve

what we earn and why should we hand it out to people who are too lazy to get a job?' Debra blazed at him as if he were accusing them of some crime.

'Gaby is studying law, she can't earn much just now, but she will, she's determined to fend for herself and have a good career,' Eloise said, breaking the eggs into the hot butter with a vengeance, leaning back to escape the fat as it spat at her.

Debra opened her mouth to speak but Lawrence got in first, 'Do you know where they are staying, Eloise?'

'No, they were in Nendaz but they didn't say where. They could have moved on. I haven't asked them, they just wanted to meet up with us.' She turned to Debra. 'I'm sure if Jerry wants you to know where he is, he'll tell you.'

'Well, *you* have Gaby's mobile number,' Debra retorted. 'So please give it to me, maybe she'll answer me as Jerry won't.'

Ken hovered about like a frightened rabbit, throwing out the occasional plea to his wife to stay calm, which she ignored.

Eloise splashed boiling butter on to the yolks of the eggs to cook them through, then she deftly tipped them into a serving dish. 'I'll have to ask Gaby,' she said, intent on her task, 'but she'll probably still be in bed, so I better wait awhile.'

She bustled round the kitchen, loading up the breakfast, and Vera, who looked as if she would burst with keeping her thoughts to herself, took the laden tray along to the living room, Eloise following with the coffee. Travis appeared, offering to help, and Lawrence was left alone with a fuming Debra and a silent Ken in the kitchen.

'I think your cook is extremely rude trying to keep me away from my nephew,' she snapped at him. 'I have every right to protect him from scheming young women.'

As she paused to take a breath, Lawrence said. 'That's up to you, but I'm sure Jerry, who is quite a bit older than Gaby, can look after himself. Now, breakfast is ready, why don't you have some before it gets cold?' He tried to steer her towards the door as if she were some mouth-foaming monster. To his relief, Ken finally asserted himself, and taking her arm and telling her he'd send a message to Jerry after breakfast and insist they meet him for lunch, he got her away from the kitchen.

When she got back to the kitchen, Eloise asked Lawrence if he wanted breakfast in here or would he brave the living room with the others.

'This has surely been one of the most traumatic chalet parties we've had and perhaps only your cooking has kept everyone from leaving.' He smiled at her, feeling as if they were two of a kind, but in the cold light of day he reasoned that was only because they both were fighting for the same thing – the future of Jacaranda.

32

It was a relief to be out on the mountains and to escape from Debra. Lawrence – bless him – suggested that she go out for the much of the day to avoid her.

Eloise met up with Saskia and the two of them went up Savoleyres, skied down the other side among the trees and took the lift up again, deciding to stop at La Marmotte for a drink before their descent to Verbier. Saskia, bursting for the loo, threw off her skis and ran inside, her hastily stacked skis clattering down in the snow, taking another pair with them.

Eloise picked them all up and put both their own pairs together a little further away so they could find them easily when they came out again. Turning, she almost bumped into Harvey. For a second, both froze – if she hadn't taken her skis off she'd have pointed them downhill and raced away from him, but there was nowhere to run now.

'Oh... Harvey, you're still here.' She stared at him in dismay.

'Y... yes, I leave tomorrow.' He glanced away and she wondered if he'd just arrived here or was leaving.

She moved away from him, 'Bon voyage, then.'

He put his hand on her arm to detain her, 'Eloise, wait a second. I didn't know you were out here. Why are you cooking at Jacaranda? I mean, I know you can cook but...'

'But I'm not good enough to cook for these super rich clients,' she finished for him. The pain at being so close to him bit deep, but anger too, anger at his leaving them and anger at him suggesting she wasn't good enough for this place.

'I would have thought you are. If they want designer food they can go to a restaurant. No, I mean why are you here at all?' He let go of her arm. She moved further away from him, desperate to get away.

'Desmond rang me to say Lawrence needed a chef. He didn't understand that the Cordon Bleu course I did hardly qualified me. But I'm glad to be here, where I was once happy.' She looked him in the eye.

He flinched, before smiling in that way she knew so well, the smile that covered deceit. She scrutinized him, taking in each part of him, the man she had so loved, the father of her beloved children, and now she saw the weakness in him. His feeble arrogance at feeling he could seduce whomever he liked, that the women in his life should be grateful for his attentions. Eloise had shut her eyes to his selfish behaviour, wanting a stable upbringing for their children. She felt sorrow at what had been lost but also a determination to not let him ruin her future.

She looked around her, the vast mountain, the blue sky and the line of trees scattered below them. She felt as if she had thrown off a heavy garment, her body now light and free.

'Keep away from Jacaranda and Aurelia,' she said, adamant that Harvey would not spoil the place that meant so much to her, take that from her too. 'She'll ruin it if she gets her hands on it, cram more buildings into the garden, spoil the atmosphere of the whole place.'

Her voice was sharp, he frowned, 'I... I don't know what you mean, Eloise?'

'Just don't get involved in any plans Aurelia has concerning the chalet. When she found out about your work I suppose she hoped you could persuade Lawrence to make changes to Jacaranda to incorporate her business.'

'She did mention something about it. She said they were only at the planning stage,' he added quickly, seeing the consternation in her expression as he confirmed her fears.

'What plans, what are you plotting Harvey?' Eloise was surprised to hear a woman's voice behind her.

She turned round and was face to face with a woman dressed in shocking pink. She was young, her face troubled, she half smiled at Eloise as if wondering if she ought to know her, ought, perhaps, to be jealous of her.

'Nothing, Petal,' Harvey said in his warmest voice.

Petal? Was that her real name or a nickname he called her?

'I'm just going inside. I'm Eloise, Harvey's ex-wife, mother of his children.' She saw the shock in Petal's eyes, the nervous way she glanced between them. 'Goodbye, Harvey,' Eloise said, 'remember what I said, Jacaranda is nothing to do with you at all, leave it be.' She turned away from him and Petal and headed towards the restaurant. Although Harvey had confirmed her fears about Aurelia trying to muscle in on Jacaranda, she felt lighter, happier than she had for years. Poor Harvey, she felt sorry for him now, caught up in his endless circle of seduction to prove whatever it was to himself, to the world.

It was warm and cosy inside the old wooden hut, the open fire welcoming after the chill of the mountain. She saw Saskia by the window, who waved when she saw her.

'Hurry up, what happened to you? I've had to guard your place like a bulldog. I've ordered mulled wine, hope that's what you want.'

'Yes, thanks.' She sat down, taking off her hat and gloves, putting them on the table in front of her. 'I... well, I bumped into Harvey,' she said.

'Harvey? I didn't see him, but then there are lots of people here.' Saskia paused to take their wine. 'Did you talk to him?'

'He's gone with a girl called Petal.'

'Petal? What sort of name is that?' Saskia giggled.

Eloise giggled too and told her what had happened. 'And now I suddenly feel free of him. The poor girl doesn't seem much older than Lizzie.'

'I thought he was after Aurelia. You said you'd seen them together.'

'Apparently, she told him of her plans to use Jacaranda for her "Tempting Delights", no doubt hoping he could help turn Jacaranda into a hideous complex for her business,' Eloise said, breathing in the spicy aroma of the mulled wine. 'I told him to keep away, he goes home tomorrow anyway.'

'That's a relief for you.' Saskia watched her carefully.

'It is. I feel I've said my goodbyes to him and can turn the page and move on.' She smiled.

'I'm so glad.' Saskia squeezed her hand. 'And it's good to see that the avalanche didn't spook you, hasn't put you off skiing,' Saskia said. 'I had a bad accident once and it took me a while to get back to the heavy skiing.'

'I felt a bit scared at first, but Gaby and Jerry wanted to meet up and they didn't want to ski anywhere near where Debra might see them so we had to ski up at the top, so I thought if they could put it behind them then so could I.' Eloise remembered the shaft of fear as she got back on the snow that first time out after the avalanche, but they'd had to ski down straight after it and that had helped her nerves. It was like the proverbial horse, get straight back on after a fall before you lose your nerve, and how terrible it would have been to have spent her last days here cooped up inside.

'You're right, and we've had a great time today.' Saskia grinned at her. 'I do like having you here, can't you stay longer, for the season even? Get a job cooking somewhere else if Lawrence has really got another chef coming out.'

Saskia's words twisted painfully through her. She knew the deal, cook at Jacaranda over Christmas and then go home. The next chef – a *proper* one – was already lined up and Eloise couldn't afford to stay out here if she had to pay for herself and find somewhere else to stay. She stared out at the snow-filled scene. Verbier and the mountains had taken her back to a comfortable place in her life, they had given her the strength to move on from Harvey, get on with her new life with optimism.

'I don't think it would be possible to stay on here.' Lawrence might let her stay at Jacaranda if there was a spare room but it wouldn't be the same and the last thing he or Jacaranda needed was a lame duck hanging around.

'Lawrence ought to keep you on as a chef, or do you have a job to go back to at home?'

'I'm a picture restorer but I took some time off. It's quite relaxed and I'd finished the project I was working on. I could take more time off, stay here, but not if I can't stay at Jacaranda and I can't do that because the new chef will need my room,' Eloise explained.

'You could stay with us, Quinn wouldn't mind,' Saskia said.

'That's kind, but you know what they say, guests and

fish go off in three days,' she laughed. 'Anyway Jacaranda's bound to change for the worse if Aurelia gets her way and I'd rather not be here for that.'

'You could help fight for it,' Saskia said. 'Apparently Aurelia's been going round saying Lawrence ought to build another chalet for him and Theo to live in, or more likely her and Lawrence with Theo dumped somewhere else, so they can let out Jacaranda.'

There was a heavy feeling in Eloise's stomach. 'Where does Aurelia live now?'

'In a miniscule apartment near Les Esserts, she spends her money on "Tempting Delights", but now she wants a bigger place, a place where she can entertain and Jacaranda would be perfect. Good for her business, I'd say,' Saskia said. 'And I suppose, whatever you think of it, it could help Lawrence financially too.'

'I don't think Lawrence wants to do that,' Eloise said hopefully, though why wouldn't he if it meant he could keep Jacaranda, especially if he needed money to pay for lawyers if Debra got difficult.

'I don't suppose he does but nor does he want to lose the chalet, though I think he makes a reasonable living from it as it is. Aurelia wants to attract a completely different kind of client with oodles and oodles of money but who are only here because they think it's the fashionable thing to do and often they have no love or understanding about the mountains and the resort. Aurelia also wants,' Saskia paused regarding her intently, 'to get her mitts on Lawrence.'

Eloise had suspected this but it hit hard. She wanted Lawrence to be happy, to have a woman in his life who loved him, but Aurelia was not the right person – it was not Lawrence or Theo she cared about, Aurelia wanted

Jacaranda. She may even get rid of Bert; Eloise had never seen her speak to him or pet him.

Saskia was watching her carefully, an annoying smile on her lips. 'Think about it, Eloise,' she said. 'Lawrence needs to work in a loving partnership for his own good as well as Jacaranda's. Who do you think is best to do that?'

'Certainly not Aurelia,' Eloise burst out.

'So stay here and fight,' Saskia said, finishing her mulled wine and saying they better be off before it got dark.

Following her to the door, Eloise thought over her words. She was about to question her further when Saskia was greeted by a couple of friends who were also leaving to ski down and they suggested they all go down together. Did Saskia mean that she must stay here and fight for Lawrence and Jacaranda? It was madness and impossible and yet was she going to just go home and leave them both to be ruined?

33

When Eloise got back to the chalet after her day's skiing with Saskia she was surprised to find Gaby racing round the garden with Bert, with the exuberance of youth. She seemed to have thrown off her feelings of despondency and was actually back here at the chalet.

'There you are at last. I didn't want to miss you,' Gaby said as Eloise got out of the jeep. Gaby ran over to her with the eagerness of a child and hugged her. Her face was flushed and shining from her scrap with Bert and Bert barked encouragingly, his tail wagging, limbs alert, poised for her to continue with their game.

'It's good to see you but why are you here? I thought' – Eloise threw a furtive glance towards the chalet, bracing herself for one of the party to appear to banish Gaby like in Victorian times, throwing fallen women to their fate – 'you were lying low.'

'We were but Debra insisted that Jerry come here and see her and he begged me to come with him, though I stayed out here with Bert in case she thrusts my return ticket at me and orders me home.' She frowned. 'It's all getting a bit hairy.'

'Does she know you're here?' Surely Bert's excited barking would alert everyone to her presence. 'What's happening with you and Jerry?'

'Debra hasn't seen me yet, but I expect Jerry will tell her I'm here.' She linked her arm through Eloise's. 'I tried to explain to Jerry that I don't want to be tied down yet and it would be best to break up, but he won't hear of it. I'm worried...' she sighed, 'that having already paid so much towards my tuition he thinks he owns me and I owe it to him to marry him and have his children.'

She had a point, Eloise thought. Being used to buying what he wanted, there was a possibility – even if he didn't realize it – that he *was* buying Gaby.

'It's usually kinder to leave a relationship that's going nowhere sooner rather than later,' Eloise said, knowing she had not obeyed this piece of advice herself, hanging on, turning a blind eye to Harvey's cheating for so long – too long – though it was a bit different, as she had been fighting to keep the family together.

'I know and I despise myself for staying on,' Gaby said. 'I should have gone straight home on Debra's ticket and broken it off there and then.'

'Maybe, but you can't just disappear, I don't know how Jerry would take it,' Eloise said, fetching her skis from the jeep and lugging them over to put away in the ski shed. She was cold and she had to get back to her cooking. Perhaps Gaby could come inside, lurk in the kitchen, though it would be impossible to continue their conversation in case they were overheard.

'I've tried to talk to him but he won't listen,' Gaby went on. 'I've thought of a way out that might work. One of my teachers at school told me I might get a scholarship to the US, but I didn't want to leave Mum, be so far away, so I didn't follow it up, but now she's got Roger, perhaps I can. What do you think?' She stood before her, her young face creased with anxiety and yet there was a light in her eyes, a surge of excitement at taking on something new.

Eloise hugged her. 'You must do what you think is right, Gaby, but don't be afraid to leave home and go and study somewhere else. It will look good on your CV.' Eloise smiled at her. 'I'll get in touch with your mother. I'd love to catch up with her again, I'm sure she'll understand. Now is probably the only time in your life you are free to travel wherever you want.'

She thought of how much she missed Kit and Lizzie, the huge void in her life now they had gone. Hard though it was, she was glad they had not stayed behind to support her. She said this to Gaby, adding, 'What I remember of your mother is she'd be the last person to stop you taking these chances. Don't worry; we mothers can cope without you, though of course we miss you terribly. Do whatever you think is right,' she repeated firmly.

'Thanks Eloise, I will.' Gaby shone with enthusiasm. 'I did think of doing part of the course there but then I thought Mum… but no, you're right, she'll be fine and perhaps she and the boys could visit, there are sometimes cheap deals around.'

The door to the chalet opened and Jerry came out; he looked slightly awkward when he saw her. 'Oh, hello, Eloise, all well with you?' He held out his hand to Gaby who, bending over and patting Bert, didn't seem to notice.

'Good to see you, Jerry.' Eloise felt sorry for him. Relationships were so complicated, tying you in and letting you go, ebb and flow like the sea. And when it was over, you had to accept it and move on.

'Oh, Jerry.' Gaby straightened up. 'Did things get sorted?'

Jerry threw Eloise an embarrassed glance. 'I'm not sure,'

he said, 'but why did you stay out here in the cold? You could have come inside.' He sounded grumpy, as if she were an annoying child, leaving Eloise to wonder if he needed someone to boss around as he felt so insecure himself. Gaby was much younger than he was, but she was too strong to let him take her over or use her to bolster his own ego. Eloise, realizing that it would be better to leave them to sort it out themselves, told Jerry she needed to go inside to get the dinner started. Jerry gave her an awkward wave before scurrying to the car he'd rented, opening the door and getting in. Gaby hugged her.

'I know what I'm going to do,' she said, 'and thanks for giving me the courage to do it.'

'You did it yourself, but keep in touch when you leave here, I'd love to know how you get on, and when Kit and Lizzie are back it would be good to all meet up again.' She watched her get into the car with Jerry and silently wished her well.

She went into the hall and before she'd even taken her boots off, she heard raised voices. The door to the living room was very slightly ajar – it needed a firm pull for the tongue of the door handle to catch – and she heard Ken say, 'Let it go, Debra, no one was hurt and these things happen in the mountains.'

Debra's voice was louder, 'If Jerry had been killed or badly injured and couldn't work in the company any more what would you have done then?'

'But he wasn't, Debra, so let's leave it, just be thankful everyone came out unscathed.'

'But we don't know that, Ken.' Debra's voice was hard and insistent as if she were losing patience with him. 'He could suffer a severe mental breakdown. He seems very nervy and anxious since it happened and mental health problems can take a long time to be resolved. He's in charge of a vital part of our business after all and we can't take chances. I've left a message for Gordon Maynard to call me to see where we stand legally, and that is that.'

Eloise was stunned at Debra's ruthless decision – she assumed this Gordon person was their lawyer. She sat there, her boots half off, Debra's words ringing in her ears. Glancing up, she saw Lawrence standing in the dusk at the top of the stairs that led to his office. His face was tense and tortured, knowing that if Debra took them to court Jacaranda could be finished.

34

Eloise was still struggling with her boots when the door to the living room was jerked open and Ken came out. His head was down as if studying the floor and he didn't see her. She froze; in a moment he would spot her and he'd surely guess that she had heard their conversation. Would he also see Lawrence lurking and listening at the top of the stairs?

'Hi Ken, good day?' She hoped she sounded upbeat and ignorant of the damning conversation she had just overheard.

'Oh, Eloise, it's you.' He shuffled in embarrassment as if he'd caught her naked instead of just bootless. She kept smiling.

'Yes, just back from a good time skiing. Did you go out today?' She sneaked a look at the stairs and to her relief saw that Lawrence was now out of sight.

'No, we didn't have time. It gets dark quite quickly at this time of the year, but I would have liked to go. I hope to get the chance tomorrow, only a couple more days left of our holiday now. Do you know the weather forecast for tomorrow?'

He was standing close to her and she could see how tense he was, though he was doing his best not to show it. He was quite a flirty man, he'd tried it on with her a few times, but she suspected that had she encouraged him he'd have run a mile. She felt sorry for him, had a sudden image of Debra cracking a whip, forcing him to submit to her will. It did not make a pretty picture.

'I don't,' she said, 'but I'll find out for you if you like.' She pushed her boots into the shelf under her seat and got up. 'Must get ready to cook the dinner.'

'I enjoy your cooking,' he said suddenly, perhaps relieved to be able to talk of a safe subject. 'What is the menu tonight?'

She had to pass him to go up the stairs to her room. Unless he moved she'd have to brush past him, but it seemed as if his feet were glued to the spot.

'Poussins stuffed with herbs and wild rice,' she said, making much of hanging up her ski jacket, hoping he'd get the message and let her pass without having to touch him to get by.

'Sounds delicious.'

'I'm glad. I hope you've enjoyed it here,' she heard herself saying as she turned to face him. 'I love Jacaranda; I used to stay here when I was a child and a couple of times with my own children when they were little. It holds many happy memories.'

'I quite believe it.' He hovered a moment and she waited for him to ask her what Jacaranda had been like all those years ago, but he did not elaborate, just smiled awkwardly and moved away. 'I'll go and have my shower.' He made for the stairs.

She waited a moment for him to be out of the way before she went upstairs herself to change.

Lawrence appeared again. 'Eloise,' he whispered, 'come down a minute.'

She followed him into his office, he gestured to the chair

by the window and closed the door. She saw the tension in his face and the anxious way he clawed back the lock of hair that fell over his forehead. She had a ridiculous urge to stroke his tension away; she pushed her hands between her knees in case they inadvertently moved to do so.

'Things don't look good.' He sat down opposite her. 'Travis informed me a few minutes ago… that Debra wishes to take legal advice over whether there's a case against Theo for taking you all skiing in a dangerous place. Ken, as we both heard through the half-open door, disagrees with her… he has skied quite a lot, whilst she knows nothing of the mountains, but it seems to me that once she gets an idea into her head she holds on to it like a dog with a bone.'

'I know, but what about Travis, might he dissuade her, side with Ken?' Eloise asked, a cold, frightened feeling settling in her stomach.

Lawrence sighed. 'I don't think so. He's a rather weak man, as I'm afraid is Ken when it comes to standing up to Debra. She has instructed Travis to act on it and so he will if he wants to keep his job.' He gave a slight laugh, 'I'd also say Travis is rather in awe of her, even has a sort of love for her.'

'Do you really think that?' Eloise was intrigued. She'd hardly seen Travis and not thought much about him. He was one of those people who were like shadows, rather sad, longing to be part of the scene, but for whatever reason unable to join in and so stayed lurking in the background.

'I do, I suppose you've hardly seen them all together, but he reminds me of a faithful and rather needy dog, utterly devoted to her.'

'And you don't think Ken can make her see sense, or even Radley?' She must take more interest in these people, though it was difficult being stuck in the kitchen.

'Oh, Radley is completely under his mother's thumb and Ken doesn't seem to feel threatened by Travis's devotion to his wife. In fact I suspect he sometimes uses him to his advantage.' Lawrence shrugged. 'You know, like asking him to do research and the like so he can get on with his own thing without Debra's interference.'

'How complicated people are,' Eloise said. 'I suppose you see a lot of odd goings-on here.' It was on the tip of her tongue to tell him about Celia and Neil's bed-hopping before she decided she better not, they might be friends of his, and anyway it was not her business to make trouble, Debra was making a good job of doing that herself. 'But what about Jerry?' She went on. 'He was there, involved in the avalanche, could even have been responsible for it. He laughed at Theo's concerns, showing off, I suppose he was trying to be macho in front of Gaby, but if he refuses to take it further, then what can Debra do?'

Lawrence stayed silent, staring out of the window. Eloise wondered what Jerry had said to Debra when he'd been here a short while ago, or what she had said to him. Had she somehow persuaded him to make a claim?

Lawrence leant back in his chair. 'The person Jerry really cares about is Gaby, he's hopelessly in love with her, and although I wasn't in the room with him and Debra – who it's been blatantly obvious thoroughly disapproves of her – I heard her say he should cooperate for Gaby's sake. She even inferred that she'd been mistaken about Gaby being just a dumb blonde after his money and she might welcome her into the family as she was obviously bright and going places.'

'You mean bribe him?' Eloise was horrified.

'Yes... I suppose so.'

'She doesn't want to marry him. She only agreed to wear his ring and say they're engaged so as not to shock the family. I've just spoken to her; she's going to try and get a scholarship, do some of her course in the US to get away from him,' Eloise said, anxiety grabbing her. She'd encouraged Gaby to leave the country, get away from Jerry, but Jerry wanted Debra's blessing on their relationship and if she gave it, her price might be for him to take her side in getting legal advice about the avalanche. If Gaby escaped him by going to study in America would that make Jerry angry and hurt enough to side with his aunt especially if he found out that she, Eloise, encouraged Gaby to leave him?

'So Jerry doesn't know this?' Lawrence frowned.

'Not unless she's told him just now.' Eloise went on to explain about Gaby's studies, 'And now I feel I might have inadvertently signed Jacaranda's death warrant when Jerry finds out I encouraged Gaby,' she finished dramatically.

Lawrence's anxiety increased and Eloise feared her interference in Gaby's escape from Jerry could make him determined to side with Debra. He could even use it as a subtle blackmail to make Gaby stay with him if he dropped his aunt's wishes to take action. Eloise struggled to find something to say to relieve the tension and blurted out that she hoped she hadn't made things worse.

'It's too late now,' Lawrence said heavily. 'I don't know how Debra's mind works, or Jerry's for that matter, but if Gaby decides to leave him for whatever reason, he could easily scuttle back under Debra's wing.'

'Gaby will do whatever she thinks best for her. She is determined to get a good career and she won't take my advice if it doesn't help her,' Eloise said lamely, moving to get up and leave the room, the dinner had to be cooked and she couldn't bear it if Lawrence was angry with her for making things worse.

'Gaby's at a difficult time in her life, making choices of getting the right degree for her career,' Lawrence said, 'and it's a pity she's got involved with Jerry and is sort of beholden to him. Sugar Dads, we never had anything like that when I was at uni.' He was silent a moment, his eyes seeming to focus on something she couldn't see. He went on slowly, 'I got involved with someone when I was a student, Georgia, Theo's mother. He was the best mistake I've ever made, but at the time it was quite a drama.'

'I can imagine.' She'd wondered about the relationship of Theo's parents but had not liked to ask. It was obvious they were not together and Theo seemed quite relaxed about it, spending time with each of them. But there was enough going on at Jacaranda now to concern Lawrence without Eloise adding to it by questioning him about his love life at uni.

But Lawrence seemed to be happy to continue with his story. 'We were fortunate that both sets of parents – well not my mother, she didn't feature much in my life, but Desmond, Maddy and Georgia's parents – supported us. It was youthful sex and exuberance I suppose, though we are still very fond of each other, but it was not enough to marry. That would have been a disaster.' He laughed. 'But I think everything worked out in the end.'

'Certainly has, Theo is lovely, you couldn't ask for better,' she said with enthusiasm.

Lawrence's story made her feel closer to him, see him in a different light. Ever since she'd arrived she'd been wary of him, knowing her cooking skills were not up to the dizzy heights he expected and afraid of letting him down. Apart from Bert and the lamb incident, which she felt he had not quite forgiven her for, he had not complained about any of the meals she had produced, though she suspected he'd be relieved when the *proper* chef arrived in a week or so and she went home.

She got up. 'I must cook the dinner and not give Debra any more reasons to make trouble. I don't know what to do about Gaby and Jerry,' she said. 'I feel bad about encouraging Gaby to go to America, but I suppose either way Jerry might side with Debra. I'd hate to have any part in harming Jacaranda.' To her horror she felt near tears, she sniffed angrily.

Lawrence noticed. 'Oh Eloise,' he said, 'don't upset yourself, how could you know you were dealing with such a megalomaniac as Debra.' He got up and put his hand on her shoulder.

She'd no idea how it happened, she must have lost her balance and fallen against him. She laid her head on his chest, feeling his heart beating and the warmth of him. He put his arm round her, perhaps to steady her or to push her away, but the feel of it was so comforting, so exciting. He bent over her head and she thought that she felt his lips kiss the top if it, but of course it could not be that, she was just imagining things.

They heard a clatter coming down the stairs, reaching the door. Theo calling, 'Lawrence, you promised a game of snooker.'

Lawrence let her go, opened the door. 'Theo... I was just talking to Eloise about the avalanche, I must question you too and she must get the dinner.'

Theo frowned, his face now anxious as he, followed by Bert, came into Lawrence's office.

Eloise escaped, running up the stairs to change out of her ski clothes, her emotions in turmoil.

35

Whatever was he thinking holding Eloise close like that, even kissing the top of her head? He could still feel the silkiness of her hair on his lips and recall the soft, flowery scent of it and the pressure of her head against his chest. He was going mad; Debra and her insistence of contacting her lawyer was causing him to behave in the most irrational way.

It was hardly surprising that it was Travis who was detailed to inform him that Debra felt it was such a serious matter that she would be seeking the necessary legal assistance. He had given the news in a monotone like a bad actor and it was obvious that Debra had convinced herself that Theo had not taken proper precautions. He'd listened with sinking heart, knowing if Debra carried out her threat he must also consult his lawyer and that could cost a fortune.

'So will you be leaving Jacaranda early?' he'd asked, they only had two more days and he'd rather they went given the circumstances, but then they'd probably ask to be refunded for the last days.

Travis had seemed surprised, 'Well I... I don't know.' He looked embarrassed, as well he might, and scuttled away, muttering that he'd 'consult with Debra'.

'So Dad, our game, we've just time before supper,' Theo

said impatiently now, turning towards the snooker table that was in the room outside the office, fitting beside the wine cellar, a deep freeze and the washing machines. Bert had made off to check out the corners of the room and to see that his bed had not been disturbed while he'd been away.

'No... in a minute, I've got to talk to you first about the avalanche.' Lawrence pulled himself together and gestured for Theo to go into his office.

Theo said plaintively, 'Not that again? You promised a game and I'm going out later.'

'I will play but I must talk first, keep you up to speed. Come in and close the door.'

'Jerry said he'd stop Debra going to a lawyer, suing me, us whatever... so not to worry.' Theo flopped down on the chair. 'She wasn't there, so it's none of her business.'

It was hard to tarnish Theo's opinion of a person he'd enjoyed spending time with but it had to be done.

'I'm sorry Theo, but it hasn't worked out that way.'

'What way? What do you mean?' Theo looked anguished.

'Debra holds the reins for this family, she probably paid out for this holiday herself. I suspect she's a better businessperson than all of them put together. It doesn't help that she knows very little about the mountains, skiing or the weather conditions, but she can get someone to find all that out and, if it's possible, to bring a case of negligence.' Lawrence sighed, he'd fight it all the way, but it would take money, wipe out the sums he'd put aside to carry out crucial maintenance on Jacaranda, not to mention be catastrophic for Jacaranda's reputation and remaining on the exclusive agency's books.

'OK, I see that, the old cow,' Theo said bitterly, 'but Jerry knows how it was. Eloise and Gaby will back me up.' He sighed, 'I'm not going to go through it all again, Dad, I've told you enough times. Surely Jerry can persuade Debra not to take action, especially as it might go badly for him, as he rushed off when I told him to wait. Eloise and Gaby heard me do it.'

'I don't know the whys and wherefores but Travis told me Jerry's agreed to support his aunt's decision to consult her lawyer to see if there is a case,' Lawrence said heavily, feeling as if he was spearing his son with a knife.

'No, he can't have!' Theo protested, his face anguished. 'He promised he wouldn't. He said she was mad and it was just one of those things that can happen in the mountains. You must have misunderstood, Dad.' He slumped back in his chair, near tears.

Lawrence longed to hold him, assure him that everything would be all right, he would deal with it, but he couldn't. Theo was an adult, accused – wrongly, he was certain – but accused all the same of a serious offence, of leading them into danger.

Debra's determination to make trouble reminded him of those disreputable insurers who cold-called people about 'their accident' on the off-chance that they had had one and could be persuaded to make a claim for it, when it hadn't crossed their minds before.

'But why would Jerry change his mind?' Theo wailed. 'He was fine about it when we talked yesterday.'

'It's Debra,' Lawrence said heavily. 'She's the one who makes the decisions. She thinks Jerry was led into a place where there was a danger of avalanches.'

'What! But I didn't know, there were no warning signs, ask

the others, ask Eloise.' Theo's face was stricken. 'Dad, Debra's mad, she doesn't even ski, how can she know anything?'

'I know, Ken has tried to dissuade her, but she's determined. I don't understand how her mind works, but perhaps she takes every opportunity to make money, that's why she's so rich,' Lawrence said, his anger rising in him, thinking of the damage this could do for Theo's ambition to become a ski guide.

'Ask Jerry; he was the one caught in it; he'll tell the truth, he must, then the lawyers will see she hasn't got a case,' Theo said with feeling. 'He said it's like falling into the sea if you're sailing, it can happen, but you can't sue unless you were pushed by someone.' Theo thumped his hand on the desk. 'She can't Dad, you'll have to sue her back for spreading lies, I suppose she's telling everyone I'm a danger to ski with and then I won't be able to train to be a ski instructor.'

There was so much to lose. He knew Theo had not been negligent, Eloise had confirmed that he had taken proper precautions before they started down, though Jerry had not listened and charged off. She had told him that she'd seen the warning flags though she didn't know if Theo had noticed them or not, but he had seen they were only a three, and, Lawrence reminded himself, he and his very experienced friends were about to go there for the powder snow themselves before they heard about the avalanche, and would have taken the same risk. Also Theo had asked the advice of a ski guide – they must try and get his name, surely his word would count for something. Lawrence asked now if Theo knew the guide.

'It was hard to see his face as he had his hat pulled down. I'll go and look at the photos at the ski office but...' Theo said desperately, 'but he could have been a private guide from somewhere else.'

'Well, we'll try.' Lawrence hoped it wasn't a private guide. They often did not know the slopes so well. He'd have to call his lawyer if Debra did go ahead with her plan, but first he'd try and find out as much as he could about the circumstances so he could make a hole in Debra's story.

'I can't believe Jerry will go ahead with Debra's mad idea, though,' Theo said now.

'It seems Debra persuaded him to side with her,' Lawrence said quietly, wishing there was a way out of all this.

'But he wouldn't really do it, he finds her quite bossy and wants to break out on his own, he probably said he'd do it to keep her quiet and get away,' Theo said, getting up to let in Bert who was scratching at the door.

Lawrence said heavily, 'I'm afraid he has agreed to go with it, Theo. You know he's in love with Gaby and Debra disapproves of her, or she did. Now she says she admires her for studying law, working hard and wanting to make a success of her life, I don't know if she really does think that having got to know Gaby better or if she's trying to get Jerry on side to support her claim. Anyway, she said Gaby would make a perfect wife for him.'

'Wife? She doesn't want to be a wife yet,' Theo protested. 'You've got it wrong Dad, Jerry wouldn't go back on his word.'

Lawrence suffered for him; it was so hard being let down by someone you thought was a friend. He was not going to go into Jerry and Gaby's bizarre relationship. 'You must ask him yourself,' he said. 'Families are complicated things, as you know, and they are in business together as well, so it could be difficult for him to go against Debra.'

'So we lose Jacaranda because of her,' Theo cried out, 'and I lose my chance at becoming a ski guide.'

'Not necessarily,' Lawrence said, feeling helpless, 'but we've got to tread carefully, see if we can resolve it another way. I suggested to Travis that they leave the chalet early; I thought they'd want to, but he seemed very surprised. I would insist they go, but then they could make more trouble by complaining to the agency.' He sighed, these certainly were the most troublesome guests they'd ever had and he longed to be shot of them.

He'd tried to contact his own lawyer earlier and found he was away until after the New Year. No doubt Debra kept a string of lawyers on standby, like a change of clothes, and would have more than a head start on them.

His mobile rang and wearily he answered it, it was Paddy, the chef he was expecting in a couple of weeks.

'Hi, mate, sorry to drop this on you, but I've been offered a job I can't refuse, working in one of the top restaurants in the world, but don't worry,' he added as he heard Lawrence's intake of breath, 'I've got a friend who'll do it, she's a great chef and she's free until the summer. I'll email you her details.'

Lawrence sighed; everything seemed to be conspiring against him and Jacaranda at once. 'OK, thanks for telling me, I'll check out her details and let her know... congrats anyway on your rise to fame.' This was another annoyance, but at least Paddy had offered him someone else and knowing him she would be a good recommendation.

'Thanks, and sorry to let you down but when you know where I'm working you'll understand,' Paddy said and rang off.

Theo, seeing his face, said, 'What now?'

Lawrence tried to digest the news; he'd been relying on

Paddy, he was a good chef and easy to get on with and had agreed to work here until the summer, but top jobs in the restaurant business were like gold dust and he couldn't blame him for taking the opportunity when it came his way. He felt crushed by anxiety though. What a year this had been, losing chefs and now Debra making trouble. The only person who could save Jacaranda seemed to be Aurelia. She'd told him she had money to invest and she could take over the catering, and after all if they were in business together he wouldn't have to pay for her food, or rely on the vagaries of chefs. He knew her and she was a good businesswoman. He'd hoped to keep things as they were but with all that had happened perhaps his only option to keep Jacaranda in these perilous circumstances was to bite the bullet and team up with Aurelia.

'It was Paddy,' he said, his voice strained with tension. 'He's been offered a wonderful job and can't come, though he's sending me the CV of a friend who can.'

Theo brightened, 'Eloise can do it. She's quite the best chef we've had, her food is sort of… well, like Maddy's was really, she makes Jacaranda seem like a home instead of some posh hotel.' He jumped up, Bert sensing excitement danced around his legs.

'No, Theo, don't say a word to her, to anyone. I need to think things over, let me read this other chef's CV, talk to her, decide the best way to go.'

Theo's enthusiasm faded, 'OK, but I'd like Eloise to stay… if she can. Now you promised me a game of snooker and we've just time before supper.'

Lawrence followed him out to the snooker table Theo's words, 'she makes Jacaranda feel like a home,' vibrating in his head.

36

Eloise watched Lawrence covertly as she made his breakfast. He seemed bowed down with anxiety, his eyes dull from lack of sleep. She fought down an overwhelming desire to put her arms round him, hold him close. She must be mad. It was being in his arms that moment that had done it; she missed being close to someone with Harvey and the children gone. It was a good thing that she'd be leaving here soon.

It helped that Vera was there, scurrying about dealing with the plates and dishes from last night's supper and dashing into the living room to lay the table for breakfast. Each time she came back into the kitchen she eyed him sharply, her face a study of disapproval until at last she said, 'It is good these people are leaving the day after tomorrow, they bring bad vibes and make you ill.'

'Nonsense, Vera, there's just a lot going on.' Lawrence poured himself another cup of coffee, drinking it black. 'But at least we have a few days off before the next lot arrive and they've been to Jacaranda before and love it.'

'Good thing too.' Vera scuttled out again with a basket of croissants. They could hear someone coming down the stairs for breakfast. Eloise wondered which one of the party it was. She didn't think it was Theo, who came down as if he were in a race, full of life and vigour, though perhaps with Debra's lawsuit hanging over him he had lost his boundless energy.

Putting the last of the bacon in a silver serving dish she'd found at the back of the cupboard, Eloise took it through to the living room to put on the hot plate to keep warm. She remembered this dish from when she'd last been here when Desmond had more help in the chalet and the silver shone. She'd cleaned it herself, finding it a far easier way to keep the breakfast warm than leaving it in the oven and having to cook the eggs as and when they were needed. Lawrence had not complained, so she'd continued with it. It made Theo laugh and say it was like Downton Abbey.

Ken had just come down and he smirked at her as she entered the living room, 'Good morning, Eloise. I trust you slept well?' His voice implied she'd been up to something far more exciting than tumbling thankfully into bed alone and falling asleep. 'Let me take that from you,' he purred, edging closer.

'I'm fine, thanks, Ken,' she smiled, walking firmly towards the hot plate with the breakfast. He was in one of his frisky moods and she was relieved Vera was in the room. She supposed he had to try and boost his ego somehow after being all but emasculated by his wife, but why did men like him think making lascivious remarks to other women, or worse still, attempting to clutch parts of them, would in the slightest way make them more manly or attractive?

'What delicious dish have you cooked for us now?' He was right behind her, bending over, and she could feel the heat of his breath in her ear.

Debra's voice cut through the room like a scythe, 'Ken, pour me some coffee.'

Eloise felt him jump away and for once she was grateful for Debra's intervention.

His voice now subdued, he said, 'I was just asking Eloise what she's cooked for us this morning.'

Eloise made her escape. 'Good morning, Debra,' she said as she passed her.

'I'd like to go shopping this morning, if anyone is free to drive me down.' Debra eyed her imperiously. 'I can't do it this afternoon as I've other things to do,' she emphasized her words, accepting a cup of coffee from Ken with barely a nod.

'I'll tell Lawrence,' Eloise muttered before escaping. She'd no idea what he was doing today, or Theo for that matter, but she suspected neither of them would want to drive Debra, be imprisoned with her in the jeep. If not, that left her to do it; she did after all need to go into the village later to shop for the dinner.

'I'm sorry, Eloise,' Lawrence said when she informed him of Debra's command. 'I've told Theo he can go skiing this morning. Keep him out of Debra's way and I'm tied up with various things that have to be done. I hate to impose on you...' He smiled at her, making her feel warm inside. The lonely, empty feeling that Harvey's departure had left in her seemed to ease whenever she was near Lawrence. But she must not become one of those tiresome women who imagined every man fancied them and felt they had to possess one like a sort of fashion accessory. Lawrence surely had a girlfriend somewhere; it could even be Aurelia, though she didn't want to give that possibility any thought.

'I'll do it,' she said with a sigh. 'I'm surprised they are still here if they think we are determined to put them in danger.'

'I know, but I think it has something to do with enjoying having us at their mercy... and not being bothered to find somewhere else or change their flights. I don't know,' Lawrence sighed, 'I'm probably being overdramatic.'

'Perhaps Ken and Travis will go with her and stay down there for lunch.' She wondered if Debra's 'various things' included consulting her lawyer but decided not to spook Lawrence by mentioning it.

'I hope so, keep her out of the way,' Lawrence said. 'Are you going to see Gaby today?'

'I don't know, we haven't made any arrangements.'

'Well if you do, try and see if she's told Jerry about her plans to study in the US. I don't want you to try and make her change her mind, I think she is doing the right thing for herself, but it might be helpful to know if she's told him and how he's taken it.' He sighed, 'My lawyer is away until after the New Year, but I thought I'd talk it over with Quinn, he's got some good contacts out here.'

'Good idea,' Eloise said. 'I might meet up with Saskia later.' She'd send her a text to see if she were free; she could do with a chat.

*

Ken and Travis set out for the day's skiing, Lawrence driving them down to Medran. An hour later Debra appeared to ask Eloise to take her down to the village. Debra sat in the jeep beside her like a queen, looking straight ahead seemingly oblivious to the snowy mountains glittering like silver in the sun and the dark green trees under the blue sky. The silence between them built up like poisonous gas.

Eloise pulled up near the square, relieved the short journey was over. 'Is this all right for you, Debra? I've a few things to do, but do you want a lift back, or are you meeting the others or something?'

'I haven't made up my mind yet, though I'll probably go

back to the chalet. My lawyer is ringing me at three and I don't want to be stuck on the mountain unable to hear him properly,' she said, rifling in her bag for her mobile, checking it, then dropping it back in a side pocket so she could find it quickly if she needed to.

Eloise warned herself to say nothing, especially about lawyers, and ignored Debra's remark. Rather grudgingly she told her to text her when she'd finished shopping and she'd give her a lift back. It was the last thing she wanted to do, but for Lawrence's sake she did not want to antagonize her further. But despite her good intentions a strong feeling of righteousness rose up in her, she could not, would not, sit back and watch Jacaranda be snatched away.

'Please Debra, stop your misguided idea of consulting your lawyer over the avalanche,' she said firmly. 'You won't win. The piste was open; there was only a small danger, as there is almost every day in the mountains, as people who are used to them know well. But your action could destroy Lawrence's business and Theo's future.'

'My dear girl, don't you tell *me* what to do,' Debra blustered, turning to face her.

Eloise ignored a shaft of fear, wondering if she'd gone too far. 'I *am* telling you. Ken warned you against it, it will harm Jacaranda, Lawrence and Theo, but it will also harm you. You'll become a laughing stock among skiers and be put down as a troublemaker amongst the other resorts. When they get to hear of it, the agency could even bar you from taking their chalets – certainly the bigger, more luxurious ones here would not welcome you,' she said wildly, not knowing whether that was true or not. 'Verbier is one of the best, most popular resorts in Europe and if people in the business take a dislike to you, other resorts will follow.' She was aware that there was probably little truth in her threats, Debra could easily book somewhere else through another name and not many people turned away good money, but she wanted to make her think twice.

Debra slumped beside her like a balloon with an air leak. She stared out of the window at the busy scene outside, skiers in bright colours carrying skis or snowboards on their way to the slopes, mothers with babies in buggies, some little children struggling with tiny skis coming back from ski school.

'I have never forgotten my childhood,' Debra said at last, her remark taking Eloise by surprise. 'Even when I'm in my lovely apartment, able to buy what I want, I worry that one day I will lose it all, be back where I started. My father was a drunk; he drove my mother to an early death. We often didn't have a meal, or new clothes, everything came from charity shops, over-washed, faded garments worn by other people, even our shoes had been worn down by other children. My sister and I were determined to have a better life, make money, and we did.' She turned to Eloise, her mouth set in a hard line, her eyes piercing through her. 'I've earned every penny I have. Ken wanted children, a houseful of them, but I only had time for one, as did my sister with Jerry. Since she passed, I have promised that I would do everything to take care of Jerry, and he could have been killed or severely injured in that avalanche.'

'But he wasn't.' Eloise hoped she sounded firm, but to her surprise she felt sorry for Debra, admired her for working so hard to make a better life for herself. 'I love Jacaranda,' she went on, 'and there's more to it than it just being a place to make money. If it were sold it would probably be stripped of all its character and warmth, turned into a soulless series of rooms, drearily done up with ugly furniture. More chalets would be squashed into the garden and no doubt a cinema, gym, even a swimming pool put in.'

'But you must move with the times, Eloise, it would make more money with those facilities,' Debra said, though her voice had lost its belligerence.

'Maybe, but it would lose so much character. There is a good swimming pool and fitness centre down here, in the village, with other people having fun, being part of the place, so much better than being stuck up alone like a recluse, out of it all in some lifeless chalet. Jacaranda is a warm and happy place, do you not feel it?' Eloise turned to her, 'No amount of money and interior decorating can make that, turn it into a home, that is priceless.'

To her horror, Debra's eyes filled with tears, she let them run down her face a moment, leaving tiny rivulets on her cheeks, before opening her bag and taking out a handkerchief and wiping them away. What could she say, should she apologize for upsetting her, had she made things worse now for Lawrence and Jacaranda?

'That's not something I really know about,' Debra said, staring ahead. 'You're lucky, Eloise, if you've had a happy family life, it's like a shield around you, I didn't have that but I have money now – financial security, which I fight to keep. I can see it's a poor exchange for a happy, loving family, but it's a life I know, and one I understand.'

'I admire you for doing so well,' Eloise meant it but her sentiments didn't give Debra carte blanche to destroy Lawrence and Theo's life. She said firmly, 'The avalanche frightened us all, but mercifully none of us were badly hurt, Jerry was even laughing and joking about it. I doubt you'll win a case of negligence or whatever, but any action could ruin Lawrence and Theo's reputation. Jacaranda has been in his family over fifty years, it was built by his grandfather, it means more to him, his father and son, than just being a place to make money, it's a home, full of happy memories, some I share. Please, Debra, think again,' she said quietly.

Debra patted her eyes, glancing into a mirror she had in her bag, before opening the door of the jeep and getting out. 'Thank you for the lift, don't wait around for me, I'll make my own way back.' She slammed the door and Eloise watched her walk away, feeling like crying herself.

Had she dug too deep where she had no right to go?

37

Eloise finished her shopping and was just about to go back to the chalet when she saw Saskia waving to her.

'Have you time for lunch?' Saskia joined her. 'I thought I'd go down to Martigny to see the art exhibition this afternoon, do you want to come?'

'Good to see you, I was going to text you, see if you were free today,' Eloise said, pleased to see her after her battle with Debra. 'I'd love to come with you, but I better take the food back to the chalet to put in the fridge.'

'I'll come up to Jacaranda with you then we could go straight to Martigny and lunch at the gallery,' Saskia said, climbing into the jeep.

As they drove up the road to Jacaranda, Eloise told her about her conversation with Debra. 'I feel dreadful now I've inadvertently unleashed bad memories for her. I really hated her, hated her for trying to ruin Jacaranda, thought her a cold mother to her son and an absolute cow to her daughter-in-law, but now I understand why.' She went on to tell Saskia about Debra's confidences.

'Well how were you to know all that about her?' Saskia retorted. 'And whatever her background, she can't go round causing mayhem for everyone else. The avalanche must have been worrying for her, but no one was hurt, so she should just be thankful and stay away from the mountains if she doesn't want to risk such a thing again.'

'I shouldn't have interfered, but we were there, just the two of us in the jeep, and I couldn't stop myself. She's bound to use top lawyers, could have a whole stable of them waiting for her demands and who will dig away, determined to find some case,' she said desperately. 'And Lawrence could be ruined, may even have to sell Jacaranda, if she goes ahead with her claim.' Eloise turned anxiously to her. 'And Theo's chances of being a ski guide will be trashed. Goodness knows what other complaints she's got up her sleeve, at least I haven't poisoned anyone with my cooking yet.' She laughed grimly, remembering Bert's theft of the lamb.

'The lawyers won't find anything to go on. After all, Theo didn't take any unnecessary risks.' Saskia turned to her.

Eloise was still worried about those warning flags. She'd told Lawrence about them and he confirmed that he'd seen them too and even if they hadn't been rushing there to help with the avalanche, they'd have taken the risk. But a lawyer trying to make a case against Theo could savage such details like a dog with a rat.

'Did he?' Saskia asked, seeing the hesitation in Eloise's eyes.

'There were some warning flags, stood at three, Theo skied past them, didn't even stop, might not have seen them. I followed him; I didn't think much about it until the avalanche hit. I've told Lawrence, but I haven't said anything to Theo or the others. If Debra succeeds in making a case it might be difficult to keep it quiet and she'll make much of it.'

'Wait and see,' Saskia said, 'the run was open and most experienced skiers would gamble on three if there's powder snow. I'd say it was just one of those things. But I'd keep quiet and not load any more on to poor Theo. Quinn thinks they are mad to try it on, but they are rich so can spend their money making life miserable for other people.'

'I couldn't bear it if they lost Jacaranda,' Eloise said anxiously.

'With luck people who have used Jacaranda before and know Lawrence and Theo will still come and tell their friends, but even if they do, he told Quinn that he needs to keep Jacaranda full during the season to make ends meet,' Saskia said.

'I know it's a difficult situation and I'm so afraid Debra could easily make trouble with this exclusive agency that Lawrence just got into and they could dump him,' Eloise told her as they arrived at the chalet. She parked and they both got out to offload the shopping.

Eloise opened the chalet door and went inside, followed by Saskia carrying another load. To her great relief only Vera was there, on her way upstairs to do the bedrooms.

'Everyone is out,' she said and then seeing Saskia smiled. 'Hello Saskia, how is Mr Quinn?' She had a soft spot for him; as he'd been involved in her rescue by suggesting Lawrence take her on.

'Fine thanks, Vera. Hope all's well with you,' Saskia said, going on into the kitchen with the box of groceries.

When the two of them were in the kitchen together, Saskia said, 'I understood that Debra and co wanted a more luxurious chalet, full of cinemas, swimming pools and such, so they didn't need to mix with the hoi polloi, and if her friends have the same tastes they won't be coming here anyway.'

'That's true, but she could still scatter stories of how her nephew was taken into danger by the son of the owner of

Jacaranda and barely escaped with his life, and that this chalet was below standard, food dreadful, all that.'

Saskia started to unpack the box of groceries, putting the butter, cheese and milk into the fridge. 'It depends if the holiday press get hold of anything negative. If she makes enough noise I can see that causing difficulties, but perhaps when she gets home she'll forget about it.'

'No such luck. I think her lawyer is ringing her this afternoon, and even though her husband's told her to drop it, and I begged her to when I drove her down earlier, I feel she's the sort of person who hates to be bossed around and she's determined to follow it through.' Eloise worried that she could have made it worse by tackling Debra this morning, uncovering bad memories she had worked so hard to overcome. 'And her son has apparently bought some publishing outfit and has said he might write an article about being here.'

'Oh no, what magazine? Quinn might know it and be able to stop it.'

'I don't know, it publishes on various things, top holiday places being one of them. I just feel everything is conspiring to ruin Jacaranda.'

'It might all come to nothing, don't stress until you have to. Come on, let's go.' She made for the door, calling goodbye to Vera.

Eloise put her fears away and they set off down to Martigny, an ancient town that was once an important trade centre in Roman times. It was not far from Verbier and was where the train came in from Geneva. Eloise suffered a pinch of nerves as she steered the jeep down the valley, she kept her eyes ahead, not looking down at the view falling away beside her. Saskia, having driven this road many times and having no fear of it, talked non-stop. Eloise tried to concentrate on that as well as her driving to quell her nerves.

They arrived in the town without mishap and parked by the art gallery and went inside to have lunch.

'Oh,' Saskia stopped suddenly, causing Eloise to almost bump into her. 'Look over there, it's Lawrence and Aurelia.'

Eloise turned to where she was pointing and saw the two of them sitting together, heads bent over something they were studying on the table in front of them. Saskia was about to go and greet them but Eloise pulled her back and out of the restaurant.

'I don't want to see them, or rather I don't want them to see me. Why would they come down here when there are so many bars and places they could go to in Verbier?' She looked back to where they sat. Lawrence was closing up his laptop.

Aurelia also had hers; she scribbled something from it on a piece of paper and handed it to him.

Saskia pulled at Eloise's arm, 'If you don't want them to see us, come away now.' She led her into the gallery. 'Appear mesmerized by the artwork, so if they come in you look surprised to see them.'

'Do you think it's something to do with Jacaranda?' Eloise whispered. She knew he was running out of options to save Jacaranda, especially if Debra was to go ahead with legal action. But would he really turn to Aurelia and her 'Tempting Delights'?

'Could be,' Saskia said. 'Lawrence was talking to Quinn about it last night. Quinn told him that perhaps he ought to go into partnership with someone else in the same business. I don't suppose he meant Aurelia. Maybe,' she looked troubled, 'he's in such a fix it's his only option if he wants to keep the chalet.'

'Oh, I do hope he's not going in with her.' Eloise felt as if a stone had lodged in the pit of her stomach. 'I wish I could talk it over with Desmond, but I can't go behind Lawrence's back. I don't want him to think I'm interfering and I don't want Desmond to feel... nor I'm sure does Lawrence, that he must put any money he might have into it when he's made his life elsewhere.'

'I see that. Quinn said Desmond turned Jacaranda over to Lawrence after Maddy died, so he probably doesn't want to get involved and stir up old memories again.' Saskia squeezed her arm. 'But perhaps you are worrying unnecessarily and Lawrence and Aurelia are here to see the exhibition like us.'

Before she could answer they heard Aurelia's distinctive voice, 'Oh, what a surprise. Lawrence, here's your little cook and Saskia.'

'Oh... hello, funny seeing you here.' Lawrence's voice was strained. He was obviously put out seeing her here.

'We came to see the exhibition,' Saskia chattered on. 'I always mean to come but so often the event is over before I get round to it. We're going to have lunch in a minute, have you been here long?'

Lawrence seemed about to say something when Aurelia slipped her arm though his, smug, as if showing off a trophy. 'We're here to discuss something important, something that will benefit both of us and Verbier too,' she smiled, a horrid cat stealing the cream kind of smile.

Lawrence said quickly, 'There's nothing decided yet, Aurelia.'

'So are we allowed to know about this plan?' Saskia said, all innocent.

'Shall we tell them?' Aurelia still hung on to his arm, a knowing smirk on her face filling Eloise with anxiety.

'There's nothing to tell.' Lawrence threw Eloise a repentant glance. 'I must hurry round the exhibition; I've got to get back. See you later, Eloise.' He moved off to the next room, dragging Aurelia with him, leaving Eloise feeling he was horrified to see her here and whatever he was up to with Aurelia he didn't want her to know.

'Let's have lunch and lots of wine.' Saskia led Eloise away. 'She's such a bitch, certainly no one will want to stay at Jacaranda if she's in charge.'

Eloise followed her in despair. What would Lawrence do when he found out that she had stirred up all Debra's past, even made her cry? No doubt she had signed Jacaranda's death warrant herself by adding to Debra's determination to get some money back for the disaster that never happened.

38

Eloise got back to Jacaranda around teatime. It was such a relief having Saskia out here; she didn't know how she would have coped without her. She'd have had no one her own age to have fun with and confide in. She wished she were with her now to act as a support in the row that was sure to come.

There were no other cars parked outside and the door to the chalet was locked. Sometimes the guests slipped the catch down by mistake when they went in, so finding it locked did not always mean no one else was there. The chalet, especially when there were guests, was rarely empty, for Vera, Lawrence or the 'chef' at the time was usually there. In the rare event of no one being there the guests were told where the key was hidden so they could let themselves in.

Eloise had her own key and she unlocked the door feeling like a thief creeping into the chalet, afraid of confronting Debra who had probably returned by now.

She had overplayed her hand by accosting Debra like that, unleashing the pain she fought so hard to forget. Consumed by a feeling of dread, Eloise wondered how her call to her lawyer had gone. Was it over, or was it going on now, here in the chalet? And would she be even more determined to take action now?

Even if Debra did nothing, she had seen Lawrence and

Aurelia together at Martigny poring over some plans and, as Saskia told her, Quinn had suggested Lawrence go in with someone else, though she was sure he didn't mean Aurelia, but all the same the two of them together could keep Jacaranda safe. Her own love for Jacaranda was irrelevant; she was going home soon.

She took off her boots, all the time straining to catch any sound of life and hearing none. The door to the living room was closed, she crept close to it and then furtively opening it, she saw that the room was empty, spotless and tidy, as if no one had been there since Vera had cleaned it that morning.

She went upstairs softly in her stockinged feet and stood on the landing listening. It did not feel as if anyone else were here. Debra could have taken her call in the village with Ken and Travis as witnesses.

Passing Lawrence's photographs, she stopped to study them. Usually she only had time to rush past them on her way to the shops or the kitchen, but now she had time to savour them. It was the black and white ones she liked best, they were so dramatic, the shadows of the trees marking the pristine snow. He was very gifted and perhaps if all else failed he could make a living from taking photographs… but she must not think like that. Saskia had told her she must try not to panic until she had to. She went into her room and lay on her bed, glad to be alone, and turned on to Facebook to see what the twins were up to.

There was a new picture of them by the Great Wall of China with a group of others. 'Here we are at Badaling, took the cable car, amazing views.' And there were close-ups of Lizzie waving and later of Kit in a group of young people, his arm round a girl. How she missed them, this was the longest time they had ever been apart. But it was wonderful for them to travel and see such amazing things. She wished she'd had a gap year when she'd been young, but she'd met Harvey. Now he was gone though she was free perhaps to travel more, not just go home and slot back into her job.

She left the twins an upbeat message, kissed them through the screen, swallowed her tears and got up to get into the shower before Theo got back. She washed her hair and changed into her jeans and pale green jersey and went cautiously downstairs to start on the dinner.

The living room door was still shut, but this time she could hear the buzz of conversation behind the door and her imagination, fired up by her guilt at upsetting Debra, sprung to life with lurid pictures of lawyers juggling vast sums of money to hit Lawrence with. She hurried past.

If only she could somehow be transported to the Great Wall and join her children, get far away from the trouble her meddling might have caused.

Theo and Vera were in the kitchen when she went in, Theo eating a large slab of Christmas cake and Vera setting a tray of cutlery and glasses needed to lay the table for dinner when the door was opened and she could get in there.

'Hi, Eloise. What did you do today?' Theo asked her.

Sign Jacaranda's death warrant, came to mind, but she said, 'Saskia and I went down to Martigny, saw the exhibition, had lunch. Did you have a good day?' She wondered if he'd seen Jerry and Gaby and what he thought of him siding with Debra over the avalanche.

'Skied with a couple of friends, though not Jerry and Gaby,' he said, his face grave. He pulled off a chunk of icing and marzipan.

Eloise felt a burn of anger; Theo had gone out of his way

to entertain them and instead of standing up for him, or even just telling the truth, Jerry had been easily swayed by his aunt to hold him to blame for leading them into an avalanche.

'I'm sorry he's not telling it as it was,' she said, 'but if it comes to it I'll stick up for you.' She squeezed his arm as she passed him, not bearing to think how much he could lose over this show of Debra's self-righteousness.

Theo finished his mouthful. 'Thanks,' he said, giving her a brave smile before leaving the room, but he was back in a moment. 'Lawrence wants a word, can you go to him when you have a minute.' He trundled back down the passage. At the same moment they heard the living room door open and the occupants go upstairs and Vera picked up her tray and scurried down the passage to lay the table before they came down again, leaving Eloise alone.

This was it. She felt as if an icy hand had grabbed her stomach, digging in its nails. Lawrence was going to be furious with her, anguished to think that she'd made things worse, upset Debra even more. She should have left well alone. Jacaranda's fate was nothing to do with her. Just because she loved this place, felt happy and at home here, there was no excuse. Jacaranda belonged to Lawrence and it was not her business to interfere, she was only 'the cook' after all.

She took off her apron sporting the 'vulgar' message and went slowly down to Lawrence's office. The door was ajar and she could see him sitting at his desk, she pushed down an urge to run and went in.

'You wanted to see me, Lawrence?'

'Yes, Eloise, come in.' He sprang up and shut the door behind her; his face was radiant, smiling at her. She couldn't understand it.

'What's happened?' She sat down gingerly on the chair by the window. Having geared herself up for his anger, she wasn't sure how to cope with his exuberance. Aurelia! That was it, they'd decided to go into business together and that would minimize any fallout from Debra's case. Though what about Theo? His reputation would still be on the line.

'I've just seen Saskia in the village and she told me you spoke to Debra in no uncertain terms this morning and...'

'Yes I did,' she interrupted him, desperate to apologize, 'and I'm sorry, I know I should have left well alone, it's none of my business after all. But we were alone together in the car and I couldn't stop myself. I'm sorry if I've made things worse, it's the last thing I meant to do.' She sat up straighter, she'd confessed it now, admitted she was guilty and he must do his worst, though why was he still smiling at her?

'But Eloise, you made her see sense. Showed her that Jacaranda means more to us than just being a business, a way of making money. I've just spoken to her... I felt I should, after what Saskia told me.' He looked slightly contrite. 'I was about to apologize for your speaking out, but she said she'd talked it over with Ken and perhaps she had been hasty. Poor woman, she told me she didn't know what a happy family and happy memories were. She's had some since she married, but making money's been her saviour. She was afraid Jerry might have some sort of delayed reaction and not be able to work or would make costly mistakes to the businesses they have.'

'She told me she is terrified of being back where she started with nothing,' Eloise said now, remembering the anguish on Debra's face. 'But I made her cry. I made *Debra* cry. I must have hurt her dreadfully and I was so afraid she'd punish me by being even more determined to get some form of compensation.' She struggled to believe Debra had changed her mind.

'Well you did the opposite, we could say it is you who has saved Jacaranda.' His smile sent a glow through her and yet still she waited for him to tell her that he was joining up with Aurelia and Jacaranda would be turned it into a hideous complex. 'So aren't you pleased? You don't look it.' He seemed disappointed.

'Of course I am,' she struggled to rally her spirits. 'I can't really believe it. I've stressed all day thinking you'd be upset with me, even send me packing.'

'Oh, Eloise, how could you think that?' he retorted. 'I don't think Theo, or Vera for that matter, would let me send you home. Theo says you've turned Jacaranda into a home, just like Maddy did.'

And what do you think? she thought but did not say. 'Oh, well… I'm glad,' she said instead. 'But you've got a new chef, a real one this time, coming out soon, so unless you keep me on as a kitchen maid,' she hoped she sounded jokey, 'I'll be going home soon anyway.'

He leant back in his chair watching her. 'I meant to ask… but as you know, everything's been so manic. Paddy, who was coming to take over from you has been offered a far better position, something that he'd be mad to turn down if he wants to further his career. He's given me the name of someone else, but I don't know her and Theo insisted I ask you first, if you could stay on for a while longer. I'll understand if you can't do it, or don't want to do it and have plans back home.'

Had she heard him correctly? Was he really asking her to stay on?

He got up and came over to her and took her hand. 'Please say yes,' he said softly

There was a brief knock on the door and Theo came in, 'The beeper is going on the oven,' he said, 'thought I ought to say in case it all burns.'

Lawrence let go of her hand and Eloise stood up.

'Thanks Theo, it means the oven is the right temperature to put in the meat.'

Lawrence moved aside to let her go. She went past him to the open door, wondering what would have happened if they had not been disturbed. She'd be foolish, she scolded herself, if she thought his touch meant anything more than extreme gratitude. She'd no idea her words had made Debra think, understand that there were some things in life that could not be bought and yet were more precious than anything.

'So, Eloise, before you go, can you stay on or must I contact this other person and tell her to come?' Lawrence called after her.

'You must stay.' Theo stood aside to let her pass.

'Yes, no... I don't know. I'll let you know after I've cooked the dinner,' she said, running up the stairs to the kitchen, knowing that the meat could wait a while longer to be put in the oven. She was running away from the emotions Lawrence had stirred up in her.

39

'I told you Eloise was a gold mine,' Desmond said when Lawrence rang to tell him the conclusion of Debra and the suing saga. He wouldn't have told him anything about it in the first place if his father had not contacted him to tell him he was delighted to receive a picture with an email from Eloise of the Christmas tree decorated with Maddy's beautiful jewelled eggs, but hearing his father's voice weakened his resolve to keep the news from him. He'd talk sense and understand his fears and Lawrence had needed to share them with someone, someone who knew and loved Jacaranda and would understand his agony. Theo was too young and inexperienced to really take on board the magnitude of Debra's action and he was the centre of the whole drama. And though Quinn was a good sounding board, there was no better person than his father to offer advice.

Desmond, having listened to the whole story, swore, saying what a pest Debra was and how he abhorred this modern fashion for threatening to take legal action over every mishap. He was highly relieved then when Lawrence telephoned him later to tell him Eloise had come to the rescue and persuaded Debra to drop the suit.

'I think it's time I visit the old place again,' Desmond said, surprising him. 'I hope Eloise will still be there. What about Easter, will there be room for me then?'

'Of course, how marvellous, I never thought we'd lure you back,' Lawrence said, 'but I don't know if Eloise will still be here then.'

'Try and persuade her. She's a great girl, she married a rotter.' Desmond went on, 'She was wasted on him, but the children are great kids, grown-up now, but at least she has them.'

'Yes... she's been marvellous,' Lawrence said, trying to ignore the burst of desire he felt for her. It was as if he'd been floundering around in a sort of fog these past years, trying to make a success of Jacaranda, channelling his feelings into being charming to the people who came to stay even if they were rude and difficult, and somehow he'd lost sight of the finer feelings of romance and love. It shocked and to a smaller extent scared him as he admitted to himself that he'd fallen in love with Eloise. He'd desired other women and had women friends, some of whom were lovers, but he had not fallen in love for years, if ever really.

Georgia, Theo's mother, didn't really count. Their flash of 'love' had not lasted, though he'd always care for her, not least for being the mother of his son. But he was being foolish, he could not be in love with Eloise, he was just grateful to her for making Jacaranda feel like a home again, producing meals that were imaginative and delicious and everyone seemed to enjoy, including him, and most important of all, she seemed to have saved Jacaranda and Theo from Debra's troublemaking.

'I'll turn up the week before Easter and stay a month or so, might even try to ski again if there's still snow and the old legs will let me,' Desmond laughed. 'Hopefully I can enjoy Eloise's cooking then.'

'I'm not sure of her plans, Desmond, but it will be so good to see you back here, Theo will be thrilled... and so will all your friends, they've been asking after you,' Lawrence said. He thought of Eloise. He had asked her if she would stay on, but she had not given him an answer. Perhaps she'd had enough of this cooking lark and, he had to admit, his often distant manner towards her, and indeed his anger with her over the whole Bert episode. Now it made him smile. He'd treated her the same way he had the other chefs. He was the boss; he paid them fairly, gave them enough time off and expected them to do their bit by producing great meals. They were not his best friend or indeed his lovers; it was solely a professional arrangement.

This job had been thrust on her out of the blue just when she was recovering from her divorce and, he'd learnt later, her children leaving for their gap year, and yet she'd kept her feelings to herself and pitched in and done her job, so he'd hardly be surprised if now she wanted to get out of here, go home to her friends and family. What a fool he'd look if he told her he'd fallen in love with her. She might even think it was a ploy to make her stay, or worse see it as a form of ridicule. No he would keep these feelings to himself. If she left he'd soon get over her, there were other women here he liked, he just hadn't made much effort lately in the love department.

But he still had business to attend to first; he had to confront Aurelia. He'd been so worried about the expense of a possible lawsuit that he had succumbed to her badgering him about how *together* they could turn Jacaranda into a money-spinner. He had agreed to meet her in Martigny, 'out of the way of prying eyes', as she'd put it. He'd never been asked to her home, barely knew where it was, but she wanted to show him the plans she had drawn up to turn Jacaranda into a profitable business for both of them.

'You won't have any more chefs running off and all the rest of it,' she'd said. 'We'll have my food, make it on the premises so it will save time and money and always be good quality,' she finished, leaving him feeling things were running away too fast, although he knew there weren't many options left if Debra went ahead with the case.

Aurelia could put money in straight away to refurbish Jacaranda and employ an architect she knew – who would charge her 'mate's rates' – to design further buildings in the garden to rent out. Although he'd agreed to see her plans, he made it clear that he was just going to look at them; he was making no decisions until he saw how Debra's threat played out.

When he saw her plans he didn't like them. There was too much involved and most of her ideas would take away Jacaranda's unique feeling of being in its own space, surrounded by the majesty and beauty of the mountains. He tried to explain that he didn't want to crowd out the place with other buildings. However well designed, they would cut off the view and, to some extent, the light.

'Get real, Lawrence, we're talking making *proper* money here, not limping along bringing in just enough so you and Theo can stay in your family chalet. In the far-off days when your father lived there money was money and went a long way. Today is different and you need to make Jacaranda pay for itself, earn its place in that agency,' she'd protested and he'd kept quiet, determined to try and find other ways to keep the chalet. Aurelia was too bossy and too controlling for him to become involved with.

Even with the fear of Debra suing him, he reasoned to

himself that if they didn't spend a fortune splashing out on all these extra rooms and buildings, they might be able to limp on. True, he wanted enough money to live comfortably, but he could do without the expensive trappings of wealth. This week with Debra and her family had shown him the downside of being mega-rich, the sense of entitlement, the fear of losing it and the loneliness of not trusting the motives of people offering friendship.

But now, thanks to Eloise, Debra was not suing them, Theo's dreams of becoming a ski instructor and guide were safe, and although money was still going to be tight, he no longer had to consider other ways to make Jacaranda pay and he could turn down Aurelia's offer to go in with him.

He must now confront her, tell her that though interested in seeing her ideas for Jacaranda – ideas he'd since discovered she'd been working on for some time, hoping to muscle in and use his chalet and the land around it to team up with her expensive takeaways and charge a fortune for it – he would not be taking up her offer to go into business.

Jacaranda being one of the oldest and most charming chalets around still needed to make a profit and he must think up more ways to make it happen, look into Quinn's suggestion of holding art classes and such. But now there was no fear of trying to turn Jacaranda into something it was not, a brand new, soulless building full of all the mod cons the very rich demanded. Jacaranda would sell itself to those who cared for warmth, good memories and a home from home.

Eloise had saved him from a damaging lawsuit. He must now put things right and hope that she would stay.

40

They were all looking at something on the table in the kitchen when Eloise came in after they had finished breakfast.

Theo turned to her, 'Come and see what Radley has done for us.'

'It's very atmospheric, a wonderful photograph.' Lawrence smiled at her.

Radley was looking rather pink and pleased with himself and Pippa was cuddling close to him.

They moved away to let Eloise in and she was surprised to see a beautiful photograph of Jacaranda caught just as the sun was setting, painting it in gold. Underneath was a short article.

Jacaranda sits like a benevolent uncle on the side of the mountain... it began, going on to describe it as a magical place, a place it was a joy to stay in.

'This is beautiful, describes it exactly,' she said, turning to him, surprised that such artistic talent was hidden in his shy character. It touched her that he had caught the chalet's unique atmosphere so well. She wondered if Debra had seen it, and if she'd think it too sentimental.

'He's brilliant at writing,' Pippa said proudly, 'it's just a pity Debra doesn't think it a good profession.'

'Now you've bought that publishing firm you can write

all you want, and this is lovely, thank you so much, Radley.' Lawrence beamed at him, making him go even pinker with embarrassed pride.

The moment was broken by Debra and Ken appearing in the hall and calling for Radley. He hurriedly snatched up the picture and pushed it at Pippa, who put it back into a large envelope while he went out to them.

Eloise was dreading seeing Debra, fearful of her reaction after she'd reduced her to tears, but she had to apologize for upsetting her. She was not to know of her difficult childhood and that she had inadvertently hit on a painful nerve. She'd acted out of panic, though, she reminded herself it had worked and Jacaranda was saved... for the moment anyway.

But what if she'd inadvertently saved it for Aurelia? The fate of Jacaranda was nothing to do with her, she reminded herself, she must accept that and move on.

This she said to Vera when they were left alone together in the kitchen. 'I feel dreadful that I made her cry,' she finished.

'Good to cry,' Vera said. 'But it must make you strong, make the changes you need to be happy.'

'But I must say something to her, apologize for upsetting her,' Eloise said. 'I didn't think, I just said what I wanted to say, I could have it made it worse. I mean, I'm only the cook.'

'So? You are allowed opinions,' Vera said scornfully. 'You did nothing wrong, just told her she could lose Lawrence Jacaranda and ruin Theo's life. It wouldn't matter to her, she'd go home and forget, and he loses everything. Rich people should do good with money not bad things.' She mopped up a small dribble of coffee with a vengeance. 'Oh... do you know that Desmond is coming for a visit?' Vera went on. 'So good he is coming back. Will you be here to see him?'

'Oh, I didn't know, Lawrence never said.' She was surprised

he hadn't told her his father was making a visit. Desmond hadn't been here for years, and she understood he'd put off coming here because he couldn't bear to think of Jacaranda without his beloved Maddy. But was she going to stay? The thought had plagued her all night. She loved it here, felt at home, complete again. It was a long time until the summer, when she was going to New Zealand to see her parents and meet up with the twins. Lawrence needed to know as soon as possible as he had another chef waiting to know if she were needed, so she must make her decision today.

It was Lawrence she wanted to be with, the thought nudged annoyingly into her mind. She had known her feelings for him for some time, though she had blocked them, warning herself that theirs was purely a professional relationship, and yet had he not held her, kissed the top of her head? But no, that was foolish; she was not going to put herself in danger of being hurt again or build up some mad scenario of him being attracted to her, even caring for her in a romantic way.

There was so much else here to make her happy though – Theo, Bert, Vera and Saskia and the mountains and the snow, so why not stay on? Her job in London could be kept on hold for a while longer. There was no one back home waiting for her and the weather would be so grey and cold. A damp sort of cold that ate into your bones, not exhilarating and beautiful like here in the mountains – and skiing, there was no skiing in London.

'I'm not sure, I have things at home,' she said lamely to Vera. After thinking it over Lawrence might decide he'd do better to employ this other chef and send her home. 'When is Desmond coming though, I would love to see him.'

'Easter, though we are full at Easter – he will have to go in Lawrence's room and Lawrence will have to go elsewhere.'

Her dark eyes flickered towards Eloise and away and she felt herself blush, which was foolish indeed. She must put a stop to this nonsense, it would be best to go home, sort out the new house, get back to her job and her life and friends back home. She would tell him that when she saw him.

Later, between mouthfuls of cereal, Theo thanked Eloise for saving him and Jacaranda. 'Dad said you made Debra see sense,' he said.

'I don't know if that is strictly true, I was afraid I said too much,' Eloise said.

Theo shrugged, 'Thanks anyway.'

He told her he was going to spend the rest of the day skiing with friends – his father had given him the day off but he would have to leave Bert behind. 'Sorry Bert,' he bent and patted him, 'but it's too far for you today.'

'I'll take him for a walk later,' Eloise said, having decided to spend the day around the chalet as a sort of farewell before she left.

'If you're sure, thanks,' Theo said. 'Tomorrow this lot are leaving, so I've got to take them to the airport.' He paused a moment before saying, 'I don't know if Jerry and Gaby are still around.'

She saw the hurt in his eyes, perhaps thinking of Jerry letting him down by siding with Debra over the avalanche.

'I haven't heard from Gaby, I think she'd have said if she'd gone home,' Eloise said, wondering what decision Gaby had made over her relationship with Jerry. She would text her later, suggest they meet up in the village. She sat down to make a list for dinner – their last one – this evening. She could hear them getting ready to leave; the chatter, the clump of ski boots. Lawrence came into the kitchen.

'I'm taking them down and then I'm skiing myself, do you

want to come with me, Eloise?' The remark was thrown out as if he felt it would be churlish not to offer.

'No thanks, I've lots to do here and Bert and I will go for a walk later. Have a good time.' She threw him a smile, hoping he couldn't see the pain in her heart. She would miss him, miss everything about the place, but that is how it was saying goodbye to places and people that had crept under your skin and become part of you.

'OK, see you later then.' He turned to go, then said, 'By the way Desmond is coming here for Easter.'

And before she could answer he'd gone. She heard the front door open, felt the cold rush of air while everyone trooped out. Then the door closed and she assumed they had all left, so she went down the passage to the stairs to go to her room. Debra was sitting on the bench putting on her boots; she looked up and saw her.

'Debra, I... I thought you'd gone with the others,' Eloise blurted.

'I'm just about to.' Debra stood up and picked up her bag.

'I... I'm really sorry if I upset you,' Eloise said in a rush, 'I didn't mean to, but thank you so much for changing your mind about taking legal action. You have saved Jacaranda.'

Debra blushed, 'I wouldn't say I've done that, but I listened to what you said and understood what you meant, and as Ken said, no one was hurt.' Debra made for the door and then she turned and faced her. 'I wanted a good and secure home for my son and I hope I've achieved it, but I see now there are things money can't buy, I'm just not sure I've done it right.'

'I'm sure you have, and Radley is very talented.' She was about to praise his beautiful photograph and article about the chalet, when she remembered his bundling it away when

Debra had called him, better to leave it. 'Anyway, thank you so much,' she added instead.

Debra just shrugged, opened the door and went out to join the others, leaving Eloise feeling sorry for her. Debra had done her best in the way she knew and she shouldn't judge her.

A few minutes later Eloise left to go down to the village to shop for the dinner. After the party left tomorrow morning they had a few quiet days before the next group – friends of Lawrence's – arrived for a long weekend, so there was not much to buy today.

She saw no one she knew in the village; Saskia had gone to Geneva with Quinn, and she thought she'd leave Gaby to get in touch with her if she wanted to. When she got back to Jacaranda she found that Vera had left, so she and Bert were alone in the chalet.

She had just finished tidying away the shopping when she heard the door of the chalet open. It was probably Debra and possibly Ken coming back and Eloise went down the passage to see, closely followed by Bert who was hoping it was Theo who'd returned. It was Aurelia. Both women stared at each other.

'Oh, Aurelia, what are you doing here?' Eloise struggled to appear composed, surprised and concerned to see her.

Aurelia quickly hid her own shock at seeing Eloise, and putting on her imperious voice, she said, 'It's OK, I just came to... measure up properly, see the space... there's so much wasted potential.'

'Measure up for what?' Eloise demanded. Had Aurelia and Lawrence decided to go into business together after all, and she had come to lay her claim? But if he was going in with her why was he not here to show her round, discuss it with her?

'I won't bore you with it,' Aurelia waved her hand dismissively as if she wouldn't understand anyway. 'I just want to look round, see the size of the bedrooms, bathrooms – see how many there are, and all that.' She turned towards the stairs.

It was not her business and yet she could not let Jacaranda go with a fight. There was something about Aurelia's stance that made her suspicious.

'Did you tell Lawrence you were coming? I would have thought he would have liked to show you around the chalet himself?' she said, moving to bar the stairs. Bert, sensing the atmosphere, growled.

'That dog's dangerous,' Aurelia said, watching him warily. 'Shut him away,' she commanded.

'He's fine; he belongs here and is just guarding the place. I think it best that you come back when Lawrence is here, see what he thinks.'

'He's off skiing now, I saw him at Medran, ready to go up.'

'So he knows you're here?'

Aurelia wouldn't look at her, she said firmly, 'As I'm here I'll just take a look around.' She took out an iPad and a tape measure from her bag and made for the stairs, a determined look on her face. 'Move out of my way please, Eloise, this is absolutely nothing to do with you, you came here to cook and I understand you leave in a few days.'

'Our guests are still here and I doubt they'd feel happy knowing a stranger was going into their rooms. I'll text Lawrence' – she took her mobile out of her pocket – 'and see what he thinks, but while I'm here alone, I will not let you go upstairs.' She began to text him.

'Just because this used to belong to your godfather it doesn't mean you belong here,' Aurelia said, her eyes spiteful. 'Jacaranda is Lawrence's now and he and I could make a real go of it, modernize it, bring in clients like these ones every time now he's with this top agency, but he's got to change things if he wants to stay there.'

Eloise struggled with her feelings. Aurelia no doubt spoke the truth, but she would not allow her to poke round the chalet without Lawrence being here. She finished her text.

Aurelia arrived to look round. Told her to wait until the guests have left and you are here

Her finger hovered over 'send' as she watched for Aurelia's reaction. 'I'll wait and see what he says.'

Aurelia's mouth twisted in anger, 'I'll come back later, I'll tell Lawrence how rude you are, acting as if you own the place and have forgotten you're only the cook, and not a good one at that. He'll be relieved, we all will, when Paddy comes back, he's the sort of chef the clients who come here expect.' She snatched at the door handle, jerked it open and stamped outside to her car without shutting it, leaving the cold air to seep in.

Eloise shut the door and deleted the text. There was no point in bothering him, spoiling his skiing. She struggled to collect her feelings. Aurelia was right, she was only the cook, and though Lawrence had asked if she would stay on as Paddy had another job, Jacaranda's fate was nothing to do with her. It was a business and perhaps Lawrence had decided that to keep it viable it would be best to make some sort of arrangement with Aurelia. After all, if all her food were here there would be no need to worry about getting and keeping a chef.

She wished now she were skiing high on some mountain surrounded by the savage beauty of nature, the snow under her feet and the feeling of liberation as she skied down with the wind in her hair and her worries blown away in the magic of it all.

Bert barked at the door, wanting to go out, and she decided to drop everything and go with him. It would only be a walk, but it would be a long one, and she needed to be outside to calm her troubled mind.

She opened the door to let him go while she put on her coat and boots and they set out. It was very cold but the sky was dazzling blue and they took the path that led to the main mountains. Either side of the path were fir trees, their branches heavy with snow. There was a stillness about the place, every so often broken by the soft fall of snow toppling from an overladen branch. Bert ran here and there, picked up a fir cone in his mouth and nudged her legs until she threw it, and he ran, barking excitedly, to bring it back to her to do again and again until she protested that she was bored of the game.

They went on up the path until they reached the top of one of the nursery slopes, the last bit of the run from the top. The skiers coming down turned on to it to ski to the bottom and home.

Ahead she saw someone coming straight towards the path they were standing on. She stood aside so the person could pass them, but Bert began to bark and run round in circles.

'Bert,' she called, going to him and bending down to calm him, 'what a fuss; other people are allowed to use this path as well as us.'

Bert broke free and ran yelping in excitement, narrowly missing being run down by the skier, who stopped and, laughing, bent down to pat him, and she realized it was Lawrence, his face covered with goggles and a scarf.

With Bert under one arm trying to lick his face, he came slowly down to where she stood.

'Eloise, out for a walk?' He put Bert down and lifted his goggles and pushed away his scarf.

'Yes,' she said, 'I've hardly done any walks since I've been here and I love this place.'

'Me too,' he said, studying her face as if he had not looked at her properly before. He said, 'Have you come to a decision about staying on. I'm sorry, I must know today, the chef Paddy recommended has been offered something else and needs to know at once.'

She was leaving, was she not? She'd stay until the next chef arrived as planned and then go home, and leave Jacaranda... and Lawrence for Aurelia. And yet she could not bear to leave. Standing here beside him in the snow at the base of the mountain surrounded by pine trees, the fresh scent of them sharp on the air, she wanted to stay, where else in the world would she feel so alive, so much a part of nature?

Lawrence bent down and took off his skis. 'It's easier to walk down from here,' he said. 'So have you made up your mind?' His voice was harsh now; he did not look at her.

'Yes.' She felt a stab of pain at his tone; she was still sore after Harvey's departure, and there was Aurelia waiting to grab Lawrence, had grabbed him already for all she knew.

'I'm going home. Of course I'll stay until the next chef arrives.'

'I see.' He looked away, his mouth set firm. 'If that's your decision. Theo will miss you, all your baking, and Bert.' He gestured towards the little dog who was playing catch the fir cone with himself.

'And will you?' The words she didn't mean to say hung in the silence. How foolish she was, she was about to make a joke only she couldn't think of one. He turned to face her.

'What do you think, Eloise?' he said quietly.

What could she say? Whatever it was it would sound wrong. 'I doubt you will,' she said, 'you won't have to worry that I'll mess up with some terrible cooking fiasco, or let Bert mangle the dinner, you'll have a real chef and it will be a relief and…'

'No,' he said and before she knew it she was in his arms, his lips fierce upon hers. She kissed him back, their passion rising, all she wanted was to stay here with him forever.

He lifted his head and gazed at her, his eyes warm with love. 'You cannot go,' he said, stroking back her hair, 'I will not let you.'

'But… I…' It felt so right being here in his arms, but if he wanted to go into business with Aurelia it couldn't work and she'd not be hurt again. 'I know that you want to – have to, upgrade Jacaranda to move with the times, and Aurelia will be a good partner, and you need a professional chef for that, I understand.'

'What?' he frowned. 'What's all this about Aurelia?'

'She came to the chalet when you'd left. Said she'd come to measure up, as she put it that you and her were going into business together… I quite understand.'

'But that's not true,' he protested. 'It's true I thought about it when I worried that I'd lose Jacaranda, but you saved us from that disaster.' He kissed her again and she felt herself melting, yielding to him, she must trust him, stop being afraid of being hurt as Harvey had hurt her.

'But Aurelia seems very determined,' she said, holding him back a moment, 'and she does have a good business of her own which could tie in well with yours.' She yearned to stay with him and yet she could not cope with Aurelia's scorn.

'She's a determined person and that's one of the reasons I'd never go in with her, I was tempted, it's true, when I thought I'd be landed with huge legal bills if Debra sued, but even then I had begun to realize it just wouldn't work, she and I in business together.' He kissed her again and she felt herself relax, she'd let her pain over the break-up of her marriage stifle her growing feelings for Lawrence. She loved him, plain and simple, and she would go with it wherever it led.

'I love you,' she said, kissing him again.' I love you, Lawrence.'

His face was radiant. 'I think I've loved you since that night Bert stole the lamb,' he laughed, 'but I hid it from myself and from you, thinking you were still in love with your ex-husband, and maybe he'd come here to try and make up.'

'No, it was a dreadful coincidence that he was here and now that is a chapter ended.'

'Come on, let's go back to Jacaranda. I want to make love to you.'

They walked back together along the path, Lawrence carrying his skis on one shoulder, his free arm round her, and Bert running beside them. Eloise felt complete, her lost and lonely feelings gone. She thought of how nervous Desmond's insistence that she could cook at Jacaranda made her and how she'd taken the challenge. He was a wily old bird, had he known all along how it would end? She laughed, joy filling her. 'Your father started this,' she said. 'Do you think he meant us to fall in love?'

'We'll have to ask him when he comes,' he said, smiling.

'I'm longing to see him, but...' She frowned as the thought hit her. 'Perhaps if you want to keep with this top agency, it may be best that you do employ a top chef.'

'I don't want to,' he protested. 'You're like Maddy, have the same gift of making a place seem like a home and that's what Jacaranda is to be in the future, a home from home.' He kissed her again. 'Kiss the Cook your apron says, and that's something I've been longing to do ever since you came.'

Acknowledgements

My sincere thanks to my agent Judith Murdoch and my editors Caroline Ridding and Sarah Ritherdon at Aria.